Beloved
Bachelor Dad

CRYSTAL GREEN

*First published in Great Britain 2002
Silhouette Books, Eton House, 18-24 Paradise Road,
Richmond, Surrey TW9 1SR*

© Chris Marie Green 2001

ISBN 0 373 24374 X

23-0902

*Printed and bound in Spain
by Litografia Rosés S.A., Barcelona*

CRYSTAL GREEN

lives in San Diego, California, where she has survived three years as a teacher of humanities. She's especially proud of her college-bound AVID (Advancement Via Individual Determination) students, who have inspired her to persevere.

When Crystal isn't writing romance, she enjoys reading, creative poetry, over-analysing movies, risking her life during police ride-alongs, petting her parents' Maltese dogs and fantasising about being a really good cook.

During school breaks, Crystal spends her time becoming re-addicted to her favourite soap operas and travelling to places far and wide. Her favourite souvenirs include travel journals—the pages reflecting everything from taking tea in London's Leicester Square to backpacking up endless mountain roads leading to the castles of Sintra, Portugal.

To Mom and Dad for encouraging a little girl who wrote some very silly stories about Indiana Jones and ill-fated cows. To Judy Duarte and Sheree WhiteFeather—our partnership is surely 'serendipitous.' To Melissa Jeglinski for guiding my fictional family to Special Edition. Lastly, thanks to Kim Nadelson and Regina Ronk for their patience and hard work.

Chapter One

He couldn't take his eyes off her.

It was noon, and the inside of Brody's Clubhouse Bar and Grill swirled with air from ceiling fans and the conditioning unit. Heat wavered over San Diego on this May day, and the guests wore rainbow-hued shorts and sleeveless shirts. As the smell of hamburgers and hops mingled in the cherrywood-laden eatery, Ray Brody mixed drinks as quickly as the servers could bring in orders.

He didn't make it a habit to look up every time a customer came in or went out, but his gaze was inexplicably drawn this time.

She was a silhouette from a cameo brooch come to life, shoulder-length hair blowing with every whir of the fan blades, and her petite figure a shadow against the frosted glass of the now-closed door.

Ray didn't like to believe in anything at first sight. In fact, he'd spent most of his life disproving the need for heart-shaped chocolate boxes and midnight-oil love letters. Suddenly he felt as if his life was about to change tracks. He had no time to call himself foolish.

As she stepped into the light, he smiled, under a strange spell. Hair so honeyed he wanted to dip his fingers into it.

For a blessed moment, Ray forgot his doubts about being a father again to his son, Trent, after a seven-year absence from his life. Stomach-churning phone calls and notes from "tsking" teachers flew from his mind. All he saw was someone close to a blush-skinned angel, hidden behind a sensible pair of glasses and a professional skirt set.

Joan, his head waitress, talked with the Cameo. She pointed at Ray. The Cameo nodded and walked toward him.

He tried not to stare, but as she came closer, he noticed more details: the way her black skirt complemented her tan and clung to the part of her waist that a man's hand could nestle in comfortably; a pair of legs that would fit nicely into thigh-highs and garters; the sculpted softness of a face as creamy as a peach; eyes like the color of the beer he had just spilled…

"Damn!" He thumped the half-empty mug onto the bar and grabbed a rag to wipe the puddle. That's the way to impress the ladies, thought Ray. You're a real Joe Cool.

He looked up again, and there she waited, close enough so he could smell citrus shampoo. A slow smile spread across his face. He caught himself, stopped the smile and wiped the bar with renewed energy.

"What can I do for you?" Use that poker face, he scolded himself. The last thing the Brody household needed was more hormones running amok. Trent was providing enough of those. Sometimes, when Ray watched his kid, he just wanted to hold him like he had when Trent was five, before his ex-wife had run off with him. But he knew his son would never tolerate that sort of intimacy. The realization left Ray feeling tapped out, empty and hollow.

He returned his attention to the Cameo, who waited patiently. With her thickly lashed eyes wide under glasses, Ray supposed she wore the kind of face you made when someone put an ice cube down the back of your shirt. "Mr. Brody?" she asked with a voice as rich as the honey of her hair.

"Yeah." He cocked his eyebrow and allowed his eyes to wander the length of her.

She blushed furiously.

She was like a painting he had once seen: a Victorian beauty, her hair in a loose bun, wearing a high-necked dress. The woman had been staring past him, thoughts inaccessible.

"Hey, Ray!" yelled Joan.

"Just a minute." He held up a finger to the Cameo, moving to the other end of the bar to answer his waitress's impatient beckoning.

The Cameo politely smiled. A mist of a smile that showed the sunshine beneath the haze. She seemed almost nervous; her foot rested on its heel, and she kept jiggling it. A paper clutched in her hand fluttered as she beat it against her leg.

In three minutes, he returned, only to see her back as she exited the Clubhouse.

The boy in him wanted to jump over the bar to give chase. The man kept his feet glued to the floor. He watched her walk out the door. It was the oddest five minutes of his life.

Why hadn't he just played it smooth? Jeez, he'd probably even been salivating because it'd been so long since someone had tickled his fancy like this.

Well, he'd just have to forget about her. Sure, she'd been pretty, but damned skittish, too. The last thing he needed in his life was to chase after a mystery woman in addition to an adolescent son. But maybe it was time for him to test the dating waters again. Go on a little fishing trip, so to speak.

It would just be much easier if his ex-wife, Cheri, would give him back those missing pieces of his heart.

Amid clinking glasses and the rattle of forks and knives, he concentrated on wiping the bar. Maybe fate was keeping his heart in shambles to punish him for his past life. After all, as hard as he'd tried, he hadn't been able to keep Cheri from leaving him, taking Trent with her as if his son was a piece of furniture she'd felt entitled to.

Then suddenly, years later—*boom.* His son was back. But this wasn't the boy he'd bounced on his knee. This was a sturdy almost-teenager, growing into the long-limbed promise of an athletic body. This was a stranger with a distrustful gaze shaded under a New York Giants cap—a gaze as blue as his mother's. Eyes a shade icier than Ray's own blue-greens. Eyes that saw the world in a whole different light.

This was the second week Trent had been living with him, and already his fears about being a parent had come true. Trent's social studies and math teachers had phoned about the youngster's tendency to disrupt class. They called him "unmotivated," "off-task," and several other teacher words Ray couldn't recall. Lord help him if he had to talk to even one more educator this year.

And, to make matters worse, Trent hated him with the usual adolescent passion. The boy blamed Ray for Cheri's abandonment.

And why not? He had been the first link in the chain leading to his ex-wife's drug habit and eventual desertion of her son. God, if he could just relive a few key moments in his life, the Brodys might have been one happy family today. But bad choices had their consequences.

Ray remembered playing catch with a son who could barely hold a Wiffle ball; he remembered smiling at the boy's towheaded sparkle and thinking, "This guy's going to be a heartbreaker." Those had been the days when hope sprung eternal, the days before he realized he would never achieve his childhood dreams. Then came the "irreconcilable differences," the divorce, the awarding of a five-year-old Trent to Cheri, the seven long years when Cheri had fled to Lord knows where, effectively cutting off all interaction between father and son. Ray had been helpless. He had spoken to everyone who knew Cheri, including her parents. No one had any clue of her and Trent's whereabouts. He even came close to hiring a private detective, but he'd been struggling just to make ends meet at the time.

Heartbroken, Ray had become a bachelor-reborn. He'd

worked odd jobs, bartending and construction mainly, and turned his melancholy frustration into an upscale sports bar in San Diego's Golden Triangle. Then suddenly, at the age of thirty-four, he had a son again.

He remembered the phone call from Cheri's parents. Yes, Cheri had left Trent with them after disappearing with a boyfriend who shared her enthusiasm for drugs. Yes, they had always known Cheri and Trent were living in New York, but didn't feel it was their place to inform Ray of his son's whereabouts. No, they did not want Trent to live with them. They had retired and already raised their *own* kids.

Poor guy. Look what his son was stuck with now. A parent with no parenting skills.

Barely contained disgust narrowed Ray's eyes. Such a close-knit family—he, Cheri and his son. No wonder the boy had the temper of a mistreated puppy. If the hand of life slapped you time and time again, you eventually learned how to snap at it.

He would not disappoint this boy another time.

Ray's eyes strayed to the door once again, fingers fisting the bar rag. What he'd give to feel free enough to run out the door to chase that Cameo. He could imagine reaching out to touch her hair, running his hands over the smooth strands, continuing down her throat, thumb resting in the hollow between the veins and the dip of her collarbone. Citrus, honey and melted amber all mingled in his memory, squeezing his heart once again with thoughts of what he probably didn't deserve.

A second chance.

"Oh, God! How could I be so spineless!" Nora Murray leaned against the brick facade of Brody's Clubhouse and tried to catch her breath. Right now, she just wanted to fade into the wall, becoming hard and uncaring.

She'd come to Brody's Clubhouse to talk to the parent of Trent Brody, her seventh-grade English student at Jefferson

Junior High. She held up the paper in her hand. Trent's essay. The reason she hadn't slept last night.

But instead of presenting Ray Brody with the heartbreaking work of his son, she'd made herself look like a total idiot in front of Trent's father. Wide shoulders, a broad chest, muscled arms… All of him only served to intimidate her, to make her feel tiny in the shadow of his towering body, leaving her to stand before him like someone had twisted her tongue into a pretzel. Running out of the restaurant as he'd gone to help his waitress. No wonder her love life was nonexistent; Nora obviously had no idea how to talk to a man.

Everyone else on earth dated people. She dated papers.

No. She wouldn't be intimidated by one good-looking guy. Well, okay, so he actually qualified as "gorgeous." But, since it was all but impossible to get a hold of him by phone, Nora was here to confront him, to discuss Trent's boozing, thieving confession of an essay. The boy had described his activities in artistic detail, exhibiting talent that a boy his age had no right to possess. But his writing skills weren't the reason Nora slumped against the building.

What was she going to do about the drinking and stealing he'd written about?

Optimism. That was the key. She was going to march right back in there and act as if she'd been teaching for years—not just four months as a student teacher. She'd ignore the distracting shortness of breath, the way her gaze couldn't help straying to the crinkles around his eyes, the smooth muscles bunching from beneath his short-sleeved shirt.

Nora sighed. She was hopeless. The only thing giving her strength right now was the promise she'd made long ago when she'd sworn she'd never again allow a man to get the best of her. Not after the way her ex-fiancé, Jared Jacobs, had treated her.

It was just that she hadn't expected a parent to be so jaw-droppingly handsome. God, she hated to sound melodramatic, but there was no other way to describe how her heart had winged through the air when she'd first laid eyes on him.

The afternoon had started well enough. But when the waitress had pointed to a crowd by the bar, all Nora had seen was a bartender who looked like he was from Australia. Now, thinking he was Australian was a major compliment denoting a ruggedness, a tacit charm conveyed across the room. Aah, yes. Blondish hair with blond streaks, killer eyes…eyes like…like the way the water in Oahu looked on postcards.

This was Trent's parent? she'd thought. Weren't normal dads supposed to wear knit sweaters and loafers, smoking a pipe and nodding sagely while reclining on a front porch swing? At that point, she'd lost her cool. Didn't know what the heck to say. Ran right out of the bar.

No wonder she felt like roadkill on the freeway of love.

Love. The word sent shivers down her spine. That sort of thing just didn't happen to Nora Murray. Love happened to other people. She had never been so lucky.

Jared had told her he loved her before ridiculing her outfits or muttering snide remarks about her makeup to his friends. Her temper still heated when she thought of him degrading her opinions, chipping away at her self-esteem sting by sting. For a while, she'd been naive enough to think Jared was merely following the patterns of boyfriends worldwide. After all, her father had treated her mom the same way. Hurled insults, aching doubts, bruised egos. They'd all been commonplace to Nora until she realized that it couldn't be normal to feel so terrible about herself.

But now she had to fight someone else's battles. A young boy needed her voice, and she was ready to wage war for him.

Nora adjusted her glasses and tapped Trent's essay against the other palm, formulating a way to go back into that bar without seeming ridiculous.

As a student teacher, she knew it would be prudent to get ahold of her adviser at the university. Unfortunately, the woman must have been allergic to returning calls. Nora had tried talking with her mentor teacher at school, Mrs. McArthur, as well. She could have predicted the advice she'd received. ''Don't get too close to the students.'' But how could she all but ignore this? Trent Brody had chosen to tell her about his problems.

If only she felt more confident about herself. As it was, she still felt like a kid on the inside as well as the outside. At age twenty-seven, she was still carded at bars. Half the students stood a few inches taller than her own five-foot-two frame—mainly the girls in the seventh grade—and students would kiddingly use her head as an elbow rest. During a parent conference, a mother had smiled tolerantly and said, ''You look like you're in high school.''

Nora constantly reminded herself that she would die for these sorts of comments when she turned forty. But in her present student teaching situation, she wanted to be a woman of the world—not an ingenue. When Nora looked in the mirror she still saw a kid. A fresh-faced girl with knowing amber eyes.

After college, while she'd scraped together enough money to return for her teaching credential, she'd waited for the hand of time to lend her face wrinkles or signs of wisdom. But upon inspecting her apple-cheeked self on the first day of student teaching, she decided that she would make up in inner strength what she lacked in an intimidating demeanor. No matter what the students thought of her.

Optimism. Forget about your issues and just concentrate on what's best for Trent Brody.

She'd just go back inside to talk to Ray Brody about this. That's all there was to it.

She took another breath, put her palm over her heart to feel its bippity-bop beat. *Forget what he looks like. Forget how his voice smoothed over your body. Forget everything but Trent.*

Shutting her eyes, Nora pictured ugly things. Bowling shoes. Gray skies. Clowns. Yeah, clowns had always made her cringe.

With new determination, she turned to the Clubhouse's door. Pressed her hand to the flat golden metal doorplate. God, she was going to be face-to-face with an Adonis. Help.

Clowns. *Remember those clowns, Nora.*

Fine. She whooshed back into the Clubhouse, feeling the breeze stirred by ceiling fans. Head high, she walked toward the bar. Toward Mr. Ray Brody, father of the wayward, essay-writing Trent.

And here she was again, heart in throat, fist on bar. She needed something to grab on to, something to keep her from falling into his seascape eyes. My word, he was tall—well-muscled and lean. A veritable dream man straight from the pages of a sports magazine. She could feel her leg begin to quiver, the vibration traveling up to places she'd rather not dwell on at this moment.

He smiled, seeming surprised, shocking Nora. He couldn't actually be glad to see her. She had to be imagining things. Men like Ray Brody dated ex-cheerleaders and girls named Muffy. They didn't light up when wide-eyed moppets like her stumbled into the room.

"Hi, again," he said, bracing his hands on the bar, leaning closer.

Nora wore her best professional face: cool smile, serious gaze, lifted chin. She'd better not crumble right in front of him. "Hello. I'm sorry for the sudden exit." She thought quickly. "I forgot something in my car."

Her gaze flicked to the bunch of his arm muscles. Oh, my. Such good, strong arms with the barest dusting of golden hair along their length. *Focus,* she said to herself. *This is serious stuff.*

She thrust out her hand. "I'm Ms. Murray, Trent's English teacher."

It was as if a stiff-lipped spirit had entered Ray Brody's body, banning the carefree playboy to the back room of the bar. He straightened his posture and stuck his hand out to shake hers. "Oh, yeah. Nice to meet you, Ms. Murray."

She'd expected fireflies to zip from her hand to her shoulder when she made contact with his skin. But his touch was an entire power station. As his smooth hand slid into hers, she leaned into the bar, needing something to balance her. God, the touch of a man's hand. *This* man's hand. He withdrew it all too soon.

This was painful. She felt like a kid, one afraid of disapproval. And from the look on his face, he'd already formed an opinion of her. His sudden switch in attitude was baffling. "Likewise. First, I wanted to tell you that it's a pleasure to have Trent in my classroom."

"Really?" Ray Brody looked downward, avoiding her gaze. "You must not know the rest of his teachers."

She ignored his pessimistic tone. *Optimism.* "So far so good, in my case. But we seem to have hit a snag."

The bar patrons cheered at the ball game on the television overhead. She tried to stay on track, but his eyes had shifted away, as if he were disinterested in what she had to say. Nora felt taken aback, slightly offended by his lack of attention. Didn't he care a whit about his own son? Maybe this was the reason Trent ran around the streets like a wolf child.

Yet now it all made sense. Nora's teeth ground together. The father owned a bar, for heaven's sake. What a big surprise: Dad owns bar, son a drunkard. Cause, effect. Such a shining example of adulthood! And restaurants were demanding; he was probably never home to help with homework, counsel his son or pay attention to him. Maybe Ray Brody was even an alcoholic. What a shame. And he'd seemed so...different.

Mr. Brody might as well have been a vision with ratty gray hair, teeming beer mug in his right hand, belly hanging over his belt and a voice like a foghorn. Oh, this would be a priceless experience. He would probably end up yelling at her just like her dad would've done. Trent's delinquency was all her fault. Education had failed his kid. Trent was her problem from 7:30 a.m. to 2:30 p.m. weekdays. She could hear it all now.

Just as she reached the peak of frustration, he returned his attention to her. How kind of him.

Ray shoved his hands into his pockets. He shouldn't have been surprised to find that Ms. Murray—who'd so graciously ruined his romantic musings of the Cameo by revealing her true identity—was having problems with his son. She'd been the lone holdout in the Trent-is-incorrigible sweepstakes. He was even finding it hard to meet her gaze. The teacher-conference butterflies were swirling around his stomach.

Ever since he was young he'd been in awe of teachers, afraid of their ruler-wielding power and stern glares. His inner child hated the notion of talking with a teacher, even if she did look as gentle and lovely as Ms. Murray.

And now she was here to tell him what all her colleagues had been breaking down his doors to say: his son was a monster, a beastie from hell. Shape him up or ship him out.

Ray knew Trent wasn't perfect—he'd felt the lash of the boy's attitude a time or two himself—but something made him want to protect his son. Defend the family honor.

When he met Ms. Murray's eyes again, he felt a certain chill. The beautiful smile that had lit her face merely moments ago had frozen. Uh-oh. He'd probably already alienated her. Damn. He'd been ticking off teachers since he'd been running around in high-top sneakers.

It occurred to Ray that maybe he wasn't acting like a parent should. But just how was a parent supposed to react? He was so out of practice, he wasn't sure.

Maybe he'd flirted too much. But who could blame him? Ms. Murray probably had men wrapped around every finger. Just his luck. The only woman he'd been really attracted to in years, and she was his son's teacher. Wasn't that illegal or something?

Get a grip, Ray. He didn't need to play nice-nice with any woman right now. He needed every speck of time and energy available just to repair his relationship with his son.

She adjusted her glasses, voice professional and aloof, eyes sparking, sending intense prickles of heat along his skin. "There are some issues I need to discuss with you as far as Trent's lifestyle goes. I'm a little worried about him."

Laughing in a bid to be civil, Ray said, "I can raise my son well enough, Ms. Murray." It made him even more defensive to realize that maybe he couldn't raise Trent that well at all.

A polite laugh, reminding him of how much he wanted to be with her in a movie theater or a walk at sunset in a park. This conversation was the last thing he wanted to be doing with someone as beautiful as the Cameo…er…Ms. Murray.

"Yes, I'm sorry," she said. "That didn't come out the way I intended."

"What exactly did you intend?" He could feel his hackles rising, an instinctive reaction caused by years of wondering what he'd done to deserve losing his son.

She held up a piece of paper. The swishing fan blades whipped the page back and forth, a beating heart pulsing between them. "I think you need to read this, Mr. Brody."

His throat closed. What could Trent have written to bring a teacher down to Ray's bar on a weekend? It had to be something awful. Something he didn't know if he was ready to deal with as a father just yet.

He made no move to take it from her, didn't have the heart to. "Could you give me the *Reader's Digest* version?"

She held it closer to him. As he looked at the words, they seemed to blur together. All he wanted to do was caress her hand again, feel the current that had traveled between them when they'd touched before. He wanted her to be the Cameo, the woman who'd entered the bar as a regular person. Not the bearer of bad news.

He accepted the paper, avoiding her touch, smoothing the page on the bar.

Before he started to read, she spoke again. "I'm sorry about this. I wish it was better news."

He looked at her, the light brown eyes sincere. Caring. But what did she know about him and his son? How could she possibly give a damn? He could take care of things himself— he hoped—without the bleeding heart of another woman to make his life more complicated.

"I don't give a damn what you wish," he said, immediately

regretting the words. He'd responded on emotion, his frayed nerves getting the best of him.

Ms. Murray lifted her chin, and Ray had to respect her bravado. "Don't kill the messenger, Mr. Brody."

He steeled himself for more of a tongue-lashing, but she merely stared him down. God, he'd hate to be one of her students, on the receiving end of all those teacher looks on a daily basis. He already missed the sunny Ms. Murray of moments ago. "Trent's got it rough right now, and I know it's no excuse for his behavior, but…" He searched for words. "I'm not sure I need to justify his actions to you. Sometimes I feel like you teachers overstep your bounds. This is a family matter. Don't be offended if I tell you not to concern yourself with us again."

She took a step backward, her lips a straight line. "No offense taken." A jaw muscle flexed.

"If there is a problem, I'll have a talk with Trent tonight," he said, watching her blush as if he'd accused her of overreacting. Come to think of it, he probably had said this in so many words. "If it's all the same to you, call me if he disrupts class or causes some real trouble. As far as giving me parental advice, I can handle that."

"Well, Mr. Brody, I think this goes beyond disrupting class." She bit her lip, and his heart gave a tiny lurch at the sight of her little pink mouth twisting in worry. He imagined running his lips over that mouth, nibbling, sucking, tasting the citrus scent of her. Just as quickly, he returned to reality.

She said, "It's just that…he's an incredible writer. I've never seen any seventh grader with Trent's talent. But you need to see what it is he's writing."

Now he knew how his own parents had felt when the teachers would call home about his school antics: setting off cherry bombs in the bathroom, playing whip-the-towel in the locker room. With a jolt, he realized that if Ms. Murray had news of this type, he would discipline his own son a heck of a lot more than his parents had served consequences to him.

If his parents had ever concerned themselves with his youth-

ful behavior, maybe they would've grounded him. Taken away
his comic books or baseballs. Instead, they'd fretted about his
boy-loving sister, all their attention going to her teenage preg-
nancy and flights from home.

He grinned humorlessly. "You're worried about Trent's talent, Ms. Murray?" To his shock, he found that his voice held
a touch of amusement.

"Not exactly, Mr. Brody. If you'd just look at…"

Too late. He'd already started to read. And what he saw
almost knocked him to the ground in anguish.

Chapter Two

Ray was at his wits' end, but he knew his troubles were just beginning when he read Trent's essay.

Story of My Life by Trent Brody

Once, long ago, I had a mom and she told me
that it's just fine to have your fun when you're
a kid. She had her own brand of fun, hanging with
dark-eyed men, smoking cigarettes in alleys echoing
sin. On a night so cold and silent, a friend and
I slipped on our fingerless gloves and stocking
caps. You could hear taxi horns honking in
the city as we kicked empty bottles down trashy
streets. Boring. This was New York, we were
supposed to be mean as snakes here. That's when
we decided to have our fun. If we didn't get caught,
we could run around the city every night like a
pack of wolves. No one ever knew what we did.
Not until now…

Stunned, he continued reading the story, allowing the paper to float out of his fingers like a lost hope when he'd finished. The essay zigzagged on a breeze to Ray's feet as he fought back his rage.

Why? Why would Trent break into a house and steal stereo equipment…? Ray couldn't believe what he'd just read. He stared at the paper, pale as an old scar against the polished wooden floor of his restaurant.

He didn't want to hate Cheri, but he couldn't stop himself. What had she taught their child? And how was he going to deal with a son who thought burglary was nothing more serious than an essay topic?

He felt, more than saw, Ms. Murray shift on the other side of the bar. Swallowing down the bitter taste of shock, he turned back to her. "I can't say you didn't try to warn me."

"I'm sorry."

Sorry for what? Sorry that he was so inept in the face of this trouble? Sorry that the adolescent hell-raiser produced by an ill-advised "first love" had shown his true colors to the world? Ray was in no mood to accept sympathy.

"Again, Ms. Murray, I'll deal with it." He stepped away from the bar, hands clenched tightly. "Thanks for your concern."

Damn. He hadn't meant that last part to sound so facetious. She'd caught on to his tone, too, from the looks of it. Her eyes narrowed slightly, back stiff and more formal than necessary.

She opened her mouth, and he couldn't help watching the shape of her lips, the deep color, the softness. Out of the corner of his eye, as if summoned by bad timing, Ray saw the focus of all his worries stroll through the front door.

One would guess Trent Brody was an angel with his baby-blue eyes and blond hair. If only they knew…

Before Ray could stop himself, he uttered a curse, causing Ms. Murray to stare at him with those Bambi-brown eyes. He wasn't sure if she was reacting to his colorful language or the sight of Trent being trailed by a cop. Probably both disgusted her equally. Boy, he'd really put on a show today.

This is unbelievable, he thought, awkwardly trying to avoid the steady gaze of his next-door neighbor, Officer Ed Sanchez. At least his friend had been the one to catch Trent doing whatever the hell he'd been up to. Ed had been Ray's friend for years, having lived across the street. Every weekend they'd find themselves kicking back on Ray's porch steps, talking sports over a bottle of beer. But, with the entrance of Trent into his life, Ray had banned the alcohol from his property. Ed still hadn't forgiven him.

The cool blue decor of Brody's Clubhouse became a little steamier as Ray shook his head and glared at his son, clenching his jaw when Trent lifted his chin in challenge. What should he do now? Should he be Mr. Rogers or Darth Vader?

He grabbed an ale-damp bar rag and throttled it. What he'd give for an instruction manual right now. Something like *How to Raise a Preteen Rabble-Rouser.* Too bad Trent hadn't come with a copy.

His son sat down on the high bar stool to the right of Ms. Murray with a thump, pants riding low on his hips, red-and-white-striped boxers peeking out. The bill of his ever-present New York Giants cap shadowed a dispassionate gaze.

Ray looked to Officer Ed for an explanation, and Ms. Murray tilted her head, staring at Trent. His son met her questioning look with a saucy grin.

"Hey, Ms. Murray. How's it goin'?"

Cool, calm and collected. Or maybe Trent hadn't committed a major crime after all.

She motioned to his hat, gentle as a mother smoothing back the stray hair on a sick child's forehead. "I have no complaints. Well, except maybe one. Could I please see you without that hat covering your face?"

Oh, God, the hat. It was the bane of Ray's existence, the subject of many an argument. Ray thought it looked thuggish and disrespectful when worn indoors. Trent maintained it was "the style." His son wouldn't give it up without a fight.

Ray almost had to clamp shut his jaw to keep it from slapping the floor when Trent removed the hat without another word. Razor-sharp layers of blond hair stuck out until Trent smoothed the strands, eyes trained on the TV behind the bar.

Officer Ed stood just behind Trent, looming over the boy's shoulder like a bad omen. "Guess who I caught taking a can of spray paint to a wall near the school?"

Trent jerked his shoulders in a pre-macho shrug. "It's not like I killed someone, man. Just get off my case."

He'd have to keep his temper in check. Especially if his son wanted to test him with cavalier remarks. But how could he walk that tightrope between discipline and the desperate need to do anything in order to get his son to love him again?

Ms. Murray watched Trent, a thoughtful purse to her mouth. In spite of the way she'd come barging in here with her unwelcome idealism, he admired the way she interacted with Trent. She didn't yell or accuse. Patience seemed to guide her responses. Maybe he should take a cue from her.

With a slight shake of his head, Ray admitted his parenting finesse was a touch rusty after Trent's seven-year absence from his life. How would his son have turned out if Cheri had run off by herself, leaving Trent with him? The thought pierced his soul.

Maybe Trent would've gotten in trouble all the same, but Ray would've done his damnedest to prevent his son from catching the eye of the law.

The static-filled roar of Ed's walkie-talkie cut the air. The officer cleared his throat and lowered the volume. He looked imposing enough in his dark police uniform, but the effect seemed to escape Trent. "Show some respect for your dad."

Ms. Murray assessed Ed. Turned back to Trent. Waited.

Waited for what? Ray almost wished she'd jump in at any time, saving him the need to bring down the hammer of discipline on his son once again. It seemed like every other day, Trent did something to earn a grounding. If it wasn't coming home after curfew, it was refusing to do his math homework. The kid thrived on challenging every rule Ray set before him.

"I'll bet cops get a lot of sex, don't they, *Officer* Sanchez?" Trent grinned.

Ed wisely ignored his remark.

Ray roughly ran a hand through his hair and pointed a stern finger into the air in front of his son's nose, making use of all his six-foot frame. "As long as you live under my roof, you'll practice respect and manners. Got it?" He frowned, daring to add, "And pull up your pants. You look like a gangbanger."

Cheri's laughing at me through my son's eyes, Ray thought.

Trent wiped his nose, reminding Ray that this was only a kid. "When I lived in New York I could say anything I wanted. Besides, if cops get some all the time, I might wanna be one."

Ms. Murray's voice softly intervened. "Mr. Brody…"

He found himself leaning toward her, drawn, in spite of his promise to stay away. He noticed customers staring in their direction. Damn. He'd been so concerned with his son that he'd failed to notice that they were the main attraction.

She continued. "Maybe you'd like to go somewhere less public?"

"Right." Of course. Leave it to a teacher to have all the answers.

Ed rested a hand on Trent's shoulder, which promptly jerked from his touch. "You're lucky I drove near your school today. If another cop had caught you, you'd be filling out papers in juvie hall, not bragging to your buddies about how your pop knows Officer Sanchez."

The boy held out his hands, as if expecting cuffs. "Then turn me in."

Ray hadn't a clue how to proceed from here. "Don't test us, Trent," he said. There. Set limits.

"Do you have an office in here?" asked Ms. Murray, prim, unruffled, more than Ray could ever deserve in a woman.

"Yeah." He flagged down his head waitress to take his place at the bar and pointed toward the back of the Clubhouse. "Come on, Trent."

His son watched a short-skirted customer sashay past. Ray

could have sworn he saw Trent go google-eyed. Great. Now he'd have to deal with more hormones?

Ed half waved to Ray. "I leave this in your capable hands." As he walked away, he gave Ray a good-luck rise of the brows.

With a resigned sigh, Trent heaved himself off of the stool and walked ahead of Ray, past laughing patrons, past the roll and click of the pool tables. Halfway to the rear of the Clubhouse, Ray noticed Ms. Murray hadn't come with them.

He looked back at the bar, where she stood, hand on hip, watching them leave. Silhouetted against the frosted window. A cameo, ladylike, calm, and a much-needed presence. Ray nodded his head toward his office, hoping she understood the invitation to join their conversation.

She stepped forward, moved into a sliver of sunlight. A smile graced her face, but he wasn't sure why the hell she was so happy.

Ray took a deep breath, motioning Trent into the office, and held the door to allow Ms. Murray to join them.

The moment Nora entered Mr. Brody's office, she noticed the baseball mementos. Golden bats, mounted balls with their white leather gleaming alongside red stitches, an unassuming amateur's uniform shirt hanging on the paneled wall in back of his desk. They all languished in this rear office, relegated to obscurity among the scent of leather gloves and brandy-tinged cigar smoke.

Trent wheeled around in Mr. Brody's stuffed leather desk chair, attitude as carefree as early summer. Mr. Brody watched as she closed the door with a muted click, something deep and burning behind his gaze.

Maybe she wasn't so attracted to him now that he'd been rude to her. A man who'd take his frustrations out on a woman—even if he had apologized—wasn't worth it, thought Nora.

And maybe she was kidding herself. He was still the same Adonis as when she'd first entered the Clubhouse. He leaned a broad shoulder against the wall, muscles streamlined under his tanned skin as he crossed his arms over a wide chest. Too bad. His looks made her job so much harder.

An uplifting sense of belonging had swallowed her whole when Mr. Brody had motioned her to join them for a private discussion. She felt needed, but it was dangerous, she knew, to get too close to this father and son. Nora wasn't equipped to help anyone.

The faint mutter of conversation and TV cheers added to the tension in the room. A squeaking chair. Her own heartbeat pounding in her ears. Who would break the silence?

Mr. Brody walked over to Trent and grabbed the chair, halting its spinning motion, forcing his son to face him. "Do you want to explain why you felt the need to pretty up a wall?"

Trent rolled his eyes and groaned. "What's the big deal, anyway? I'm a first-timer. It's nothing to get weird about."

Nora watched the two of them, their body language so much the same, their tempers a match. She almost felt like an observer, one who was much too involved in the life of these strangers. She shouldn't have been there. She shouldn't have been getting this involved.

Yet here she was, once again, unable to resist a man who was all wrong for her. She'd known it with Jared. She knew it now.

Mr. Brody straightened again, crossing his arms over his broad chest. "You're in junior high now. That means it's time to act responsibly. And you have the chance to start over here in a new school, a new town. Don't blow it. Do we understand each other?"

Trent shrugged. "I guess."

"Good. No more tagging. Or anything worse."

"I was just being creative. Ms. Murray said that creativity is the closest we can get to feeling like a god."

"What the hell…what are you talking about?"

Nora wanted to find a nice dark spot in the room and hide. She cleared her throat and straightened her black skirt. "I encourage the students to exercise their creativity. But—" she lowered her brows at Trent "—I don't expect them to break the law while doing it."

"I'm still asking why you were spraying a wall," said Mr. Brody. He'd returned his attention to his son, thank goodness. Nora had almost felt guilty for a moment there.

"She likes us to take chances," Trent said, not looking at either of them. "Wants us to be artists. Showed us a video about kids who make graffiti into art. She wanted to *inspire* us."

With the way this kid twisted words, he'd make a fine law-yer someday. Nora could hardly believe how Trent was the one who'd been wearing a cop as a fashion accessory, and she was the one who was getting the third degree.

She addressed Mr. Brody. "Wasn't there an essay to talk about?"

He leaned his arm on the chair, presenting himself and his son as some sort of male united front. If it wasn't for the grim line of his mouth, she'd have been amused by the masculine preening.

"I'd sort of like to hear about this video," he said.

"What about it?" She'd defend her teaching ideas to the death. Just as she'd been ready to fight for Trent, the little turncoat.

Mr. Brody lifted up an arm in a half shrug, unsettling Nora with the gesture's indifferent sexiness. Arm muscles stretching with the slight move, shirt tightening across his chest. Her mind was definitely in the wrong place.

"First, I guess I'm flabbergasted that Trent's even remotely interested in something that has to do with school," he said.

The boy shot him a miffed look, but Mr. Brody ignored it. "I'm also surprised that a teacher could so liberally classify graffiti as art. Did you know some of the businesses in this area have problems with taggers? The owners spend hundreds of dollars in time and labor repainting their buildings and signs after an 'artist' takes a spray can to their property."

Nora could feel her temper rising. Her face had probably turned six shades of red in the last minute. She wouldn't be scolded by a man who couldn't even keep his son under control. "It was a video about kids beautifying their neighborhood. I made it clear that it wasn't being shown to encourage tagging and such. The message was positive—"

"It was cool," interjected Trent.

Mr. Brody pointed a finger near his son's face, silencing him. It was obvious Trent had respect for his dad. The shine of his eyes proved it. Trouble was, whenever Mr. Brody looked at him, the approval disappeared, as if Trent hated to admit his feelings.

Mr. Brody had to have a lot of courage to take over the raising of his son. When Nora told people what she did for a living—teaching junior high—they usually got a look on their faces reserved for news of a family member's death. Then they backed away a few steps before saying, "Really?" As if to deal with kids of this age, one needed to have the fortitude of a lion tamer.

Well, Ray Brody certainly had a strength about him. And no matter how rough-edged he'd been with her earlier, she couldn't help feeling an attraction for him.

He looked pointedly at Trent. "Good try, but you're not off the hook. Maybe your punishment should be painting buildings."

"Oh, man. I said I wouldn't do it again."

She put her hands on hips. "Excuse me. The essay?" She dragged out the last word as if it were a piece of gum stuck on the bottom of her shoe.

"Right." Mr. Brody moved across the room, each step thumping her heart a little louder, until he stood next to her. Arm to arm.

She barely came to below his shoulder, low enough to look up at him as if he stood on a soapbox.

Soap and man, mixed with the office's slightly brandied aroma. Her eyelashes swept over her gaze, allowing her a moment of enjoyment. Instinct encouraged her to grab his arm, lead it around her shoulders, so she could grab him by the waist. Bury her head against his chest. Rub against him like a kitten. But common sense told her it wasn't such a hot idea.

Fighting a tingle at his nearness, she tilted her head to see his face. Bay-water eyes met hers, wary and deep-running all at the same time.

"The essay?" she repeated.

His gaze cleared. "Uh, yeah. With all the excitement I left it in the bar."

Trent leaned forward in the chair, sunburn staining his cheeks. "So you brought my paper, Ms. Murray?"

The troublemaker was excited. Did he enjoy stirring up this sort of emergency? Maybe he was putting his father through every test he could imagine. Seventh graders excelled at that sort of thing.

"Yes, of course I did." She wasn't sure what to say beyond that.

"We're worried." Mr. Brody had taken the words right out of her mouth, thank goodness, since she hadn't been able to find them.

The use of the word *we* almost made her smile. She liked the thought of being a "we" with Ray Brody. "We" could fit them together nicely, body to body, pulse to pulse.

Trent sighed heavily and stood. "I'm not so bad anymore."

Mr. Brody spread out his hands. Nora noticed their corded strength, like bands of harnessed rage under the tanned skin. Those hands could float over her body and make her neck arch back in pleasure. Or they could roughly shake her shoulders out of these daydreams.

He said, "I'm not saying you're bad. I just want to know why you feel the need to drink and fly in the face of the law."

Trent shoved his ball cap over his head, cutting off all access to his eyes. Nora's heart sank, because she knew the conversation had run its course. The boy came out from behind the desk and walked toward the door, hesitating when he reached his father.

Mr. Brody clenched his hands, but he didn't reach out to

stop Trent. His son seemed to realize that his progress wouldn't be halted. He slammed the door on his way out.

"Where's he going?" asked Nora.

Mr. Brody shoved his hands in the pockets of his Docker-style pants, jaw tight. "This happens all the time. He flies out of the Clubhouse, waits outside until I come looking for him and, after we have more words, comes back inside to inhale a hamburger or two."

"Oh." So who controlled whom in this situation? Pointing out that Trent ruled Mr. Brody's life didn't seem prudent at the moment, not with the way his hands were fisting in a mock strangle. "Mr. Brody—"

"Why don't you call me Ray?"

Protectively, Nora crossed her arms. She didn't know if she could call him by his first name. It seemed too intimate. Then again, she could be making a big deal out of nothing.

Ignore his request. That's what she'd do for now. "It's probably a good idea to have Trent cool down, I suppose. He was in no mood to talk when he flew out of here."

"Yeah. That's exactly how his mother would've reacted." A shadow passed over his eyes, a dark cloud over the blue of an ocean.

Trent had written in his essay about his parents' divorce, and, from the looks of it, the process had been bitter for both son and father. Something perverse inside Nora wanted to hear more about Mr. Brody's...*Ray's* ex-wife. About their marriage and divorce. Then again, she really didn't want to know more about him at all. Too much information would only lead to her becoming more involved than she should be.

He'd calmed down, relaxed his balled fists. "This, too, shall pass. We usually have one monster argument per day, then a little bit of peace. I think we've reached our quota for the time being." Ray actually smiled.

Nora fought her answering grin, but her body won over her mind. Physically, she was screaming "Yes!" Mentally, she heard the broken-record skip of a memory. "You're worthless, worthless, worthless...." Those had been the words her dad screamed at her mom, then they'd become a mantra repeated after her breakup with Jared.

She couldn't give in to this man's charm. Obviously, he was all wrong for her—a messed-up home life, a hot-button temper. Yet she couldn't help drowning in his gaze, shivering as his shirt brushed her shoulder. Why was she always attracted to the wrong man? And when would the pattern stop?

Nora vanquished her smile by tightening her lips. "Well, Mr....Ray. I've done what I came here to do, I suppose. Not that I wanted to ruin your day."

"It wasn't entirely ruined."

His soft voice startled her. She almost didn't want to look at him to see if she was reading more into his statement than he intended.

But his gaze was locked onto her, troubled, with a touch of the old playboy she'd first met this afternoon. If she had any confidence in herself whatsoever, she would've languished under his interest. But why would a guy like Ray Brody be flirting with her? It was crazy.

She reached up to adjust her glasses. As he raised his hand to help, she darted backward. He jerked back his hand in response, clearly embarrassed, judging from the ruddy blush creeping up his neck.

"Sorry," he muttered.

"Not a problem," she said, much too quickly. "These things are always slipping down my nose. I need new ones."

Ray could've clobbered himself over the head. What the hell had he been doing just now? He'd been fantasizing about touching her, that's what. And when his hand had reached out to her of its own accord, she'd bolted backward like a frightened animal. What did he expect? They were practically strangers. He couldn't expect her to cuddle up to him.

Besides, he'd already thrown one woman's life into chaos. Why ruin another? Cheri had dedicated her life to making his miserable, and, in the process, Trent had been caught in the middle, mangled by their poor choices. Ms. Murray didn't need his deadly touch, and, certainly, Trent didn't need a re-peat of Ray's marital disaster.

Ms. Murray stared at him, head tilted to the side, consid-ering. God, he didn't need to be read. She wouldn't like what she saw, anyway. Maybe it was time to dismiss her from his life, his thoughts.

"I've got a restaurant to run," he said, abruptly stepping toward the door.

"Of course."

As he held open the door, she breezed by him, sending a whiff of citrus whirling through his senses. Again, without thinking, he placed his palm on her waist, guiding her out. And his hand *did* fit perfectly.

This time she didn't jump away. She stiffened, kindling a playful desire for him to tickle her or, better yet, run his fingers over her hip, belly, upward to the curve of her breast. Back in his college-athlete days, he would have done it, too.

He was still touching her, beginning to think a stolen caress wasn't such a bad idea, until she stopped walking, staring dag-gers at his hand. Slowly, she grabbed his index finger as if it was a used tissue, and removed the appendage.

He couldn't believe it. The gall. The queen of repression, with her fortresslike glasses, prim glances and stay-away at-titude. Thank God she was leaving. As she regally strolled out the front door, he told himself he was glad to see her go.

He leaned against his office door and ran a hand through his hair. If he was so glad to see her go, why was his libido screaming at her to come back?

Chapter Three

Nora hoped she wouldn't have to see Ray Brody ever again.

Amid blessed silence and the stale gym smell of a typical junior high classroom, Nora puttered around, setting up her lessons for the next day.

She rubbed her arms, recalling the way he'd watched her at the bar, almost devouring her with his gaze. *Intense,* that was the word. Although it had been a few days since she'd seen him, she still couldn't erase him from her mind. She kept remembering how he loomed over her, his water-tinted eyes churning, his jaw flexing…. Stop! She needed to forget about Ray Brody and his problems—if she could.

Now was the time of day she could let down her hair and relax. She grabbed a cherry sucker and rolled it around in her mouth as she unplaited her braid until it clouded around her shoulders in waves. Just as she finished gathering her canvas backpack and papers, a soft knock sounded on the door.

It was late afternoon, the campus wind blowing with silence, so who could be visiting? Cautiously, she cracked open the door.

He stood outside, shoulders filling the doorway, hands in pockets, watching her beneath rakishly raised brows. She blinked. The vision turned into a man who looked annoyed. Of course. Who but Ray Brody had cornered the market on crankiness?

She almost spit the candy into the air. Calmly, she reached up and removed it. "Hello, Mr. Brody." Her voice shook. She felt her knee "doing the chicken," as she and her roommate Josie called it. She felt so nervous that her leg wiggled back and forth of its own accord. She covered herself with the door, feeling vulnerable under his steady gaze. Shouldn't he be at home while she gathered her thoughts for the day? This assault didn't seem fair.

"Ms. Murray. Am I catching you at a bad time?" He seemed so damned collected, like a creature with ice water for blood.

A slow burn had started in her tummy and was languidly spreading outward, freezing her. It made her angry to know Ray Brody could have this sort of effect on her. "It's not a bad time at all. I always like to talk with parents."

His smile said that he knew she was lock-stock-and-barrel full of bluster. He lifted an eyebrow and raised his chin at the same time, in effect asking if he could enter.

Curiosity nagged her. Why was he here? Nora opened the door wide and had the sudden prickly feeling that she'd invited something exciting to cross her threshold. Exciting and maybe dangerous.

What if the world were different, and Ray Brody had come here to flirt with her? What if? She could imagine sidling up to him, running her nails over his flat stomach, his toned chest. Hey, if the bad girls did it, why couldn't she? She wondered what sort of response she would get. A sharp laugh, a shove, a curse? Or would his eyes glaze over, a prelude to him winding a tendril of her hair around his finger and leading her lips to his?

Nora's heart double-fluttered. Right. As if a man with his looks would glance twice at a prim schoolmarm like her.

Shaking any fanciful notions out of her head, she said, "I'm sorry—not altogether here at this time of the day, you know." She threw the sucker into the trash can and prayed that her mouth wasn't too red.

Her knee jerked. She sat in the nearest chair, crossing her can-can leg behind the demure one while adjusting her wire rims.

He sat near her. She closed her eyes a moment, catching the scent of soap and clean laundry. When she opened them again, she glanced sideways, hoping that her appraisal of him was subtle. Her breath caught as she perused his tanned skin and the way it brightened his tropical-water eyes, his sandy hair just brushing a slightly tattered and limp shirt collar. She wondered if he'd just yanked it out of the closet in a got-to-get-to-work hurry mode. Then she moved lower, to the space opened by the shirt buttons. A smattering of hair peeked out, light and sunny upon a broad chest. The chest led to his waist, nipped and firm, perhaps a product of the baseball objects she'd seen in his Clubhouse office. His leg muscles strained under khaki pants that were creaseless, but suitably casual—like a day on the golf course messing around, until the rich snobs waiting their turn behind you tapped shiny Rolexes and stiffened their squared jaws in irritation.

Nora blinked and pushed up her glasses. Long ago—an almost-forgotten lifetime ago—she had looked at golf courses from the Rolex side. A time when Jared had ridiculed her beginner's golf swing as easily as her own father had jeered at her mom's housekeeping skills. She contained a shiver and swallowed away the heavy lump in her throat.

"Ms. Murray, I came to apologize for the way I treated you in the Clubhouse. And I thought I'd talk to you about Trent. I know that you spend more time with him than Mrs. McArthur does, even though Trent says you're just a student teacher."

Her eyes widened. Startled by the comment, she could only

think to nod her head as if she had been complimented. *Just a student teacher!* She was so angry, she couldn't bring herself to ask why he'd come to her classroom. Maybe he planned to deride her in a typical male fashion. If so, he'd gotten a good start.

He continued, tone smooth and pleasant, much to Nora's surprise. He probably hadn't realized he'd offended her. "Trent admires you, talks about you all the time. I guess I was feeling a little envious."

Nora put a hand on her chest, taken aback by his candor. "I try to be a good influence on the students, Mr. Brody."

Sigh. If only this conversation concerned favorite books and foods—first-date chatter—instead of a subject so professional. Then she could just reach over and touch his hand, soft as a ladybug sweeping over a blade of grass.

Fate did play mean tricks.

His eyes strayed to the area of her hand and lingered. With thumb and forefinger, he scratched the slight blond stubble on his face and almost hid a grin. Clearing his throat, he straightened his mouth. "I thought maybe you could give me a hand."

Nora blushed, trying not to dwell on double entendres and the direction his gaze had taken. Yet she allowed her hand to linger over her chest, fingers brushing over cotton. It was wicked of her, that was the truth. But she enjoyed the way his eyes burned as he watched. Burning for her?

This man could be an even poorer error in judgment than Jared had been, she thought. *Just think of how his temper flares. Just think of all the problems that make his life stressful. You don't want to be with him, Nora. So don't waste your time dreaming about it.*

Ray shifted in his seat. "I should tell you more about Trent. His mom recently packed him off to live with me in San Diego—I haven't had any contact with him since he was five years old. See, my ex-wife took off with Trent years ago. I haven't had the chance to be a real father to him until now. I understand that it's been hard on him. You know, it's tough enough just to move to a new place.''

"He's fairly quiet. But he does his work," she said, following the advice of her textbooks, trying to stay positive.

Ray touched the back of her chair. The patch of skin nearest his hand tingled. "I'm sorry again. When you came into the Clubhouse I wasn't in the best of moods. It's been like that since Trent came." He laughed without much humor to back it up. "Not that I don't love him. I'm glad I finally have him home. The thing is, I don't really know what I mean anymore. Every word I say manages to be twisted around until it chokes me."

Walking this tightrope between teacher and human proved almost impossible for Nora. As teacher, her duty was to professionally steer clear of the emotional problems and refer them to a counselor; at least, that's what McArthur told her. As a human, she just wanted to brush his blondish hair back with her fingers. She wanted to massage his temples, near the crinkles of those vivid eyes. She wanted to make him happy.

And she wanted to reward him for his honesty in talking with her. Trust was a tenuous thing, as easily broken as the thread of a spiderweb. He cared about his son, wanted to mend their splintered relationship. Nora ached to help. But how? What in the world could she do to assuage Ray Brody's pain?

My word. Such explosive feelings. She had no right to them. Not after she'd had such a disastrous first relationship with Jared. Nora didn't trust herself enough to become involved with another man.

She wiggled her ankle, then stopped, thinking the movement too annoying. "I know how it feels to be confused about all this. Kids this age seem to scramble everything around them...almost like magnets when they get too close to videotapes."

He chuckled, and she relaxed. He was absolutely devastating to her good intentions when he smiled, showing white teeth against the gold of his skin. As she smoothed back a stray lock of her hair, she told herself to pull her guts together. She should act like a career woman. No more apologizing.

He still reached out and touched her arm. She froze, feeling caught between the bruising stirrings of memory and the fire-burn of desire. He let his hand drop and shrugged. "Thanks for being kind to Trent. I know you wouldn't have tried so hard to help him if you didn't care about your students. You'll be one hell of a teacher."

His blue-green eyes stroked over her legs. Without thinking, she crossed them, moved them slowly back and forth.

Relaxing back into his chair, he said, "I'm sorry my attitude chased you out of the Clubhouse so soon. The Padres played a great game, you know."

She wouldn't have stayed for the world. Not after she'd treated his hand on her waist like a creepy insect that needed removal. Abruptly, she cleared her throat and straightened her legs. "I had to be someplace, anyway."

"Away from me, I suppose." He grinned.

She surprised herself by lifting her hands in a flirty, dismissive gesture. She didn't know if she could handle anymore of this light talk. Ultimately, if she got her hopes up, she'd be disappointed. Probably he flirted this way with every woman who walked into his restaurant. Nora Murray was nothing special to him.

So don't even hope, she thought.

But what harm would a little coquetry do? She decided to test the waters. To drop the repressed scholar act.

"You know," she said, "when I met you in the Clubhouse, I imagined you as an irresponsible parent—a guy who owned a bar and threw back brewskis with his son in a sad attempt to bond." At his startled laugh, she smiled and shrugged. "No, no. I'm just trying to tell you that I know I was wrong. Your coming here today says a lot. You truly care about Trent."

"Thanks for noticing."

When they locked gazes, she could have sworn his eyes had gone soft and tender. The thought gave her stomach a carnival-ride turn.

He said, "When I first saw you at the Clubhouse, I had no idea…"

With a jolt, she realized that he perceived a different woman than she saw in the mirror each day.

In turn, that mirror image wagged its finger at her. *Don't get personally involved in their lives, Nora. Remember Jared. Remember your dad.*

Mentally, she erased the warning. "I'll do whatever I can to help." She leaned toward him, realizing too late that her lips were parted, eyes wide, skin giving off heat. Now she'd done it. Been way too obvious. He'd probably laugh now. Walk right out the door and tell the PTA about Ms. Murray's unprofessional conference demeanor.

Was she mistaken when she interpreted his gaze as "interested"?

Probably.

He looked at his watch, cursing under his breath, and stood. Nora followed suit, somewhat thankful for an interruption, and made a show of straightening her skirt, once again the professional.

"Okay, then. Thanks for listening," he said.

In what must have been a hot flash, Nora imagined throwing herself at his wide shoulders while he dragged her out the door. She would run her hands over the bulk of his back, down his hard stomach—

God, what a rich fantasy life she led. "Thank you for coming, Mr. Brody."

He grinned and put his hand on the doorknob. "It's Ray."

"Oh. All right. *Ray.*" She barely contained another smile, then regretted having done so. It had been a long time between spontaneous smiles for her.

But why couldn't she allow herself to have some fun? To feel worthy of a man's lingering gaze? Nora only wished she'd never followed in her mom's footsteps, letting a man demean her until she ached. She'd seen her father belittle her mom, and she'd thought it was natural. The way a male should treat a female in his innate caveman dominance.

But when she'd dated Jared, become *engaged* to Jared, she'd taken a good look at other couples. The men hadn't sat their women in a corner while they played poker until three in the morning. They hadn't cut off their girlfriends' speeches in the middle of a philosophical thought, sarcastically saying, "Have another drink, would you, Nora?" They hadn't deemed it their right to flirt with other women across a crowded party, only to curse their loved ones when confronted with evidence of their boorish behavior.

Yes, she'd thought she was close to worthless when she'd gone out with Jared. But the night he'd raised a hand to her, she'd thrown his ring in his face and left forever.

Her smile disappeared all too soon. There was something she still needed to give Ray. She wanted to slap her forehead. Focus. She'd never allow her "man here alone with me?" hormones to take control of her mind again.

He hesitated, locking gazes with her. What passed between them forced Nora to flinch. She put both hands behind her back, once again the career-minded teacher. His eyes dimmed, and he turned back to the door.

Nora couldn't contain herself any longer. "Wait! I can't just let you go without saying one more thing! I'm worried about your son. How often does he drink? And does he usually burglarize houses? He's young enough to be swayed from this kind of life—" she paused, feeling his first name raring to get past her lips "—Ray."

Ray stopped. Just halted. Froze. "When he came out here to California, I had no idea he'd have these sorts of problems."

She searched the desks and found Trent's latest essay. As she held up the paper, it looked as though an aftershock was shaking her hand. She handed him the essay. "Look at his latest masterpiece. He refuses to take any sort of responsibility for the things he does."

He gave her a suspicious gaze, then scanned his son's work. Nora paced, trying to seem busy, poking at books on her desk.

Ray seemed so engrossed with the essay that he didn't even look up. Finally, he turned the last page and met her eyes.

"I just can't believe he's acting out like this."

"Of course." She crossed her arms, ready for the anger. Why hadn't she broached this subject when he first stepped into the room?

"Please, Ms. Murray. I don't need you to Sally Sunshine me."

Heat danced on her cheeks, burning. She wasn't about to take the blame for someone else's sins.

Ray made as if he were about to throw the paper to the ground, arm muscles straining with obvious anger, but he pulled up and looked at the ceiling. Nora didn't dare say a word. In the little experience she had with men, she'd learned enough to fade into the background when a male was hurt.

In her mind's eye, seen through the fog of childhood, she could still see her mom flying across the room, crashing into the dining table chairs from the force of her father's fist.

Ray opened the door, stopped.

Forgetting her anger, Nora said, "I wish I could help." She'd give anything to make things better for Trent. And that was her problem. Even her roommate Josie accused her of being far too altruistic.

As he looked back over his shoulder, still white-knuckling the doorknob, Nora's heart melted for him.

He smiled, the corners of his mouth pulling down like a wilted dream. "I'd do anything in the world to help my boy. I just wish he'd give me the chance...." His voice choked off.

Then, as if he'd said too much, he thrust open the door. "Thanks for your time, Ms. Murray." And he was gone.

In the silence of her classroom, she whispered, "My name is Nora."

Chapter Four

The next night, in spite of the fact that it was only six-fifteen, Nora had already scrubbed off her makeup and slipped into a lacy, white linen nightie that was more *Little House on the Prairie* than Frederick's of Hollywood style. Nights were nice, allowing her to lounge in her apartment, a modest place, decorated with the heavy hand of college remnants and fairy dust left over from Nora and her roommate's young dreams. Degas prints lined the walls and oriental-flavored knickknacks rested in corners and on shelves. During their time as college roommates, she and Josie had collected the furniture piecemeal, during the days when they thought throwing dinner parties might be fun. Now there was no time, no inclination for Martha Stewart-style soirees.

Nora settled into the pillows of her secondhand couch, adjusted her glasses and picked out today's student work from a box teeming with paper. Right away, she sorted through the stack in search of Trent Brody's writing workshop response.

He'd been a model student this afternoon, leading her to

wonder if his father had read Trent the riot act. Ray Brody had sure been steamed enough to do something with Trent's attitude. Hopefully, the boy had turned a corner and would no longer act out. He'd even smiled at her today.

Okay, so it'd been a sly smile, and Nora had gone over to his desk to see what mischief was brewing this time. But he'd been diligently working away, baseball hat tucked in his backpack like a discarded habit. She'd smiled back and kept her eye on him for the remainder of class.

Now, if only her *other* problem could vanish so easily. That certain Ray Brody factor. She was finding it near impossible to erase his touch on her fingers. In fact, she'd found herself rubbing those fingers over her lips a time or two, immersed in a daydream in which she was pure, never knowing another man's touch. Never living with biting memories that kept her from loving anyone.

Nora stared at the papers in her hands, wondering exactly when she'd allowed her job to eclipse her soul. She'd avoided emotions for so long that it was hard to confront them. As a matter of fact, even if she hated to admit it, every time Ray Brody had reached out to touch her, she'd erected a barrier. Body language. Her job. It was all a front to stay out of love. Forever.

It hurt too much.

Her roommate, Josie, wandered into the room and grabbed the *TV Guide,* flipping her long blond hair over her shoulder. "Why the long face, Nor?"

Nora sat up on the couch, hoping her expression wouldn't further reveal her turmoil. Back to the grindstone. "My workload is awful, Josie. Just awful."

Her friend tossed the guide into a magazine rack. She was a study in efficient body language; the act of throwing the publication not only cleared Josie's hands, it indicated her level of disgust. Ever since Nora had known her—throughout college, throughout the disastrous dating scene afterward—Josie had been her cheerleader. Her rock. Too bad Josie could never replace the confidence she'd never really had. "You and teaching. It's turned you bipolar," she said.

"I won't *ever* lose control. Believe me." Nora punched a couch pillow and burrowed her head into its softness.

Josie patted her friend's head. "Why are you trying to save the world? Go hug a tree instead."

Nora sat up and ran a palm over her eyes. Saving the world was tiring. "You know I love what I do. And I'm so broke. I got my loan bill today…." She let the sentence fade, then brightened. "But yesterday some of the older teachers were telling me about golden handshakes."

Ah, yes, the good old golden handshake. If a teacher should choose to retire next year, they would get a nice severance package. What this meant was that there would be positions opening up at Jefferson Junior High. And Nora intended to pick up where the retiring teachers left off.

Nora felt happier already. She imagined decorating her own classroom with colorful posters and student work. It would be her second home. Jefferson Junior High. The name rang of permanence and contentment. Yes, if it made her feel better, if it protected her, she'd welcome workaholism in lieu of another broken heart.

In the meantime, maybe she could cut down to one meal per day to save money.

Josie bypassed all discussion about golden handshakes and lifted her finger like a flashing lightbulb idea. "Hey, now. Go to a pawn store and cash in on that vulgar grandma bracelet of yours."

Chin lowered, Nora shot her roommate her most lethal teacher stare. "Not on your life. You know Gran Murray gave that to me."

Gran Murray lived in the Midwest, a surrogate mother from afar. She'd found out too late about the abusive relationship between her mom and father, not until after Nora's mom had died from cancer. Nora's mom had kept secrets well.

The bracelet Josie referred to had been a fourteen-karat gift for Nora's engagement. It was also a symbol of what Nora would never have. Love.

"And where're you going to wear that statement of opulence? The opera? The next ball you attend?" Josie thumbed her nose, making her distaste clear.

Nora felt her eyes drift into a fog of dreaminess. Truthfully, she had fantasized about donning her grandmother's diamond bracelet to places as exciting as Monte Carlo or even a silk-swept white wedding.

As if reading Nora's mind, Josie broke in. "Just get rid of the thing. You could feed a small village with it."

"Oh, now the guilt trip."

A Cheshire cat grin stretched over Josie's mouth. "Listen to the voice of reason here. You already know that Prince Charming doesn't exist."

Nora blushed, thinking about how she had learned that lesson the hard way with Jared.

"You gleaned enough to know that any guy who dresses like a prince is hiding creep underwear."

Nora could feel herself blushing. "Maybe not all guys are bad."

"Oh, isn't this a switch? Who is it? Tell me all!"

What to do? To give voice to her fantasies would only make them more real. But Nora told Josie just about everything. But dare she tell her about a certain lean, tall man who, in spite of his stubborn streak, still managed to catch her fancy? "It's no big deal. Just some cute guy who owns Brody's Clubhouse Bar and Grill."

Josie sighed, green eyes shining. "A businessman. What's he like?"

Nora launched into a description, leaving herself breathless. It was almost embarrassing. "And his name's Ray Brody."

"So what are your plans? How're you going to capture this guy?"

Nora frowned. "Please. Like it's even a possibility, Josie. A man like him…"

"Yes?" Josie put her hands on her hips, daring Nora to denigrate herself.

"Nothing."

"Hmm." Josie checked her watch. "Well, Murray, my social life is calling. Don't work too hard, okay?"

"Sure." She'd only work hard enough to keep her mind off Ray Brody. Josie shut the door, making Nora aware of the lack of sound in their apartment. In her life.

Nora found herself alone once again.

Ray went to work behind the bar that night only to encounter the last thing he needed—an attractive blonde who was sizing him up and making him uncomfortable. As if he needed more woman-worries right now.

The five o'clock news blared over the TVs as he felt her stare. He was much too preoccupied with Trent's latest essay—and a pair of golden eyes that haunted his every thought—to care. He hoped he could go home early to talk to Trent since he hadn't seen his son since this morning, when, once again, he'd tried to talk to Trent about that essay. Rolling his eyes, his son had simply slammed down a glass of milk and, wordless, had sprinted out the door, dairy mustache and all.

Damn me, he thought, remembering how Ms. Murray had counseled Trent. Hell, she got along with his son better than he did. And it was no mystery why; Ray had figuratively tossed dirt and smeared it all over the Cameo yesterday. What luck with people he had. He felt like the Evel Knievel of relationships—so many broken bones after too many stunts.

Ray shook his head as he wondered whether Ms. Murray even remembered Evel Knievel. She seemed young, but she carried herself with an air of maturity when her sunshine smile wasn't peeking through her professional facade. It was too bad she was Trent's teacher and not a real person.

Real person? Ray thought to himself, She was real enough. Real enough to touch if he'd dared. She had lips soft enough to make the cherry-red sucker remnants look like a vamp's lipstick. Her eyes were so direct, yet so innocent. Her legs…well, when one of them wasn't trembling they were *gams,* not *legs.*

Ray hadn't realized he could still make a woman's legs shake. He'd only gone to her classroom to discuss Trent, to apologize for his attitude during their first encounter and perhaps revel in her nearness just a little longer. But she'd caught him off guard once again.

Actually, he admitted, his ego had taken him by the belt and led him to the classroom. And for that hour, his mind had whirled in a blur of citrus shampoo and silky stockings.

Out of the corner of his eye, he saw the blonde still assessing him. He pulled at his collar, peering around the Clubhouse, hoping another server could help her. But no luck.

He wandered over to her. "What would you like?"

She pursed her pink lips and inspected every inch of him. When Ms. Murray had looked at him in a way that made him heat up, he'd felt good. Confident. Right now, he merely felt like a side of beef.

The blonde finished her perusal. "I'd like a martini, please." As an afterthought, she added, "Shaken, not stirred."

Ray nodded and reached for a glass. No matter where he moved, *dodged,* her eyes followed him. Inventory eyes. Recording his actions, his clothes, every hair on his head.

She laughed, causing Ray to furrow his brow. Was his obvious discomfort amusing?

"I might as well introduce myself," she said. "I'm Josie. Josie Bailey. And I'd like to ask you a couple questions."

Ray only hoped the interrogation wouldn't strip him as bare as her gaze had done.

Nora wanted to throttle Josie.

The nerve. Her roommate had phoned, giggling. "Come pick me up, Nor. I've been drinking too many martinis. Oh, and by the way, I'm here talking with Ray Brody."

After getting over the shock and surprised anger, Nora had resisted playing chauffeur. Then she remembered that Josie had driven her car when she'd left the apartment. No drunk driving; it was a simple choice to pick up her roommate.

Now, as she stood outside the bar and grill, peering through the window, the Brody's Clubhouse frosted logo and blue curtains blocked most of her sight. She caught a glimpse of Josie in the corner, tapping her fingers against the table and checking her wristwatch. But she couldn't see Ray.

Of course, Josie wouldn't be outside. She'd force her to come in, to face Ray Brody. Well, Nora hadn't sprayed on perfume and applied red lipstick for nothing. If she saw him, fine. If not, better than fine.

Encouraged by Ray Brody's apparent absence, Nora decided to slip inside, grab Josie and make a run for her car. She tiptoed through the door under the cover of a rock and roll song, sneaked across the polished floor and seized Josie's arm.

But Nora had forgotten something. When God had built Josie, He'd added some features that didn't come with your standard human body. Not many humans had eyes in the back of their scalps.

Five feet away from victory, Josie turned around. "Nor!"

Nora hung her head in defeat. Maybe she could borrow Josie's extraordinary powers for moments when she had her back turned to write on the blackboard, and the students threw spitballs at one another.

"I'm going to jump-start your love life!" Josie said. "Get ready for the ride!"

"Let's go, Josie. *Now.*"

Her roommate didn't budge. "Listen, Nor. What a hunk! Here's the scoop. He's not married. His wife left him years ago. She disappeared with that student of yours. Trent. Yeah. Just up and vanished. What a harpy, huh? He dates and stuff so I figured—"

Nora tapped her fingers against the table. "Figured what? Besides, I knew all that, so you've wasted your time."

"Hardly. I told Ray Brody about this lovely girl I know who's single and searching and—"

Oh, no. What did Ray think? That she'd sent out a spy? She wanted to give Josie a good talking-to. "You didn't!"

"Yessiree, Bob. I did."

A throttling would be too kind for Josie. "You didn't say my name, did you?"

"Pshhh. Give me some credit. I'm wily. You're Nora. Just plain Nora."

She exhaled. Thank goodness. "Great, now I can escape undetected. Let's go."

Josie crossed her arms like a five-year-old, fake whistling since she couldn't whistle in the first place. Her eyes lit up when she saw something behind Nora.

Nora's heart hit the floor before Josie could even tell her what was lurking in the shadows.

"Ray!" Josie stood up. Like a ringmaster, she presented her friend with a sweep of her arm.

"Meet your Love Connection—Nora Murray."

Nora turned around and lowered her gaze, peering up through the dark hedges of her lashes at Ray, who was looking so smug with a smile and a casual stance. He seemed so cool, so calm, standing there, hovering over her until she wanted to shrink into the woodwork or stand toe-to-toe with him. Her lips curled up in one corner.

She'd let it be known she was not here by choice.

Ray was relieved to see the Cameo. Josie had been trying to set him up with her friend Nora. Ray had no idea she'd been talking about Ms. Murray. He was pleasantly surprised.

But, evidently, she wasn't so pleased. She was like a kitty, ready to bolt. Before now, he had only seen her in skirts, but he had to admit, she did wonders for a pair of jeans as well. None of *his* teachers had ever looked like this. The sight of her beat his heart so that it sounded like a drumroll, clenched his stomach with nerves and possibilities.

It didn't help that he'd just gotten off the phone to check up on Trent, who'd given him a hard time about having nothing but curdled milk, tuna, bread and cheese in the refrigerator.

After grudgingly agreeing to eat a tuna sandwich for dinner, his son had scooted off to watch his favorite TV program. Ray was content that Trent had actually come in before curfew tonight. Thus, his flippant mood.

Now Nora. She seemed nervous. Maybe he'd play a little, make her regret calling him "Mr. Brody" instead of "Ray." Taking his time, he walked over to her, extending his hand in greeting.

Nora hesitated, and he wondered if she was going to refuse his welcome. Maybe she felt offended by the gesture, taking it as sarcasm. After all, they'd already met a couple of times. Her eyes narrowed. She accepted his offer, softly laying her hand in his.

He absently stroked the valley between her thumb and index finger with his thumb, reveling in the soft texture of her skin. Feeling the heat pulse between them.

Teeth gritted, she pulled away her hand and brushed her jeans. He had ample opportunity to gaze upon the old jeans hugging her bottom—and what a bottom. He thought his hands would cup it nicely if he were to pull her in for a kiss.

His eyes traveled up, across her flat stomach, to the tight red sleeveless top that should've been on the blacklist of every teacher. She was as innocent and appealing as a fifties beauty decked out in cherry-lollipop lipstick. Yeah, that was right. Even in provocative clothes she was a kitten.

"So," Ray said. "I didn't think you'd be back so soon, Ms. Murray. Or, Nora. You do prefer Nora, don't you?" He grinned and put his hands in the pockets of his khakis.

I prefer Nora, he thought. Even if she doesn't prefer me.

"I would prefer to leave this place—" Nora crossed her arms "—Mr. Brody. I'm just here to pick up my drunken ward."

Out of the corner of his eye, he saw Josie settle back into the cushions of the booth. "Fasten your seat belts," she giggled. "It's going to be a bumpy night."

Chapter Five

After the trio took a seat in one of the Clubhouse's cozy upholstered booths, Ray sat near Nora, draping his arm across the seat by her shoulders. Something like an electric force field buzzed in the narrow space separating their skin.

At that moment, if a spaceship had landed in front of Nora, beamed her up and introduced her to aliens who promised her eight years full of probing and experimentation, she would've gladly accepted the offer if it meant escape. It was one of those moments when she literally wanted to shrivel up and die. Or better yet, she wanted Josie to shrivel up and die.

But Josie reclined across the table, apparently not as drunk as she pretended, not even slurring a word. When she caught Nora evaluating her, Josie merely winked. Meddling roommate. Nora didn't know whether to hug her for the matchmaking scheme or throw her furniture off their apartment balcony.

Nora subtly shifted in her seat, longing to leave the bar. Josie had forced a situation Nora didn't want to deal with, and now Ray must've known that Nora had talked about him to her roommate. Otherwise, Josie wouldn't have strolled into the Clubhouse to start shooting questions at him.

What could Nora do? Acting as if she wasn't interested in him wasn't an option—Josie had seen to that.

Nora chased back a frown. The choice was obvious. She had to leave before he could touch her as he had in her classroom. She'd cut off this relationship before it even started. That way her choice in men couldn't get her in trouble as it had with Jared.

Yet here she was, sitting next to Ray Brody, not moving an inch. She was about to do something ill-advised, like running her fingers along his clean-shaven jawline, or maybe even stroking a palm over his muscled chest. Softly, subtly hinting she wanted more than a parent-teacher relationship.

Ray said, "Your roommate is quite a matchmaker."

His voice sent her romantic thoughts fluttering to the corners of her mind—a hundred flapping, confused butterflies. She resisted looking at him, even though he sat mere inches from her side. He still had his toned arm hanging over the back of her seat, and she took great pains to lean forward so as not to make any body contact. Wisdom demanded she distance herself from temptation.

"She likes to think she excels in the art of connection," she said to the air in front of her.

He tapped the back of her seat, and she felt a tingle run up her spine. "All right, Nora. I'm going to lay it on the line."

She found his fingers cupping her chin, turning her head toward him. Her heart lurched, twirling just behind her eyes to blur her sight. His eyes flashed with amusement as she lightly pushed his hand away.

A muffled laugh, fading into the distance, signaled Josie's departure from the table. Nora was relieved. Now she could give Ray Brody a piece of her mind. She lowered her chin and looked sternly at Ray, trying to project a yes-what-is-it attitude.

As a heat-tinged bayou song lazed from the jukebox, Ray

sighed. "So things haven't ended up so well between us. I've insulted you. I've made you feel like you have no right to be interested in Trent when I should be thanking you for caring. I've accused you of encouraging crime in the hearts of America's youth. Am I leaving anything out?"

Not even your charm can win me over.

"I'm sorry," he said, then laughed softly. "Aren't we always apologizing to each other?"

She felt her forehead crease as she raised her eyebrows, sucked in her cheeks, tapped her foot. He was making it too easy for her to inch closer to him. No, no way. She couldn't be within a foot of him without her emotions going all goofy. "Now that we're practically spewing apologies, should I apologize for anything I've done?" There. Firmness, like a stop sign.

He looked away and smiled. "No."

The soft hairs on the back of her neck waved like grass in a breeze because she could still feel his arm behind her shoulders. Unthinkingly, she leaned back. As her bare shoulder touched his firm biceps, his sparse blond arm hairs brushed her skin. He felt warm. Warm enough to burrow into and forget about her worries. Warm enough to enfold her, sending heartbeats of comfort and tenderness into her body.

She stiffened and shifted her position so that she faced him. "I think we can work together if there's no animosity between us."

"You're not giving up yet?" asked Ray.

"Nothing scares me."

She felt him watching her and, for a brave moment, she turned her head to meet his gaze. Puzzlement and maybe even admiration mixed in his eyes. Her heart gave a confused hop.

What was this conversation with Ray amounting to? Were they being civil again? And how long could the peace last this time? She recalled the quicksilver change in his demeanor yesterday after he had Trent's confession in hand. From experience, she knew it was best to shy away from moods that could alter like a summer storm. Moods like Jared's, her father's. Her own.

But her body wouldn't obey her memories. Ray Brody's nearness felt too intoxicating. It was nice to feel his powerful body, the heat of his skin. She leaned into his arm once more, purposely this time. "I'm sorry for thinking that you would be a big, sloppy beer hound when I met you."

His arm snuggled closer. "I'm sorry for imagining that you were Polly Playground."

"You're really into this sunshine-and-playground-name thing, aren't you?" she asked, a grin on her face. Was this her, Nora Murray, making small talk?

"That talent is well developed when I'm around you."

"Yes, well, I inspire people in different ways." She kind of liked the feeling of flirting. If that's what this was. Maybe she could get really good at it, too.

His eyebrow cocked above the pool of his Hawaiian-water eyes, causing the veins in her throat to thrum. Obviously, his male radar detected the spark of flirtation. Fingers crept closer to her bare shoulder, hovering, the pads waiting to smooth over her tan.

"How do you find the time to lie in the sun, Nora?"

Oh, the sound of her first name coming from his mouth. Maybe this feeling was the reason cats couldn't help purring. As his thumb pressed into her shoulder blade, her head buzzed.

"How do you find time to come up with lines designed to distract my attention?"

For a minute, doubts ceased to loom over Nora's thoughts. They were two people, cozied next to each other in a sports grill, the strains of a rock song now encasing them in a different world.

She watched his mouth—the way his slight stubble surrounded it like short spurts of gold, the cupid bow of his top lip capping the fullness of the bottom. She wondered if his lips would heat her skin, or if they would leave her cold as a diamond ring.

Ray was grinning at her. "What's so funny?" she asked, her fantasy moment fading at his apparent amusement.

The tips of his fingers had joined his thumb in its play. Tingles from her shoulder traveled down her body like thick, warm fumes.

"Nothing's funny." His eyes grew serious for a splinter of a second, then warmed. "You make me smile. I haven't smiled in a while."

Me, neither, she thought. The last time she remembered really smiling was when she and her childhood friend, Tommy, had hidden in his tree house, scratching poetry into the wooden walls. How they'd laughed that summer when she was thirteen. Dandelion seeds floating through the air, making them sneeze and shiver. The adventurous "whoo" of a train as it chugged by their homes, clickity-clacking into places they could only long to visit. Beach-tanned legs pumping up and down as they rode their ten-speed bikes to the corner convenience store to freeze their brains by drinking cherry slushes too quickly. Yin and yang. That's what they'd been.

Until a drunk, one who kept the town gossips busy with his frequent benders, had run over Tommy. The criminal had left town, dismissed on some inexplicable technicality of justice.

Tommy's mother had wailed as they'd lowered her son's coffin into his grave. Nora's silent scream had lasted for years.

Why can't you just forget the past, Nora? Why can't you live here in the moment, with a man who's devoting all his attention to you?

She pushed her thoughts away, determined to ignore the empty feeling that threatened to engulf her.

Ray was still smiling, a little more softly now, as if he was aware of her pain. "I'll try not to tickle your funny bone quite so much." Gently, his fingers smoothed down the round of her shoulder to the indentation just below, and she caught her breath.

The drunk hadn't even given Tommy time to say goodbye to her or his family. She hated the man for killing her happiness, her cricket-hum summer nights with a good friend. She hated the dark, empty spot he'd left in her life.

Abruptly, Nora leaned forward and set her elbows on the table. Ray seemed distant due to this sudden freeze. Much to her dismay, he put his arm on the back of his own seat.

Civility replaced the touching, the tentative smiles. "Well. This is a very nice business you have here." Nora peered around the bar, noting the cherry wood, brass and vintage decorations.

Ray's voice was formal. "I bought the place after the original owner decided to take up deep-sea fishing."

"Oh?" Despite her skittish reaction, she really wanted his fingers back on her skin.

"Yeah. But I had a hand in building it. Right from the ground up. In fact—" he gestured toward the bar "—my main duty was to build that bar over there."

"It looks wonderful." She smiled wanly, estimating just how long she could continue this inane conversation. "It just gleams in the light."

"Yeah."

There was a thick pause while she wondered if they were on a first- or last-name basis right now. Nora or Ms. Murray? She wanted to hear him say her first name again.

The slight ice on their discussion remained. She decided to broach the subject of Trent once again. It finally seemed an appropriate matter since her moment of lighthearted flirting had long since passed. Besides, an idea was forming in her mind.

"Here's the thing." Nora turned to Ray once again. As she struggled to make eye contact, she felt herself warming around the area of her stomach. "I think we can straighten Trent out before he's swallowed by crime."

As if adjusting to the shift of subject, Ray tilted his body away from her ever so slightly. "How do you suggest we do that?"

"Hmm." What could she say? She had no children herself, and, surely, her parents hadn't been wonderful role models.

Maybe she could learn from them how *not* to raise a child. But how would she have liked to have been raised?

Picnics at the ballpark playing baseball, family vacations to amusement parks and natural wonders, steak dinners around the kitchen table, the smell of freshly cut grass while strolling with her mother during the late hours of a summer night. It sounded like a dream. She grinned, wondering if she could convert her fantasies into Trent's reality. "He needs someone to spend time with him. Help him with homework. Go to the beach. Eat a home-cooked dinner with him." Ray almost interrupted, but she stopped him. "I know. You've got a restaurant to run. We can settle your priorities another time."

"Are you preaching to me?"

Nora groaned. Another shattered truce. "Not at all. Do you want my help or not?"

He tightened his lips and watched her mouth. "Yes, I do."

"Good. Because if you blow it with me, you won't get another shot." She changed her tack and looked at him from beneath her lashes. "Let's try this again. What if I spent some time with him? I'm not talking about baby-sitting, but maybe a tutoring session that turns into a movie or a meal?"

"You're volunteering to take a lot on, Ms. Murray."

Yes, she was digging herself in deeper and deeper. How would she make time for this? But it was too late; she had made the offer. It would be like being a Big Sister, like volunteer work. She could always make time for a good cause.

Especially for Trent…and his father, a voice said in her head.

"What kind of person would I be if I stood by and watched a kid ruin his life? Now, if I'm making a sacrifice, you'll need to make one as well. Why don't you consider hiring someone to take over a few of your hours here at the Clubhouse?" She watched him expectantly.

Ray squeezed his eyes shut as if he were in pain. He opened them, and they seemed as clear as mountain water. "How many hours?"

She leaned on her chin and tapped her finger on the table.

His stubbornness could've been charming if it wasn't so irritating.

"Okay. Yes, I can do that. I would *love* to do that."

"Great!" What had she just done?

Well, genius, said the voice of reason. *With one fell swoop you've cut out all your free time and inserted yourself into an alliance with a man you should steer clear of. Good work and good luck.*

Nora grinned, proud of herself in spite of the doubts. She imagined the successes Trent would achieve, the places he'd go. She stuck out her hand. "Shake on it? Or should I get a knife to cut open our hands for a blood oath?"

"No more *Tom Sawyer* for you, young lady," Ray chuckled. He accepted her gesture. "Project Trent, under way."

Her hand felt so natural in his larger, slightly callused one. It felt so warm, so secure.

"Nora?" Ray said softly.

They still held hands. In fact, she wouldn't have minded if he never let go. Right now she didn't care if her eyes were glazed over like an idiot's. The feel of him was so comforting.

"Ready?" asked Josie, who'd obviously sensed the high point of her and Ray's conversation and was attempting to rescue Nora from anticlimatic disappointment.

She stood reluctantly. "We start Project Trent tomorrow." Nora could've sat and stared at him for hours longer, but maybe Josie was saving her from looking like a complete lust-struck dullard. "I'll do homework with him after school tomorrow, so don't panic when he's late arriving home."

Ray just nodded, his smile almost hidden by the hand that covered his mouth. Nora hoped she was the reason behind his grin.

As they left the bar, Nora slapped a hand to her forehead. What had she gotten herself into?

Josie marched over to the passenger door and waited for Nora to unlock it. "He likes you."

Nora shrugged. "Nah. We were just talking shop."

They climbed into the car, and as the engine sputtered to

life, Nora caught Josie grinning at her. She lightly pushed her roommate's arm and drove out of the misted parking lot.

When Nora looked at her friend once again, Josie had already shouldered into the worn leather seat and shut her eyes. Always one to have the last word, Nora heard a muffled "Shop shmop" before Josie's breathing evened out.

She allowed a slight bit of happiness to settle over her. It was a welcome change. She enjoyed contributing to someone's life in a positive way.

She couldn't stop smiling. Tomorrow would be a brand-new day.

On the way home, as Ray turned his Range Rover around the corner and onto his street, he tried his best to remind himself that Nora—God, how he loved that pure, simple name—was only volunteering to be Trent's tutor. Not Ray's fantasy girl come to life.

Actually, having Nora involved with Trent on more than a school-day basis was a dream come true. Maybe his son's bad behavior would dissipate under his teacher's kind words and nurturing. Maybe she could be the mother figure Trent had never had.

Ray shook himself. He hadn't meant "mother" in the sense that Nora would be his *wife,* for Pete's sake. He'd only meant that Nora would provide Trent with some guidance and stability, a gentle mentoring hand to help him through rough times. Ray couldn't stomach the thought of disappointing Nora in an actual relationship as he had disappointed Cheri.

His gaze blurred. The feel of Nora's sun-warmed shoulder. The faint perfume of her hair. He felt like a teenager, standing at his locker to moon over the pinups taped inside.

But the pinups now looked like a Victorian cameo. Somehow, the dopey, short-breathed feeling of adulation felt right.

Cool off, Ray. Just take a cold shower.

When he arrived home he locked the car and creaked open his front door. Silent and dark. No TV. No radio. No Trent.

Just as he almost cursed, he saw that the door to his son's

room was shut. Could it be that the boy had already turned in? No, Ray thought. That was too good to be true.

But there he was, his son, cuddled up in his covers, the open window blowing a cool coastal breeze through a room bereft of decoration. White walls shone in the moon glow, so stark that Ray felt empty inside. He would really have to get Trent some posters to make him feel at home. They could go shopping. Actually, maybe he could leave that to Nora.

He smiled as he thought about Nora's proposition. What a woman. She already had faint red rings around her eyes from lack of sleep, yet she'd volunteered to keep Trent on the straight and narrow. How could she care so much about a kid who wasn't even hers?

Ah, he reminded himself. In a sense, Trent *was* hers. It must be hard being a teacher, letting those kids go year after year, never really knowing how they turned out, if you had any effect on them. And he had no doubt that Nora would affect many kids in her lifetime.

But first things first. Ray walked over to Trent's side, noting how innocent the twelve-year-old looked when he slept. A little blond angel. He laughed and thought that all parents must call their slumbering children "angels." It was a different story when they awakened.

He reached out and gingerly touched Trent's head, his throat going dry. Aside from an awkward hug the two had exchanged when the boy had arrived at the airport, Ray had never really touched Trent. Now it was beginning to feel natural to lay a hand on his shoulder. To feel only slightly rebuffed when his son flinched.

He thought back to their first meeting: Trent stumbling out of the plane tunnel with his carry-on luggage, that tentative hug, the silence of not knowing what to say after seven long years apart.

On the ride home, Ray had started to apologize, to explain Cheri's abandonment and the broken marriage. But his voice had died after Trent emphatically turned away to look out the car window.

Sure, Ray had eventually explained the separation over TV dinners and in between spats, but judging from Trent's glacial eyes, the frigid stares, Ray didn't know if he truly understood.

So many years wasted. *Why, Cheri? Why did you have to run off? Were you merely being cruel to me? Well, guess what,* he fumed. *Guess who you hurt most of all?* He had "tomcatted" around for seven years, a bachelor with an unspoken past. Life could have been worse for him. But Trent had probably had a series of "uncles," men who watched him with derision in their eyes. *Who did you hurt, Cheri?*

Ray shut the window quietly and looked back at his son. *No more disappointments, kid.*

Tomorrow he would ask Joan, the waitress, if she would accept the job of Clubhouse manager. It would all but kill him to give someone else control of his very own Clubhouse, but he knew it was time to put the bar down a notch on his list of priorities.

There you go, Ms. Murray, he thought.

Full-time father at your service.

He gently ran his index finger down his son's cheek, wishing he could get away with this sort of uninhibited emotion when Trent was awake. If only his son could realize how Ray spent sleepless nights worrying about him.

Tomorrow would be a good day to finally discuss that essay, first thing in the morning before Trent escaped out the door. But would his son retreat even further into his shell if confronted yet again?

Ray feared the very thought of Trent's withdrawal, but he had to take the chance, lay down the law. He had a theory that his son needed structure, *wanted* structure.

And how would Trent react to Nora's tutoring plan? Would he run away, hurl hateful words at him, tear down his room in a rage? Ray and Nora had to give her plan a try, or else Trent might one day find himself in serious trouble.

Ray shoved his hands in his pockets, backing away from the bed, scared to death that tomorrow would bring more pain to their already awkward lives.

He wished Nora the best of luck.

Chapter Six

The afternoon sun spit heat off Ray's driveway as he toiled in his workshoplike garage. A rack of tools perched over an unpainted wooden table, upon which a basketball backboard reclined. He was so immersed in his task—and daydreams of a certain honey-haired teacher—that he failed to notice that he'd aimed the hammer straight for his thumb.

"Damn it to hell!"

Ray threw the tool away as his digit throbbed in pain. He just couldn't concentrate on his carpentry, not with Joan ruling the Clubhouse and Nora running around town with Trent in tow.

Nora had called right after school let out, informing Ray that she'd talked with Trent. And he was actually agreeable to studying together. After Ray had overcome his surprise, Nora had further related that they would be going to the library.

Never in his life would Ray have predicted that Trent would step foot into a quiet place filled ceiling to floor with books.

Nora must've been pretty persuasive to accomplish such a feat. He was impressed as hell.

Altogether, Nora seemed to be having better luck with his son than he had. Ray's planned essay talk of this morning had fizzled when Trent had scooted out of the house at an ungodly hour. The little munchkin had probably guessed Ray's intention to attempt another serious conversation with him.

With Nora's success, Ray should've been dancing in the streets. Yet instead, he'd managed to nearly pound off a thumb. Noting how red it still was, he shook it out, cursing under his breath.

It was 6:30 p.m., and he hadn't seen hide nor hair of either of them. To make matters more stressful, Joan had accepted the manager's position today, and the Clubhouse was her own. He shouldn't have been nervous; after all, Joan was the one who ran the place when he was sick or took a rare day off.

Ray cradled his pulsing thumb, which now seemed to thump in his head. Images of pink gingham froufrou curtains framing the Brody's Clubhouse window logo made his spine shudder. Sappy top-forty music on the jukebox, drinks with tiny umbrellas, a Chippendales calendar hanging on his office wall…

Maybe he would just call Joan one more time.

A cherry-red car pulled up in the driveway. He stepped out of the garage, rotating the wounded thumb as Trent hopped out of the car.

"Hey!" his son yelled, bouncing up to Ray.

Taken aback, Ray could only look at Nora wonderingly.

She sauntered over to him, a smug grin on her face. The setting sun burnished her hair to a dark honey ale, and although it was tied back, he again had the urge to wrap a strand around his finger.

"So, Trent tells me that tonight he had the first square meal he's had in…how long?"

"Since I was a sparkle in my dad's eye."

Ray winced. "Where did you hear that?" He peered at Nora.

"Don't look at me." She spread her hands.

Trent swung his backpack low to the ground as he laughed. Ray's heart almost burst with happiness. The smell of barbecue wafted over the cooling air, and the sound of a lawn mower made it seem as if they had a normal suburban life.

Trent said, "Cheri used to say stuff like that. And that's tame. You should have heard some of the jokes—"

"Maybe in a couple of years, son," Ray said. Not even the mention of his ex-wife's name could put a damper on his spirits at the moment. Also, the fact that Trent called Cheri by her first name didn't faze him; the first time he had heard her name come out of his son's mouth Ray had almost jumped out of his skin.

"I should probably get going." Nora turned to Trent. "See you next time."

"Right, Ms. Murray. Thanks for everything."

Ray put a hand on Trent's shoulder. The boy started slightly, as if he had never been touched before. Ray lightened his hold, but kept contact. He wouldn't allow his son to know how much it hurt whenever he tried to draw away. What he'd give to keep the smile on his face.

"Son, why don't you run inside. I bought you something today. It's on your bed."

Trent's blue eyes lit up as he smiled. He waved to Nora and sprinted inside the house.

"What is it?" she asked.

"Just a basketball. I've been trying to work on the backboard, but…" He held out a hand, his thumb an angry red.

"Oh," Nora breathed. He thought he saw concern behind the glasses, in those amber eyes, as she reached out to touch his hand. He clenched his other hand. Just as their skin made contact, she jerked her hand away and used it to smooth down her skirt. She cleared her throat. "Maybe you should put some ice on that."

So close, yet so far away. When it came to touching, she was as tentative as his son. "It won't kill me."

They faced each other awkwardly. Nora's cheeks pinked as

she bit her lip. Ray had to stifle the urge to reach out, to feel that burning skin, soft as a peach.

She must have seen something in his eyes, because she stepped back and put a hand to her throat. "Just so you know, it turned out very well today. We ate dinner, as he said. But before that, we went to the library. It's pretty small, but I wanted him to know it was there." She smiled. "Just in case."

"Maybe he'll manage to find his way there again. Someday."

Her eyes brightened even more, and Ray's breath caught in his chest. God, she was beautiful. And he couldn't have her. Not if he respected Nora Murray. Her life seemed to be going just fine without him stepping in to ruin it.

Again, he remembered his own female teachers. Especially Mrs. Carrigan with her soft blue sweaters and tiny bird-ankles. In fifth grade he had told himself that someday he would marry a girl just like his gentle-smiling teacher.

Those dreams had barely gained speed before his dad bothered to look up from the morning paper, laughed and told Ray that he would never be good enough for a lady like Mrs. Carrigan. But Nora seemed different, almost accessible now. After all, he was no longer a spike-haired, mischief-in-the-eyes kid.

And she was close enough to touch. If she'd just let him.

Nora cleared her throat, and Ray wiped the grin from his face.

"So are you saying that maybe there's hope for Trent?" He held his breath, hoping for the best, knowing in his heart that it was possible. How many daggered looks could Trent throw at him before he realized that Ray cared too much to merely ignore them? They could be a family, a unit. Something Ray had been longing for all his life.

He remembered when Cheri had become pregnant, the feel of the baby—Trent—kicking in her belly. Ray's hand had absorbed every shot with wonder at the life he and his wife had created. When Ray had been young, he'd never felt a part of his family. Emotionally, his parents had paid more attention to his top-of-her-class sister, who'd returned the favor by getting pregnant at the age of sixteen. After she'd left home, the Brodys had wandered around their house like zombies: eating, sleeping, existing.

But not Ray. Ray had wanted to be a baseball star. He'd spend hours at the local baseball field, after the sun had set, shagging batted balls and lying on his back, elbows beneath his head counting the stars. He didn't need a family. He had baseball.

All that had changed when he went to college. He saw moms and dads, brothers and sisters visiting his teammates at the dorms, attending their games. When Ray invited his parents, there was always an excuse not to come.

That's when he'd met Cheri, who promised to not only *be* his family, but to give him one as well. He'd lived in this fantasy for a while, but, after Trent was born, their marriage had crumbled, shattering Ray's dreams.

From that point on, he'd armored his heart, making sure no chinks were visible. He'd never be open to hurt again. Vulnerable. Idiotic. He'd always protect himself, and his son, from another Cheri.

As Ray watched Nora talk, he steeled himself, appreciating her good intentions, yet unwilling to allow himself to expect more than this parent-teacher relationship.

"I think with some TLC we've got a good shot at turning Trent around." She raised her eyebrows, grinned and headed to her car. Ray walked beside her, thinking about how beautiful she looked when she smiled. And thinking about the man who would be lucky enough to come home to her every night, a man who couldn't possibly carry the baggage Ray Brody did.

"Can I reimburse you for the supper?" he asked.

She seemed to consider the offer, then blushed. "Oh, no. Don't worry about it. It was a cheap meal." A worried little wrinkle perched between her brows.

He bent closer to her. "I guess I owe you a dinner, then."

Eyes downcast, she said, "No problem, Mr. Brody. Really."

His hormones wanted to ask her if she could stay for a while—stay for the whole night. But he knew it wasn't possible. You just didn't make advances to your son's teacher and expect to maintain a professional working relationship. Or could you?

Forget it, he thought. Making love with her would only allow her access to his soul. He couldn't let that happen.

"Are you sure you don't want to stay to…shoot some hoops?"

She said, "It sounds like fun, but I have to be going."

"Are you sure about that?" The words had escaped him before he even realized he'd spoken.

She spread her hands helplessly, taking a step forward while doing so. "Do you accept rain checks?"

Anything from her. He grinned. "I suppose, if you're that adamant about leaving."

She hadn't retreated. In fact, she was so close now that he could see the lighter slivers of sunny-gold highlighting her eyes, the slight indentation above her lip, an eyelash that had fallen on the curve of her cheek. He reached out to brush it off, but stopped himself, remembering how she'd reacted when he'd tried to catch her glasses during their first meeting in the Clubhouse.

Her gaze lit on his hand, which was, by now, poised near her waist. Slowly, she scanned up his arm, his chest, her scrutiny like a trail of hot flame cooling to ash. Finally, she met his eyes, her cheeks flushed.

If he hadn't thought she was interested before, he knew so now. Unfortunately, the closer she came, the more he needed to withdraw. Past experience had made wariness a necessity.

But nobody had informed his body of the hard rules Ray needed to enforce for his own peace of mind. For Trent's emotional safety.

As Nora shyly lowered her chin and sucked her bottom lip, biting it, Ray felt himself tucking his misgivings into a dusty corner of his mind.

He extended his hand to her hair, relieved and elated when

she stayed motionless under his touch. Smooth, soft as the look she was giving him. He wasn't terribly surprised that her locks had the consistency of silk, as well as the subtly sweet smell that was a combination of orange, peach and something indefinable—something that urged him to slide his other hand to her cheek to thumb away the stray eyelash.

She closed her eyes, lids fluttering as he slid a finger under the frame of her glasses to graze her temple. Her skin felt heated, like peaches warming under the sun. Touching Nora was like getting a taste of wasted youth—what could've been if he hadn't made so many mistakes.

What would it mean if he kissed Nora? Ray had the feeling that she wasn't a woman to take such a thing lightly.

He leaned over, willing to see if kissing her would mean the end of the world as he knew it.

She wrenched away from him, the sudden movement leaving scarlet finger streaks on her face. The marks burned white as she reddened further. God, he hoped he hadn't accidentally hurt her, left a mark. He'd hate himself.

"I've got to grade papers, Mr. Brody." She pushed up her glasses.

Damn those things. He wanted to slide them off her face, to talk to her without the display-case essence between them. But how could he blame her for pulling away? What would an upstanding teacher want to do with an inept parent like him? Deep inside, she was probably laughing at his inappropriate advances.

He stood up, hands stuffed in pants pockets. "Are you okay, Ms. Murray?" he managed to ask, nodding toward the fading finger marks. Fool. Idiot.

A wan smile answered him. "Yes." She laid a hand on her face. It slid, almost memorizing the streaks. She straightened her posture, a whole new Nora. The one he'd met in the Clubhouse. "Back home for me. No rest for the wicked, I'm afraid."

Still, she hadn't moved. Did she want to prolong his discomfort for as long as humanly possible?

"Bye, Ray."

She'd whispered the farewell, so quiet he'd barely heard her. He turned away first, and went inside the house. He couldn't watch her walk away.

When Nora whooshed into her apartment, she leaned against the door, out of breath. She'd run all the way up the stairs, just steps ahead of her regret.

What had she been thinking, almost allowing Ray to kiss her? My God, she'd probably been making cow eyes at him. The thought of her behavior at his home gave her a stomach-ache.

How would she face him again? How could she keep her mind on Trent's problems when a dozen of her own resurfaced every time she got near Ray Brody?

Nora didn't want to think about the ramifications of having a physical relationship with him. Things would definitely end for the worse, as they had before. Life was just that way—she latched onto the wrong men. Nora didn't want to add Ray to her list of bad decisions.

She peered around the living room, hoping Josie wasn't hiding in some corner, waiting to ask a million questions about her day with Trent. *Think. Just think about the trouble you could get yourself into with this man, Nora.* But maybe her problem was that she thought too much.

No, looking before leaping was a better option than finding your heart left crushed in your hand. She'd take thinking over hurting any day of the week.

That settled, Nora tiptoed to her bedroom and quietly shut her door to the world.

Chapter Seven

Ray couldn't believe he was doing this.

Yet here he was, arms loaded with bags of Chinese food, moving through a slight wind to join his son and Nora at an after-school study session at the beach.

The smell of sand and salt mingled with the aroma of vegetable lo mein, egg rolls, fried shrimp and beef broccoli, driving Ray to the brink of animal hunger. He'd been fighting the urge to devour the food ever since he'd picked it up after leaving the Clubhouse.

He'd been surprised yet pleased to hear Trent's voice on the phone, asking him to come to the beach to eat dinner and watch the boy surf. Oh, yeah, Ray thought, and he did mention an extra guest who'd be present.

Evidently, Nora and Trent had decided to forgo the library and the classroom to work on his son's social studies project. He wondered if Nora knew he'd be here. Probably not, he thought. Trent was full of surprises, things like writing wicked essays and an unwelcome talent for tagging walls.

He spied his son and teacher reclining on the shore. Instinctively, his gaze sought Nora. At this distance, she was an enticing honey-and-coral blur against the wavering heat rising from the sand.

Trent stood up abruptly and smiled, flagging him down with a waving arm. He looked wave-soaked, hair scooped up into stiff, salt-watered blond tufts. As Ray drew closer, he saw Nora's hand fly to the top buttons of her bright sleeveless blouse, a nervous gesture, he supposed. Obviously, she hadn't known he'd be here. Well, surprise, surprise.

Did he make her that nervous? After the way he'd all but thrown himself at her the other day, who could blame the woman? If he were a member of the opposite sex, he'd have turned tail and skedaddled, too.

Except Nora had almost accepted his near-kiss.

Females. They confused the hell out of him, and that's the reason he needed to steer clear of Nora Murray.

He arrived at their shocking pink blanket, noting the black-gold-silver star glow of sand dotting Nora's skin. She wore her hair in one of those braid hairstyles today, the strands drawn back from her face except for a few stray curls bobbing with the wind. A bottle of tropical-scented sun lotion rested against the sleek muscle line of her thigh.

Trent's voice knocked Ray out of staring mode. He hadn't even looked Nora in the face yet. Coward.

"What kind of food is that?" Trent stood on his tiptoes. Ray watched Trent realize that his excitement was "uncool" as his son suddenly averted his eyes and leaned against the surfboard planted upright in the sand.

Ray finally gathered his confidence and grinned at Nora in what he hoped was a nonchalant manner. Now that he could get a better look at her, he thought she looked gorgeous, as usual. Toasty bare legs tucked under her shorts and coral blouse opened at the throat to reveal a bit of skin. His ears tingled just thinking about the tender area connecting the throat and chest. As his gaze moved back up to her face, he saw she was inspecting him as well.

Suddenly, he got all self-conscious. Ray hoped that he hadn't splashed on too much aftershave following his shower. Women were supposed to love the stuff; at least, that's what his head waitress had told him. He didn't wear it much, but now was as good a time as any to start.

Gruffly, he said, "It's Chinese. I hope you don't mind, Ms. Murray."

"No. I love it," she said with a smile that warmed his stomach. "Trent just finished his studying. Good timing, Mr. Brody."

As sunshine glinted off her glasses, Ray noticed her surreptitiously surveying the beach. Was she looking for a way out? Maybe the recollection of his almost-kiss was making her uncomfortable. He'd know for sure if he could just see beyond those damned glasses; he wanted to whip them from her face and run a finger over her lips just to distract her. And maybe Ray even wanted to bring back the moment when his fingers had lifted the stray eyelash from her face, expectation hanging in the air like the forever-fall of a lost feather.

After one last glance at her aloof Victorian profile, he grinned and settled a discreet distance from her, far enough so his son wouldn't think anything of it, near enough to sense her skin prickle his own.

The brown bags of food were already under attack from the forces of Trent. The boy happily plopped onto the blanket and for several minutes proceeded to stuff lo mein noodles into his mouth. His head suddenly tilted toward Ray as he sniffed the air.

"God. Did you use cologne?"

Ray laughed uncomfortably, looked at Nora—who might have been pretending not to have heard—and mussed Trent's hair. "The waitresses rubbed those magazine samples on me. Guess I'd better run the next time I spy a woman reading one." He gave Trent's head one last, *hard* muss.

The boy understood that he had committed some sort of faux pas, but, instead of the requisite sheepish look that would have won forgiveness, he cackled quietly.

"Hey, Trent. If you're done eating, why don't you make like shark bait."

"Still hungry."

The kid was incorrigible, Ray thought. It had been pretty cute when Ray was like that at Trent's age, but now he knew how his parents must have felt when he had used his own smart-aleck mouth to ruffle their feathers. Even if they'd never been around to comment.

Nora stirred, and Ray's attention focused solely on the warmth of her proximity. She said, "Won't you have to wait to go in the water now, Trent? You're not supposed to swim after you eat. At least, that's what my mom always said."

"I always go in the water after I eat," Trent said, his jaw set. "Nothing happens."

Nora watched Ray as he tried to seem unconcerned. Sure, he'd heard the advice about swimming cramps, but he'd always thought it was an old wives' tale.

"Maybe you'd better sit out for a half hour," Ray said, glancing at Nora for a second opinion. Was she thinking he was an inept father? Hell, he'd suffered through the same thoughts many times himself.

"Sounds about right," she said, a sun-baked smile giving him confidence.

Trent polished off the last of his portion of food. "I want to go now." He stood and yanked up his trunks, which had slipped low on his hips.

It was on the tip of Ray's tongue to order Trent to stay, but he decided against it. Knowing his son's personality, an order would probably encourage Trent to disobey. Maybe his son needed to make up his own mind.

"I hope you don't sink like a stone. Good luck."

As Trent stuffed the board under his arm, he eyed his father warily. It seemed as if the boy was rethinking his position. With one last defiant gaze, he ran to the water's edge, splashed through low waves, and hopped on the board to paddle into deeper water.

Ray tried to keep his poker face, but he worried. Weren't

parents supposed to worry most of the time, anyway? He figured Trent probably wasn't a strong surfer—not unless they had wave pools in New York. But the boy could swim; he had been a water baby, floating around in many a hotel pool during the short time after his birth when Ray and Cheri had relocated from place to place, job to job.

"You don't think he's going to drown?" asked Nora, voice soft. He caught the smile disappearing from her face just as the sun dipped behind a cloud, stealing the gleam off her glasses.

He felt a keen cut of embarrassment at what Nora must be thinking right now. He was a man who couldn't even get his son to obey. A failure.

"I'll keep my eye on him." Ray stabbed at his food as Nora played with hers. He could sense her disapproval. But why should he care so much? Trent was *his* son.

They watched Trent while he bobbed in the ocean, waiting for the perfect wave. He focused on his son's safety, but, at the same time, Ray couldn't help wondering if Nora was as aware of him as he was of her. Was the arm next to his as alive with heat? Did her stomach tighten, pinwheeling as if it were at the top of the first roller coaster hill?

Damn, she scattered him like a puzzle. On one hand, he knew he should keep a professional distance from her; she was here to help his child, not because this was some sort of date. On the other hand, he wanted to run his knuckles over her upper arm just to see if goose bumps would tease the soft blond down. He felt a little too carnal for his own comfort.

As he leaned back on his elbows, he took another opportunity to caress Nora with his eyes. He couldn't help himself. As the sun leaped from its lone-cloud cover, the streaky sky shadowed her. Slight gusts of wind lifted her hair as if an invisible hand toyed with it. Her eyes fixed on Trent, guarding him.

She must have felt Ray's scrutiny, because she smiled at him and tentatively leaned on her side. He noticed that her blouse fell open at the collar, revealing a lacy white bra against sun-melted smooth skin.

He could imagine running his lips along that smooth curve of her breast, using his tongue to stroke the underside, sliding upward to take her hardened nipple into his mouth. All the while, he'd be coaxing her shirt away from her beach-warmed body, listening to the whisper of cloth against skin, basking in her orange-peel scent.

He could almost feel his hands encircling her waist, thumb swishing around the inside of her belly button, making her laugh as if she had no cares in the world. He'd trace his hands up her torso, over her firm breasts, kneading them, causing him to ache for her.

Ray turned away, fighting to be a gentleman. He was straining against his pants already, just from a fantasy. What would happen in real life? He didn't know if he'd survive reality.

He willed himself to calm, trying to focus on anything but Nora, even if he could hear her soft breathing next to him. Out of control. He was worse than a teenager.

A brunette wearing well-filled exercise gear jogged by their camp. She gave Ray the come-hither look of a calendar girl. He realized that he was relaxing on a…pink…blanket.

He saw Nora watching the jogger, lips tight and expressionless.

Jealousy? He wished. Envy would've meant interest on Nora's part. But since she'd pulled away from his kiss, he wasn't sure if she'd ever allow him to fulfill his down-boy fantasies.

When Ray realized he was more into Nora's reaction than the jogger herself, he fell back onto the blanket and rubbed his palms over his eyes. He was a goner, all right.

He expected Nora to tear into him for even looking in the jogger's direction: *Do you think she's attractive with that huge chest? Why? You're sickening. All men are sickening.* It's what Cheri would have said to him. Even when they'd been married, when he'd been a faithful husband, she'd accused him of ogling other women. In hindsight, Ray attributed her sharp tongue to a guilty conscience. After all, she'd been doing more than looking when it came to other men.

He tightened his jaw. No more thoughts of Cheri. *No more thoughts of your screwed-up life.*

When he looked at Nora, he was prepared for the worst—an accusation, a "how could you" stamped on her frown. Instead, he saw Nora's laughing face, surrounded by a halo of the setting sun.

"Could she be a little more obvious?" she asked.

"Oh. Was that some sort of invitation? I didn't notice." He attempted to pull off an innocuous face.

Nora tucked a tendril of hair behind an ear. Ray attempted to keep his gaze away from the gape of her blouse.

"Why don't you jog after her?"

He grinned. Definite jealousy tinged her tone. It made him feel wanted, cared for in a primal way. "No, thanks."

His hands were full enough.

She scanned the beach again, and he did the same. Trent still waited for a wave, but three little surfers, a few years younger than Trent, had joined his vigil. They talked as if they were comfortable, and Ray wondered if these were his son's surf teachers, his friends. Sadness slipped down into his heart. He wished his boy could be happy.

He looked at Nora and caught her watching him. She bit a lip and lowered her gaze. He could almost read her mind as she clutched the collar together, shutting off the view of her bra, stifling herself back into that Victorian corset of emotion and slowly sitting upright. He followed suit.

Damn, he wanted more. It wasn't enough to preview her body—Ray wanted to experience all of her, without the top, the shorts, the white-lace bra. *All.*

"I keep thinking that I'm going to run into a parent out in public—and it'll be at the worst possible moment," she said, watching the ocean.

He understood her meaning. "Aren't you allowed to have fun? It's your time off."

She nodded and busied herself by cleaning up the last of

dinner. "I guess I'm sort of a public figure. I can't consort with certain people. No offense."

"None taken." Maybe he should have been miffed, but instead he saw an opportunity to find out more about her: What shadowed her eyes? How had she become so good at dealing with kids? Why did she withdraw every time he took a step closer to her? Maybe he didn't want to hear the answers, or maybe he'd feel even more admiration for her gentle spirit.

He decided to start out with an easy question. "Why did you become a teacher if you feel…I don't know…is *persecuted* the right word?"

While she laughed, she forcefully shoved the containers into bags. "No. Not the right word at all. I think I was destined to become a leader of others."

He raised his brows at this lofty statement. Maybe Nora had some sort of power trip tied to her teaching. If so, he didn't want to know. But instinct told him he'd misjudged her words.

"That sounds really odd," she continued, shrugging one bare shoulder, "like I've had God's finger touch me or something. But, have you ever had a moment, a sort of epiphany?"

"Yeah," he said, remembering the very physical *epiphany* he had experienced on a college baseball field. That certain *epiphany* had changed the direction of his life forever—it had blown out one of his knees, shattering any hopes of going on to a career in professional sports.

"Well, I don't want to bore you with my blather," she said.

Ray didn't think about his next move. He reached out and used his finger to lightly graze her cheek, to gently slip off her glasses. The effect was like feeling the sun beaming on his face after throwing open a window. "You are anything but boring."

In her eyes, he saw the decision to stay. He knew she was somewhat paranoid about being seen in public with the "wrong person," but he also knew that she was a fighter. It was intriguing to watch the battle. If only she didn't feel so strongly about being seen with the wrong guy…a parent. She'd made her preferences clear enough.

She flicked a gaze toward the water-bound Trent, then looked at Ray's arm, but she didn't move. In a whisper that barely rose above the surf, she said, "I made my choice at a funeral when I was about thirteen. I suppose that's where most of us get our deep thoughts. My eleven-year-old friend was in that casket."

"God."

"Yes. It was bad." She hesitated, took a deep breath. Almost didn't say anything more. Then something seemed to change her mind. Nora's eyes grew misty. "A drunk driver killed him while he rode his bike home one afternoon. People used to think he was a hell-raiser, sort of like Trent, I guess. But he was the sharpest kid."

He nodded and let his hand drop to the blanket, where he leaned closer. He wished he could take every one of Nora's bad experiences, fill his hands with them and crush them until they turned to dust.

She continued. "Even though he was younger than I was, we used to write poetry together during the summer. He wrote these poems that could break your heart. When he died I lost hope for a little while. He had so little time, and he just blew it by hanging out with 'the punks,' smoking cigarettes in bathrooms."

She shook her head and hardened her jaw. "His death was just senseless. There's no other explanation. At the funeral, I stood next to his father. While we walked away he put his arm around me and said, 'You were good with him, Nora. You brought out the best in him, what little there was.'" She paused. An odd sense of wonder tinged her tone. "His father was so nice to me."

She cleared her throat, resumed her matter-of-fact voice. "Of course, I didn't believe what he'd said—I believed that everyone has good in them. He would have written those poems even if I hadn't been there.

"So I sat in the car, staring at the flowers and the people in black when it hit me—not everyone is optimistic. When I look at kids, I see people who need road signs, something to guide them.''

Ray watched his son floating on the ocean, waiting for that wave.

Nora added, ''Not everyone thinks that there's a good seed in themselves that just needs to be watered. Am I making sense?''

Ray quietly said, ''Yes.''

''I realized that maybe I wanted to water seeds. If you know what I mean. I never questioned my future. It just took a while for me to get around to realizing my goal.'' She looked down.

Nora, the savior of our generations, he thought. I wish your optimism could touch me.

He wondered how the young boy's death had affected her future besides careerwise. An event so sad had to have left its mark in other ways. ''Did they ever catch the drunk driver?'' he asked, hoping to draw her out.

Nora leaned back her head, closed her eyes. Ray's heart squeezed like a fist when a tear fought its way past her lashes and down her cheek.

''He never got what he deserved.''

Her bitterness should've surprised him, yet, considering the subject, it was appropriate. But was this the same Nora who thought that with ''a little TLC,'' Trent would turn out all right? He couldn't think of anything to say that would match her passionate opinion, so he settled for platitudes. ''Sometimes the slime of humanity manages to ooze out of the worst situations.''

When she looked him straight in the eye, the amber colors had morphed into shards of hellfire.

''The man driving that car was my father.''

Chapter Eight

Why had she told him that?

Nora gritted her teeth, expecting Ray to react as everyone else in her neighborhood had—finger-pointing, frosty glares, sneers reminding her that her father had ruined yet another life. Tommy's life.

She'd never gotten over the feeling of worthlessness. Daughter of the community's biggest monster. It was a label she'd lived with for years. Teaching wasn't only a job for Nora, it was a saving grace. Maybe, if she could touch enough young lives, she could erase the sins of her family.

Tommy's mother and father had been about the only people in her neighborhood who hadn't shunned her. But she couldn't stand to see the pain in their eyes every time she said hello. Eventually, they'd taken to ignoring each other. Eventually, she'd gone off to college, long after her father had left town.

She didn't want to see Ray's reaction to her outburst. He'd probably be disgusted with her, just like the neighbors from her Midwestern hometown.

The never-ending whirl of the surf masked their silence. After an eternal moment, he spoke. "I'm sorry about that, Nora."

Sincere. But, oh, how deep and philosophical of him. She mentally shook a finger at her thoughts. What had she expected? An earth-shattering realization that would yank her out of this low self-esteem? She'd done everything possible to remedy her confidence problem herself. Becoming a teacher had only been a small part of her therapy. She couldn't rely on a man she hardly knew to make her feel better about the world.

Yet it'd been so easy to confide in him. Surely that meant something.

He said, "People have a way of disappointing others. You aren't alone."

His was the voice of experience. Trent's essay had clued her in to his dark moments. Maybe if anyone would understand her pain, it'd be Ray Brody. "Sometimes I feel very alone."

His pinkie finger nestled near hers. When he spoke, his words cracked in half. "There's a thing called marriage. Why haven't you thought of ending your loneliness in that way?"

"You're recommending the holy state of matrimony? How optimistic of you." Oh, acid. Maybe she shouldn't talk anymore, not until she'd gotten a hold of her emotions.

His smile hinted at long, sleepless nights of reflection. "I'm just wondering why you've never found someone."

She gave a short laugh. "Haven't found the lucky guy yet, I suppose."

"Maybe you have, and you don't know it." He smiled. "Somewhere along the line, I mean."

She warmed at his comment, then thought of Jared. What if he'd been her best chance at love? She wanted to tell Ray all about him, how he'd made her think twice about ever having another relationship. The beach lent an atmosphere of revelation, of soul-searching truth. Maybe, if nothing else, Ray Brody could be a good friend.

Here goes. "A few years ago, I thought I'd found Mr. Right."

"Really?" His eyes lit up, then dimmed. "What kind of guy was he to have lost you?"

"How flattering for you to think the loss was his."

For a second, a certain longing passed across his features. "Unless you're hiding a serial killer inside that sunny personality of yours, I'd think Mr. Right had something to do with your relationship ending."

She could imagine falling for a man with the comfort skills of Ray Brody. He actually made her believe for a minute that she was something special. "I left him." Sigh. "Jared Jacobs. Let's make a long story short and say it wasn't a match made in heaven."

"How long did it last?"

Too long. "A couple years. We were engaged."

He paused, ran his long fingers down her forearm. The breath left her body at the unexpected caress.

As if he hadn't done anything to throw her off balance, Ray continued with his questions. "What ended it? You couldn't agree on a china pattern, the caterer canceled…?"

She wasn't prepared to tell him everything. Especially about the near-slap that knocked some sense into Nora's brain. She'd never, ever allow a man to handle her the way her father had treated her mom.

Never.

"Let's just say we outgrew each other. I know better now."

Or did she? Ray had leaned in closer. So close his broad shoulders blocked the low wind, sheltering her from fluttering sand pebbles. What if he tried to kiss her? Would she freak out, an invisible leash woven of guilt and self-preservation yanking her backward?

Out of the corner of her eye, she looked to the ocean, searching for Trent. Still waiting for the waves with his friends, unconcerned about what his father and teacher were doing on the beach.

His voice was low. "We've all made bad decisions, Nora."

She couldn't take it anymore. Nuzzling up to him, she buried her nose under the line of his jaw, moving up along his cheek, her lashes scratching stubble. She hesitated, lips a breath away from his. "I don't..."

He rubbed his mouth over hers, lower lip parting, delving, until she took it into her mouth. She sucked on it until he shifted his weight, his fingers strumming her neck veins, his mouth taking all of hers in a soft kiss edged with need.

For the first time in her life, a man—*this* man—made her feel...wanted. Maybe he wasn't her savior, but, at this moment, with his lips tasting hers, his hands roaming her shoulders and showering sparks over her skin, he was her universe. But when the kiss stopped—and it would have to—he'd still be another man she wouldn't dare trust.

Breathless, they both came up for air, forehead to forehead, nose to nose. Her hand had somehow landed on his shoulder, fingers digging into his polo shirt. She'd never forget this, the smell of salt water and clean cologne mingling to stir her thoughts into a mishmash of confusion.

"Nora..."

She allowed herself the pleasure of brushing her fingers down his solid chest, then backed away to look at him. His skin was flushed, his eyes wild as a tropical storm. The sight struck fear into her heart. Or maybe it wasn't fear, merely trepidation. Whatever it was, it sent tingles all over her body.

Trent hadn't caught the wave yet. When she looked toward the pack of boys straddling their surfboards, the effect was similar to the alarm clock beeping in the warm, cozy dark of morning. *Wake up, Nora. No more sweet dreams.*

She casually scooted to the edge of the blanket, far from temptation. "I don't think I'm the only one with a life story. How about you?" My God, her voice held a note of deep, scratchy hunger, a reminder of his mouth on hers. Just like the stubble burn on her face.

Ray straightened up, trying to rein in the call of the wild. How could she just end the kiss, flit away and act as if nothing had happened? His heart was still hammering in his ears, his muscles still rigid from what could have been if the beach blanket had been a bed, and they'd been alone.

Well, Brody, he thought. Should have enjoyed it while it lasted.

He could smell her scent on him. Citrus. Tangy, a swirl of sweet and bitter, just like Nora.

He took a deep breath, exhaled. Calmed himself. "You read Trent's masterwork. That's the story of my life, too."

"Surely there's more."

He caught her running fingers over her lips. Shyly, she looked down at the blanket, the pink glow reflecting off her face.

She'd been very candid with him about her father. The conversation had created a connection, played out in their kiss. But did Ray really want to go into the nitty-gritty details of his own life? No, not really. They didn't need to dwell on more ugliness.

She cleared her throat awkwardly and said, "I'm sorry. I'm used to knowing everyone's business, being a teacher."

He'd have to worm his way out of disclosing any of his life story—it was too depressing to talk about right now; he wanted to enjoy the moment with Nora. A barefoot stroll over a bed of hot coals seemed more appealing to him than a discussion about his life. He spied a book by her leg and reached for it.

Nora, obviously thinking that he was grabbing her thigh, jumped. He held up the novel, a grin on his mouth, as she said, "Oh," and laughed, a delicate, ice-breaking sound that mingled with the waves to wash his soul clean.

"This is one of my favorites," he said, thumbing through the pages, now sticky with salt and sand.

Nora's amber eyes brightened like the colors of a kaleidoscope. "It's my second time reading it. It's so humorous. And sad."

"Just like life, huh? Guts and all."

When he looked at her again, she narrowed her eyes, reading him. Great, now she wanted to make his mind into her summer literacy project.

"What?" he asked, laughing.

"I don't know. You're…" She waved her hands about, sifting through thoughts.

"Hard to comprehend? That's intentional." It was the only way to keep a wall between himself and the continual heartbreak the world offered.

Nora turned onto her stomach, facing Trent and his buddies, who splashed water at one another. "So many of our first impressions are wrong. I…I just think it's, well, great that you're well-read."

In her comment, he heard the question, *Why* is a guy like you so well-read? He was half-disappointed that she thought literature to be beyond his bar-owner experience and half-flattered that she found him intriguing. *Ray Brody: Man of Many Mysteries,* he thought sarcastically. He'd make a great novel.

Drawing circles in the sand, Nora seemed speculative. "I don't know. Maybe you're some sort of superhero who leads a double life." When she looked up, a sparkle filled her crystal-amber eyes. It was a nice change from the shadows.

"Don't get your hopes up."

She laughed ruefully. "Don't worry about that."

The dark side strikes again. He didn't want to be the man who brought out the sadness; he wanted to conquer it.

Continuing, she said, "So you're not even going to throw me a bone? Some little juicy piece of meat to appease my love of a good riddle?"

What the hell. "What do you want to know?"

She looked sideways and grinned. "I know. Give me your life story."

"Too much to ask." Wasn't there some way to avoid this line of questioning?

"Too little to tell? I doubt it."

Ray fervently wished Trent would rudely interrupt them with his surf-rat friends.

"Well," she said. "Maybe I can help you out. Born where?"

"Morro Bay, California."

"Any major childhood distinctions? Nondistinctions?"

He looked at the shrouded sky, thinking. *Let's see, Dad raised us by absentee ballot, Mom slaved at two lousy jobs, my sister got pregnant and left home when she was sixteen: just an average childhood.*

"Nothing special." He spied some sand twinkling on her upper arm and playfully brushed it away. He couldn't keep his hands off her.

She rubbed her arm, paused, but thankfully moved on. Was that a blush or sunburn flaming on her cheeks? Ray couldn't be sure, but if she felt half the heat he did, they'd both spontaneously combust.

"All right, then. College? Now, this should be interesting."

"Why?"

"Didn't college shape you?"

More than you know, he thought. "San Diego State."

"Me, too!" she said, putting her hand on his thigh momentarily. When she realized what she had done, she retreated, leaving an imprint on his skin that felt like the ice-burn of muscle rub. "What was your major?"

He laughed, not out of courtesy, but irony. She'd love *this* one. "I think I should explain…"

Nora's eyebrows arched. "All right."

He sighed. "I went into college on a baseball scholarship. Shortstop. Hot bat."

"Oh."

"To make a long story short, I was injured on the field. It was the oddest thing, too. The other team's catcher did it. Two innings before, I had slid into home on a close play. He blocked the plate, and I had no choice but to, ah, bowl him over."

"Ouch. Did you hurt him?"

"I was fine, thank you." He grinned.

She giggled low in her throat, and he noticed a little dimple on the left side of her mouth. He longed to run his lips over it.

Down boy, down.

"His pride hurt more than anything else, but he was an actor. Rolled around in the dirt for a minute before giving me a death look and limping to the dugout. Anyway, he came back into the game and managed to hit a double. I was covering second and—what do you know—he felt healthy enough to take out my legs."

Unexpectedly, Ray shivered. Why didn't the years dull these damned memories? But he could still feel the cleat, the flames in his knee, then the numb cold of knowing that his life was as good as over.

"I tore a ligament and broke a bone." He patted his right knee. "So don't ask questions on my limping days."

She held up two fingers. "Scout's honor."

He could tell by the tone of her voice that she didn't realize how serious the injury could be to a player. Yet he also realized that she was compassionate just the same. That was just Nora's way.

He shrugged. "It was my epiphany—knowing my baseball days were finished. No Show for Ray Brody."

"So what happened next?"

A muscle flexed in his jaw. "Now we come to your answer. I had declared English as a major."

A laugh bubbled as she clapped her hands. "I knew it. Siblings under the skin."

She was laughing, and he was the cause. It made him feel good. "Well, it was only because I thought I'd never have to use it. Remember, I had dollar signs and stadiums in my eyes. I just enjoyed reading and analyzing—the work was really easy for me. Of course, I've never used the damn major in my entire adult life." Ray shrugged to himself, recalling days of soup and bread for dinner, nights of living in cheap housing. "Ultimately, I became a carpenter and the respectable man you see before you."

He wondered if Nora had noticed the omission of Cheri from any of his ruminations.

As he opened his mouth to continue, Nora murmured, "I think Trent found the Wave." She stood up to get a better view.

Thankful that Nora had stopped him before he could reveal any more about himself, Ray watched his son carving across a gel-like slice of water as it carried him to the shore. He was a natural-born athlete, he thought, pride making him smile.

Trent wobbled, roared like a twister and tripped into the ocean as the Wave won the contest. He popped back above the water, and he whipped his head around to get the hair out of his eyes. He sent a "thumbs-up" their way, then pulled the leash to retrieve his board.

When Nora was around, the boy seemed different: a normal, twelve-year-old kid, impressing people with his impetuous antics. Ray only wished she could always be there.

As he turned to Nora to say something, she stood like an Easter Island statue.

"I've got to go," she said. Before he could ask why, she'd grabbed her book and glasses.

"I'll get the blanket later!" she called, as she power-walked toward her car.

He watched her, already feeling the world was less interesting. With her went a certain disappointment. Kissing was all they were probably ever going to do.

Three young boys walked past the pink blanket, burping and pumping their armpits to make rude noises. One of them looked in Nora's direction and said, "That looks like Ms. Murray."

As the guys craned their necks to get a better view, Ray frowned, knowing that he and Nora would be chasing each other for a long time to come.

But wasn't she worth it?

With a doesn't-it-beat-all grin, he sat back down on the blanket, thinking he could get used to soft colors and newly breathtaking sunsets. Everything suddenly seemed more vivid. Even kisses had the shade of red, of wanting more.

The boys had halted their progress, staring after Nora, and for a moment, Ray felt anxious for her. Had they recognized her? One boy cuffed another.

"Don't be dumb," he said, resuming his underarm symphony. "Teachers don't go to the beach."

Eleven o'clock at night, and Trent still hadn't come home.

Ray stood up from the couch one more time and peered out the front window. After the surf session today with Nora, everything had been great between father and son. On the way home, Trent hadn't stopped talking about the huge wave he'd caught, and how he would do it again someday soon.

Ray had felt closer to his son than ever before. They'd shared something, and Trent was obviously proud that his father had been at the beach to see him in a moment of glory.

They'd eaten a nuked apple pie in companionable silence, Ray noticing that, every once in a while, a fleeting, blinding smile would light on Trent's face. Things had been so hunky-dory, in fact, that Ray had allowed Trent to go skateboarding with his surf-rat friends until eight o'clock, an hour later than the newly imposed curfew.

What a fool. He should've known his son would take advantage of the situation. Anger built inside him until he was afraid of how he'd react when Trent finally came strolling through the front door.

A flicker of panic worried him. What if Trent didn't come back? What if he'd run away for some unexplainable reason? Or, worse yet, what if someone had harmed his boy?

He remembered Nora's story from this afternoon; how her father had run down an eleven-year-old boy on a bike, killing him. The expression on her face had been horrific, a terror he'd wanted to smooth away with the right words. Except Ray hadn't been able to find the right words. He'd failed in that respect.

But when she'd leaned into him for a kiss—that touch of

her lips that had just about torn open his soul, making it bleed once again—Ray had felt that maybe, just maybe, he had the power to heal her.

Then she'd left him standing on her pink blanket. And that was that. He'd have to forget her.

Ray leaned against the side of the window, trying to see through the darkness beyond the pool of light on the driveway. He couldn't stand the thought of Trent's absence from his life. Just when they'd been reunited and things were starting to look up.

Dammit, he couldn't stand here like this, waiting, wondering. He started to pace the floor, running his hands through his hair every time concern reared up and kicked his conscience.

The roll of skateboard wheels clicking across every sidewalk crack alerted Ray to Trent's coming. He moved to the window again, squinting into the night, watching as Trent skated into light from the garage door. His son flipped up the board, catching it with his hands, tucking his baseball cap into a wide pocket in his long shorts before setting down the board and entering the house.

The fact that Trent had taken off his hat before coming in their home was all but lost on Ray as he stood in front of his son, hands on hips, rage welling up within him. "It's after eleven, Trent. Where the hell…where have you been?"

"Jeez, do you have to cuss?"

He fisted his hands, unclenched them. "That's not the issue, Trent. I said you were to be here at eight."

Trent shrugged. "I forgot what time it was."

So nonchalant, as if Ray hadn't been sitting here imagining every worst-case scenario possible. "You forgot? Surely your fertile mind can invent a better story."

"Not really, because it's the truth. I'm here now, okay?" He started to reach into one of his pockets. "Check this out. I was over at Jerry's and his grandpa showed us how to—"

"Boy, this is serious." Ray was doing his best not to grab a handful of Trent's shirt to drag him to his room. He hadn't wanted to cuss again, so he'd resorted to "boy." It'd sounded dirtier than he'd intended. "I thought you were in some ditch somewhere, or maybe kidnapped."

Ray expected his son to roll his eyes; it would've been a typical response. Instead, Trent's lip trembled, then stopped, making Ray wonder if it'd ever happened.

"I can take care of myself," Trent said. "You and Ms. Murray need to chill."

"We need to chill?" Ray wanted to tear out his hair. "Do you have any respect for my feelings whatsoever?"

"I guess."

How would Nora have handled this situation? Did she get this frustrated with her preteen time bombs in class? Ray would've given anything to have her by his side right now, defusing the situation. She'd know exactly what to do. "Trent, I've no choice but to ground you."

His son's eyes narrowed into blue slits of anger, like the hottest part of a flame. "You can't ground me."

"Bet on it. No TV for a week, and when you come home from school, you're to go to your room. And no listening to your stereo."

Trent's hand was still in his pocket, not having moved for the duration. He slid out his fist, grasping an object until his knuckles turned white. "Here," he said, spiking the item to the carpet, stalking away to his room. His voice trailed after him. "It's all yours."

His door slammed, causing Ray to jerk in reaction. Had he done the right thing? Or should he apologize because he'd been harsh?

Dammit, he'd reacted out of panic for his son's well-being. It was the protective parent coming out in him. And all he got in exchange for his concern was Trent's temper and a piece of wood he'd thrown down in a fit of pique.

Where was Nora when he needed her?

Shaking his head, Ray picked up the object from the floor. His heart plummeted to his feet.

He held a roughly whittled totem featuring waves, the sun

and two figures watching over a smaller one. The artistry was crude, but it tore at Ray's gut. Trent had wanted to give him a gift he'd made, and Ray had rejected it without a glance.

When he knocked on his son's door to apologize for his hastiness, his answer was a muffled "Go away."

"Thank you, Trent. This is…great." He waited to hear a shuffle, a sign of movement, anything telling him Trent would open the door to talk with him.

Louder this time. "I said go away."

And he did. Grounded in his own room for the night.

Nora would've known what to do.

Chapter Nine

The next day, Nora bopped her head back and forth to the beat of an eighties song on the radio. An involuntary shiver scrunched her shoulders, puckering her cream short-sleeved blouse under the safety belt. Here she was, at the ripe old age of twenty-seven, reliving "oldies" songs from her high school years. Her students hadn't even been born when some of these songs originally hit the airwaves.

Time to grow up, Nora, dear, said a grandmotherly voice in her head. *You're going to age, just like every other mortal.*

A stop sign loomed in front of her. She sucked in her breath and pumped her brakes, swinging her right arm over to the near-empty passenger's seat in a protective motherlike gesture. With the motor purring, she widened her eyes, imagining a phantom child in the seat next to her.

But instead of a chubby-cheeked youngster she saw Trent's homework spread like a fan over the white upholstery.

Had Ray's kiss made her totally lose her perspective? Was

the feel of his skin against hers strong enough to wipe away years of avoiding her craving for a baby?

Or maybe her estrogen flare-up was just another indication of how much she wanted a real family. If it was up to her to start one, she'd certainly raise her children to love themselves, no matter what life held.

"Don't be ridiculous," she chided herself, jamming on the gas pedal, throwing her head back against the seat. If she hadn't known any better, she would have said that Ray Brody had shoved her maternal instincts into overdrive.

"The last thing you need is a child, Nora Murray." She tried to get back into the swing of the techno music, but feeling suddenly like a teeny-bopper, she snapped off the radio. "Your plate is already overflowing with bundles of pubescent joy."

She continued driving to the Brody house. Trent had been absent from school today and, per the verbal contract—or impossible dream, depending on how you looked at it—with Mr. Brody, Nora felt responsible for keeping her student up-to-date on any homework.

Okay, so maybe she was going overboard. Would she have gone from class to class, checking to see if Trent's other teachers had homework for him if he were any other student?

Based on Nora's lack of free time, she would have answered negatively. But she had made a deal with Mr. Brody...*Ray*. And she would stick by her word even if she passed away from sleep deprivation.

Her car turned into the trimmed-grass street where the Brodys resided, then skidded to a halt by the address white-washed onto the curb.

Absently, she tucked stray honey strands into the twist of her hairstyle and pressed her lips together, rubbing until any red lipstick remnants came back to life.

What if Ray was home? Worse, what if he wasn't?

She hated to admit the extent to which she wanted to see those bayview-blue eyes, the slight cupid-bow arch of his lips. Memories of yesterday's sunset beach picnic rushed back to

Nora with the force of a sandstorm, bringing the burn of the wind and his stubble back to her skin, her lips. Was she getting too close to him? The voices in her head said, "Absolutely." Her heart said, "You could get a lot closer, babe."

But what if those Jefferson Junior High students had seen her on the beach? They'd been a physical reminder of what she needed to avoid. Ray.

Without thinking, she'd scrambled out of range, back to her car, in such a haste that she'd left her pink blanket.

What would have been the harm? Didn't teachers have the right to go to the beach as well as anyone else? Of course they could.

A rush of breath. There, good. She was ready for anything.

The click of her heels on the driveway boomed like shots as she walked to the front door. God, they probably thought a Clydesdale had come to visit.

Her crisp knock on the wooden door was equally nerve-racking. After a second knock, she found herself face-to-face with Ray Brody. For a moment, everything they'd talked about yesterday—their epiphanies, she thought, mentally rolling her eyes—came flooding over her, heating her face. She had revealed too much; she just knew it.

Her gaze couldn't help straying to his mouth, remembering its softness, tenderness. And now he'd probably play it cold and distant. At least, she hoped he would. If he was as lovable as he'd been yesterday at the beach, she'd be in big trouble.

It took her a moment to realize that his breath came in drawn-out gasps, a hammer jutted from his hand, and…oh, my…

He wasn't wearing a shirt.

Struggling to maintain eye contact, Nora tried not to allow her smile to be too wide. "Good afternoon, Mr.…Ray."

A thin sweat-sheen glistened on his skin, wetting the slight hairs on his chest. The expanse of his shoulders made her feel that he could protect her from anything. How long had it been since she had found herself this close to a bare male torso?

What would he do if she reached out to run her fingers over his lean stomach?

Don't think about your chest against his, she thought to herself, thinking about it, anyway. It was the best feeling in the world, to feel a man's muscles against your own, his hairs tickling your skin, friction so strong that you couldn't help burying your face into his neck.

Ray nodded and wore what seemed to be a surprised smile on his lips. "Nora."

Her name was almost her undoing. She could imagine a parallel universe in which Nora Murray tore off her glasses, let loose her hair, undid the constraining top button of her blouse and threw herself at Ray.

She blinked, twice, several times. Adjusted her glasses. Shoving his son's assignments at him, she said, "I thought I'd bring Trent's homework since he wasn't at school today. How is he, by the way?"

Not being able to stand the effort anymore, she slid her eyes down to his chest. She found that he had slipped his hammer into a belt loop on his faded jeans. When he reached out for the papers, Nora slowly let her gaze roam back up, up to…the stormy look on his face.

He flipped through the homework. "I hate to tell you, Nora, but Trent went to school this morning. Same as usual."

"Oh?" She set her jaw, wondering if Ray was going to be difficult again. Was he planning on calling her a liar about his son's absence today?

Leaning against the door frame, he ran a hand through his blondish hair. Didn't he realize he was half-naked?

"I'll get to the bottom of it. Trent will not be ditching class…not ever again." He shook his head. "I don't know what goes through his head sometimes."

She didn't like the cynical curve of his brow. "What's wrong?"

He belted the papers against the door frame, gritting his teeth. "We had it out again last night. He came in about three hours after curfew."

"And you let him know of your displeasure, of course."

"Yeah. But—" he stepped away from the door, still talking, and reappeared with a wooden object "—he'd been at a friend's house making this for me."

Her heart twisted at the sight of the beach-inspired picture. "That's sweet."

"Unfortunately, I'd already sent him to his room. I tried talking to him this morning at breakfast, but he was stone silent."

"You don't think he did anything rash," she said, again trying so very hard to keep her eyes on his face. She gave him the wooden picture, trying to avoid his touch. Success, but disappointment came with it. "Like running away, for instance?"

"My instinct says he's just playing a mean trick on me. Ditching. A 'there, I'll show you' gesture."

She nodded, relieved. "Sounds like Trent." Then, reflexively, she gazed at his chest again.

Maybe he knew what was going through her mind. All the dirty little thoughts of a fallen angel. He took his time answering.

"I felt so guilty about grounding him that I let Trent go surfing when he came home. He shouldn't be back for a while. Boy, what a sucker I am." He grinned. "I was a heartbeat away from calling you for advice last night."

"Really." A late-night parenting call from Ray Brody. Romance at its best.

He took a step back. "Walk to the store with me? I'm out of sugar."

Her brow furrowed as she wondered about his strange comment. Of course. He probably didn't feel like talking about Trent, and this was his way of avoiding it. She made a show of looking at her watch. "Well, sugar is one of those emergency items. I suppose I could go."

Naturally she would go. The more minutes she could pass with Ray, the happier she would be. They could be friendly, keep the relationship on professional terms.

But she really hoped he'd keep his shirt off.

"Good. Be right back. Come in." He left, his lean-hard form backing into the darkened hallway.

Stepping over the threshold, Nora folded her hands behind her back and scanned the living room as she waited for Ray.

Yes, it was the domain of a male, all right. Mismatched furniture, TV given the place of honor, a stereo hunched in the corner below a louvered, noncurtained window… She could really do a makeover here.

Nora wanted to throttle these overwhelming homemaker urges, but, on the other hand, they felt right. She could see herself straightening the picture of the sailboat above the TV. Choosing samples of new carpeting. Kicking her foot as she sat in a lawn chair on the back porch while Ray barbecued and Trent ran around the lawn.

Nora stroked her hand over the well-worn material of the upholstered couch. If it were up to her, she'd have accented its tan color with a comforter draped over the back, throw pillows tucked into the corners.

She sighed, letting her fancies get the best of her. Was this what was commonly referred to as a "nesting urge"? Whatever it was, it ran against her better instincts.

When she focused, Ray stood in front of her, a blue shirt covering what God surely intended for the world to see.

She forced a cheery smile. Professional Pollyanna once again. "Off it…um, we go."

As they walked to the store, Ray was aware of the gap between them. A fluffy, white Maltese dog scuttled through a hole, emphasizing their distance. The owner darted around them, chasing the pooch down the lawn-lined sidewalk, past white-picket fences and fizzling sprinklers.

He wondered how a guy like him had ever gotten into the neighborhood.

Ray didn't want to think about Trent's latest stunt right now. He wanted to think about Nora, and the way she had made him feel as her gaze had driven over his chest. Ray hated to flex his testosterone, but, damn, it felt good to be appreciated.

He'd detected the troubled lift of Nora's brow earlier. She probably suspected that he wanted to avoid a talk with Trent about his misbehavior. And she was right. The little manipulator would probably take advantage of him again.

"Thanks for taking the time to bring the work over." Out of the corner of his eye, he could see that she just about came to his shoulder. A stray hair kept brushing his upper arm; he only wished she would undo all the strands so he could smell that citrus scent of hers all the better. "It took a lot of effort for you to do that."

She spread her hands apart. No big thing, her gesture said. "It's part of our deal, right?"

"Right." A portion of him felt as though he needed to keep the conversation rolling; it had that first-date tinge of filling every minute with banter. Then again, part of him felt a certain comfort level with Nora. He'd been impressed with her willingness to open up with him about her father, her ex-fiancé. He hadn't been as honest with her about Cheri last night.

"I've never walked to the store before," he said, without quite thinking beforehand. Damn, Brody, he thought. That sounded idiotic.

"Oh? First time for everything."

He closed his eyes, hoping that she didn't see where his thoughts were taking him. He'd already imagined a first time with Nora. And a second time. Et ceteras.

They both started to speak at the same moment, then laughed as he gestured for her to go first.

"I was just going to say what a beautiful afternoon it is."

"Yeah. The weather's been great." What he had meant to say earlier was that he hadn't ever walked to the store with Cheri. They'd always gone their separate ways. They'd driven cars to the store, in a hurry to get back home and continue their stilted conversations and heated arguments. Strolling to the corner store as the late-afternoon wind cooled the sidewalks was something you did if you read self-help books. Appreciating life had never been high on his list of priorities.

But walking with Nora was almost a metaphor of something he could have. Something he'd never experienced in this lifetime. Something he wanted with all of his heart.

They arrived at the neighborhood market. While they ambled down the short aisles, he picked up his sugar, then some eggs, whole wheat bread, low-fat milk, granola bars and orange juice. He didn't want Nora to know that a healthy meal around the Brody household consisted of pizza and soda pop.

Each of them carried a paper bag on the return stroll. If Ray had been driving by in a car, he would have mistaken him and Nora for a couple, ready to stock their refrigerator and run to the bedroom in a fit of passion.

He smiled. Maybe the passion was all inside his head. What made him think that this prim, bespectacled schoolteacher next to him, quietly carrying her baguette-topped grocery bag, felt any emotions for him whatsoever? Maybe he was fantasizing too much.

Aside from their kiss yesterday, he saw no further indication that she wanted to pursue a relationship. And maybe that was for the best.

As they approached his house, a titter sounded next to him. Then more laughter. He watched her, wondering what could possibly be so funny.

"Private joke?" He brushed against her, and the giggling ended on a gasp.

"I don't know." She cleared her throat, giggled again. "I was just wondering if domestic service is in my job description."

"Maybe I'll ask at the next PTA meeting."

He stepped in front of her as she began to laugh again. She bumped into him.

"Oh, sorry." He stepped out of the way and dipped into a bow. "After you."

Nose in the air, she affected a regal walk. "I do say. Thank you."

They were acting like a couple of dorky kids, but he hadn't felt this lighthearted since college, when his whole life had spread ahead of him like an empty, glorious highway. Caught in the moment, he used his free hand to tug on a lock of Nora's hair.

"You know," he said, winding the honey tendril around a finger, "you really ought to wear your hair down again some day. Like you did at the Clubhouse."

The laughter ebbed in her eyes, molten amber. "It just gets in the way." She stood still, waiting for him to follow up.

He slowly unwound the strand to make a corkscrew, which fluttered out in the bare wind. Reaching behind her, at the nape of her neck, he drew at the ribbon that held her hair in its twist.

Mouth agape, Nora shot her hands over his, dropping her grocery bag in the process. In the blur of a moment, Ray heard the crunch of shattered eggs and the crack and splash of broken glass.... Afterward, he saw the shield Nora erected, barring her arms across her chest and stepping backward, as if deflecting an anticipated harsh word for her error.

His concern must have been a fraction of what was mirrored on Nora's face. Her bottom lip trembled and pupils blanketed her gaze. Immediately, she fell down to her knees, scrambling to piece together the damage.

"I'm sorry," she murmured, fumbling with the tear in her sopping bag. "I'll go back and get more, I promise."

Ray bent next to her, his hand gently encircling her wrist like a bracelet. "No harm done. Don't worry about it." His finger lifted her chin so her fear-filled eyes met the strength he hoped was in his.

People didn't react this way.

Not unless they'd learned to.

Nora could've burrowed into the ground.

As she felt sticky orange juice and egg on her hands, she remembered how Jared would've reacted if she'd dropped his grocery bag. Protecting herself from a verbal dressing-down, backing off had been pure instinct, shielding herself from memory. Why had Ray been there to see it?

She nudged her chin away from his hand. The fight-or-flight beat of her heart hadn't subsided yet. "I'm sorry," she repeated.

An empty anger flitted through his eyes. Suspicion. Who treated you so badly? he seemed to be asking.

It took one wounded person to find another. From what Nora knew from reading Trent's essay, Ray had felt his share of pain.

Glass scraped across the sidewalk as she cleaned her mess.

Jared had merely followed in her father's footsteps. And, in a sick way, she'd become her mom, repeating the pattern of choosing the wrong man. Sure, Jared had dressed like royalty, all style, public manners and private demons. But it took more than polish to make a boy into a prince.

Nora knew what it felt like to have someone call her stupid, good-for-nothing white trash. She knew how it felt to be taken out to dinner at a restaurant with valet parking and red-velvet upholstery flickering under candlelight, to feel the knife of embarrassment when Jared had "made fun" of her for not knowing what crème brûlée was. To have him to turn to the waiter, wink and bellow, "I guess they don't serve crème brûlée in trailer parks."

To feel the stain of shame cover her skin as she avoided the waiter's disdainful glance as she ordered a bowl of chocolate ice cream. Never mind that she had never even stepped foot in a trailer park. She didn't understand what was wrong with living in one in the first place. The remark had hit home because, to Jared, anyone who hadn't been born with a silver spoon in her mouth was lower-level and, thus, subject to ridicule. He wanted her to feel lucky to be in his company.

And, like a young, inexperienced fool, she had fallen into his trap. Just as her mom had fallen into her father's.

Once, and only once, she'd asked her mom why they didn't leave. Nora had been too young to keep questions to herself.

Her mom had merely shaken her head and whispered, "Hopefully you'll never understand."

Nora didn't believe her mom loved her father, but she'd depended on him. Her mom hadn't possessed any skills or the confidence to obtain any. She'd been a pale shadow, traveling through the house by hugging the walls, trying to remain invisible.

As for Nora, her father had pretty much ignored her most of the time. And she'd learned to hide from his drunken rages. Every time she'd hear his slurred yelling, she'd fade, feeling stabs of guilt from being unable to protect her mom.

After college, Jared had attracted Nora with his flashy charm. The lure of his promises held her in thrall until she realized that, compared to the people around them, Jared didn't treat her very well. But after the way her father treated her mother, she thought Jared's treatment of her was normal. Thank God she'd finally wised up and found the courage to leave him.

The sting of a glass cut brought Nora's attention back to the present. Forget about it, she thought. Forget that part of your life.

She stood up. "I'm just so stressed out lately. Shaky. You know?"

"Nora…"

"It's getting late. I've really got to go."

He stopped her by cradling her shaking hand in his. God, she couldn't stop trembling as his thumb ran over her cut.

"You're hurt."

She shrugged. "It's no big deal. Really. I've got a bandage in the car."

With one last caress, Ray picked up what was left of the bag and motioned with his head in the direction of his house. "I've got bandages, too. You're coming inside with me."

And, with that, he waited for her to stand next to him. He smiled and they walked up his driveway, silence reigning over Nora's doubts.

Chapter Ten

The front door stood ajar when Ray and Nora entered his home. Reclining on the couch, engrossed in a television show, Trent swung his leg.

"Where have you guys been?" he asked, spying the ruined grocery bag Ray carried.

Ray settled his thumbs in his jeans belt loops. "I want to ask you the same thing." As Trent merely shrugged, Ray left Nora standing by the door while he went to the kitchen. She heard a thud, the smack of the refrigerator opening and closing, then the whoosh of water in the sink. Briefly, she stuck the cut finger into her mouth, tasting the tang of her blood.

Trent sat up in the chair. "What's up with him?"

Nora opened her mouth to speak. "Trent, what did you—"

"Do you have an answer for me yet?" Ray asked as he ambled out of the kitchen. He shot a meaningful look to Trent.

The boy quirked his mouth—such a Ray-like thing to do, thought Nora—and returned his attention to the TV.

Ray sighed and took hold of Nora's elbow, leading her down into the darkness of the hallway.

"Really, Ray, I can handle this cut." She wished he'd go back to talk with his son.

Ray clenched his jaw until she could see the muscle working. Maybe he was just trying to control his temper. "Don't worry. I want to give Trent all my attention just as soon as we've finished here."

When they entered a bathroom, Ray opened the medicine cabinet mirror and sifted through aspirin and cough drops, finally drawing out a crushed box of bandages. A dissatisfied frown on his lips, he searched some more until he found ointment. The sight was almost comical—this large manly man poring through small jars and boxes—but she was hardly in a laughing mood.

"Ray, I can do this by myself...." Nora's breath tightened as he put his hands on her waist and lifted her to the sink counter. Embarrassed, feeling like a small child, she crossed her ankles and absently wiggled her feet. He was taking care of her, treating her like the fragile eggshells she'd crushed on the walk home. It made her feel precious, cared for. Such a strange, scary experience.

From the living room, she heard Trent ask another question. "Hey, can Ms. Murray stay for macaroni and cheese?"

Ray turned on the hot water faucet and gently reclaimed Nora's hand. "We'll ask her in a minute." His brow furrowed, and his blue-green eyes bore into the cut until she almost believed he could heal with a glance.

She nudged her glasses up. "My mommy says I have to be home before dark, Mr. Brody."

By natural law, his eyelashes shouldn't have been allowed to be so long. They dusted over his eyes, a golden brown glinting in the subdued light that poured through the shower window. Nora tried valiantly to control the speed of her breathing, but his presence threatened to shock her body.

"We'll get you cleaned up and back home soon enough, Nora." He touched her knees and turned her toward the sink, leading her finger under the warm water. The feel of it threw heat down her body, settling into her lower belly, stirring there like a whirlpool.

His hands had stayed on her knees, and he was so close that the knees rested against his hip. She was almost straining with the effort of keeping the contact minimal, but she finally gave up, allowing herself to enjoy the sound of her stockings swishing against his jeans.

Using his thumb to test the cut, he rubbed soap over the wound, burning it. Then, with one swift move that startled Nora's heart, he kept hold of her hand and bent down below the sink to grab a thick towel. While he dried her skin, she inadvertently clutched his shoulder.

The crooked grin on his face caused her to blush, but he continued his job, now smoothing ointment over the cut.

Nora cleared her throat. "Lost my balance there."

He chuckled. "I'll be more gentle, then."

She didn't know if she could take "more gentle." Already she could feel her leg warming up for its chicken dance, the jerky nervous motion she detested.

As Ray wrapped a bandage around the cut, she attempted to stamp out the tension in the room. Inane conversation, that should do it.

"Oh, my pink blanket," she announced, as if it were the most important subject in the world.

Even though he had finished his ministrations, his hand still held hers. She could feel her heartbeat throbbing through her wrist, under his thumb. He was probably getting a real laugh out of her. Out-of-control Nora. Can't keep hold of a grocery bag or her emotions.

"Yeah, I've got it in my car."

She felt her legs opening as he moved between them. Looking down, as if from a cloud, she saw her knees on either side of his hips. His hands folded into her hair, and she felt his breath by her ear.

"We can get it later."

Her skirt had slid up her thighs, and, without thinking, she wrapped her leg around his, drawing him closer, feeling him between her legs.

He didn't skip a beat, drawing her to his lips to kiss her. Where that first kiss at the beach had been tentative, tender, this one was urgent and demanding. She slid her hands down his chest, molding them to his back, feeling every bunch of sinew as his tongue entered her mouth.

Warm and slick, she matched him thrust for thrust. He moved closer, evidence of his desire straining against the thin material of her skirt.

He held her so tenderly, so securely, she never wanted him to let go. She could live forever nestled against his firm chest, breathing in his scent, feeling dizzy under his caresses.

Nora moved her hips, longing to get closer to him, to twine her legs around his, never letting go. What would it be like to have him inside her, joined for all time like a never-ending circle? The thought shivered somewhere deep within her soul, stirring memories best left stilled.

As he pressed the small of her back toward his body, heat throbbed in her belly, spreading like a rising sun, racing under her skin until the breath left her lungs.

With a gasp, she broke away from his mouth, unable to breathe. She took his earlobe between her lips, licking it, teasing it with her teeth. He groaned softly in response, burying his face in her neck, quivering her skin with warm, harsh breaths.

She wanted to cradle his head, run her fingers through his sandy hair, tell him she cared about him. Cared way too much.

What would he say? Would he look at her with a knowing gaze, mutter something along the lines of "Do you actually think *I* could make you happy?" Her heart dropped in time to his lips traveling up the veins of her throat. This couldn't happen. Not if she valued the safe haven she'd created for herself.

Nora's sensitive classroom hearing caught footsteps coming down the hallway. Quickly, she pushed Ray away and dropped to the floor, adjusting her skirt and glasses.

Trent stuck his head in the doorway. "I'm making mac and cheese." He watched both of them, and Nora could have sworn that he knew exactly what had transpired. Heck, the window had even begun to fog around the edges.

"Come with me, Trent." Ray brushed past his son and Trent went after him, leaving Nora to breathe a sigh. Her body was still throbbing and, already, they were onto another dilemma.

"What do you want me to say?" she heard Trent yell.

She caught up to them in the family room, the TV's hum in the background. Ray stood with his arms crossed while his son mirrored him. Nora wondered if Ray realized how crazy his son was about him. Maybe Trent didn't let his father know about his feelings outright, but to her, his need to be loved was obvious.

Ray spread his hands. "Do I really need to say it, Trent?"

"Yeah."

A short laugh followed as Ray fell onto the couch and clicked off the TV by remote. Trent sat on the arm of a kick-back chair, jogging his leg.

Nora, who had at first felt out of place, realized that she was to play teacher right now, so she sat next to Ray while Trent watched her with suspicion. She was all too aware of the heat that still wavered between them. Ignore it, she thought.

"I missed you at school today," she said. "Your dad has your homework."

"Oh," said Trent, as if the big mystery had been solved. Didn't he realize that skipping school wasn't anything to take lightly?

"Trent, remember that talk we had with Officer Sanchez?" Ray leaned forward, trying to catch the drift of his son's smile. Nora could see firm lines etched around his mouth, as if he were straining to hold back his anger. For a moment, her heart jumped, recalling her father and how he'd dealt with rage.

Trent slid down into the chair, pulling back the lever so he reclined. He looked as if he didn't have a care in the world. "Yeah. But that was about tagging. I haven't been tagging."

"It was also about staying out of trouble."

"What did I do that was so bad? A bunch of kids had ditch day today." His fingers occupied themselves by picking at his New York Giants T-shirt.

Nora leaned forward. "Does that make it right for you, Trent?" Echoes of Gran Murray's voice washed over her. *If a bunch of your friends jumped off a cliff, would you do it, too?* She knew enough not to use that line on her students. They had heard it one too many times, and it was ineffective. Sometimes she thought that these kids were hardened to everything, and it scared her, sapped at her hope.

The youngster shrugged. "All we did was hang out."

"What am I going to do with you?" Ray ran a hand through his sandy hair.

Nora watched his son, watched his blue eyes widen, perhaps expecting the worst. She wondered how the boy's mom would have handled this situation.

As if reading her mind, Trent said, "Cheri wouldn't have cared. She let me ditch all the time."

That was the last straw. Nora couldn't stand to see Trent chipping away at his father's self-confidence in this manner. Lavalike anger pushed the words out of her mouth.

"Did you enjoy living with your mother, Trent?" She paused, waiting for him to make eye contact. When he did, she continued. "According to that essay you wrote, you didn't sound too thrilled."

"It was fiction, okay, Ms. Murray?"

She smiled, trying to hold back the sharp remarks that were bursting to get out. "Let's not lie to each other. I think we have a more respectful relationship than that."

Ray sighed, and she looked at him, his mouth turned down, eyes suddenly hooded. "I don't want to argue about this again, Trent."

"What?" Trent said. "That Cheri ditched you, too? She ditches everybody, man." His nose scrunched, and Nora realized that the stench of burnt noodles hung in the room. "Oh, great. Now dinner is toast."

As Trent leaped out of his chair, Ray called, "We'll talk later."

A moment stretched between them until he chuckled, none too comfortably. "Welcome to the Brody house."

Nora's smile felt wobbly. "He'll come around. I've heard of kids who have run away from home before even talking to their parents." At Ray's startled expression, she touched his muscled arm, leaving it to linger even after the first burn. "Don't worry—he likes you. He's cooking you dinner, for heaven's sake."

"I don't know. I'm just sorry about what he revealed to you."

"What do you mean?"

His eyes held depths of sadness, regret. "You shouldn't have to hear about my ex-wife."

"Too late." She grinned and realized that her hand still settled on his arm. Reluctantly, she drew it back. "I care about what happens to Trent."

She almost shrank into herself when she caught the intensity of his eyes. "Do you care?" he asked.

Her voice carried on a whisper. "Yes." She cared more than she would admit. Investing too many emotions meant a world of trouble. If she cared, she'd risk getting hurt yet again. She'd be much more effective if she could look at this situation with an unbiased eye. Cold and judgmental. That's what they needed, a referee.

But that just wasn't her style, and she knew it. She swallowed. "So, do you think his mom will come back?"

Ray shut his eyes. "Not to me. She was always a wanderer."

Nora tried not to let her relief be too obvious. In the next breath, she wondered what he meant by "wandering." Why would anyone ever stray from this man?

"But I don't know about Trent. Cheri always had a way of wanting to hurt me."

Before she could stop herself, Nora murmured, "She's crazy."

His eyes connected with hers, but she was too aware of the burnt macaroni smell wafting from the kitchen to fall into his gaze. She'd been hurt too many times to risk falling for this man.

Steeling herself, she said, "Caring is my job, Mr. Brody."

Ray frowned, and Nora felt the air change from intimate to professional. Had she just pushed him back forever?

You'll never be happy if you don't embrace it, said her grandmother's voice. The sparkle of the diamond bracelet— her wedding bracelet—glinted in her thoughts. At this rate, Gran Murray would never get to see her dance with the jewelry shimmering on her wrist.

Trent strolled into the room, cutting the tension between Ray and Nora. "I burned dinner. Can't we just have pizza?"

"Wonderful," said Ray, avoiding her gaze. "Another pizza night."

"Well," she said, rising from the couch. "Time for my dinner, too. Bye, guys."

"Hey, you can stay for pizza!"

Ray looked at her. "Fine with me." He ran his hand over his mouth, reminding Nora of their last kiss. The heat, the almost-got-caught scariness of it.

Tempting, but she knew she couldn't stay. It'd just be one more step toward getting her heart broken. "I've got some plans. But thanks for the invitation."

She caught Ray's skeptical expression. But she really did have plans. Grading papers over just-add-water risotto. It wasn't as appealing as pizza, but it was safer.

"Thanks for the homework, Ms. Murray," he said, shooting a look at Trent, who'd turned on the TV and tuned them out. The boy lifted his hand in an absent farewell.

"You're welcome." Nora headed outside, followed by Ray. He shut the door behind them, immediately reaching out to rub her arms. She froze.

"This can never happen again," she said, part of her really meaning it.

"This? You don't want me to rub away your goose bumps?" He squeezed her arms gently, sending a jolt through her.

"You know what I mean."

"Yeah, I guess I do." He dropped his large hands and put them in his pockets, looked away.

She propped up her glasses. "Well, good luck with Trent tonight. Who knows what he has in store for you."

When he met her eyes again, she detected a longing so fierce she almost ran away. But she'd been running her whole life, hadn't she? Why couldn't she bring herself to accept his need, his touch?

He shocked her by withdrawing his hand from a pocket and lifting her chin to meet his gaze. "Will I ever get to see you again? Not the teacher, not Ms. Murray. I'm talking about Nora."

Why would he want to? She couldn't understand. "I'll help Trent with anything he needs, but we can't sneak around, kissing in bathrooms."

He looked back at the window, and she followed his line of sight. They were lucky Trent wasn't spying on them.

"So this is a new way of saying you just want to be friends?"

She couldn't read his expression since he'd turned away, but she needed to protect herself, tell him the truth right now. "Actually, we can be associates. People who have one young boy in common. Nothing else."

He nodded, hands back in pockets, watching her now. "So that's that."

What, was she an idiot? Ray couldn't remotely be like her father or Jared. So why was she still running? "That's that."

"Then I guess it's goodbye."

When he took his hand out of his pocket, Nora's heart fluttered, thinking—hoping—he'd touch her again. But he was opening his door. Walking away from her.

The door closed softly, but to Nora, it sounded like a slam.

Chapter Eleven

Days later, Nora was still experiencing Ray-tingles. Time or distance hadn't soothed her adrenaline-choked body. She could only lie on her bed, staring at the ceiling.

Heart beating like the cadence of an automatic weapon, she exhaled and forced herself to calm down. She'd been thinking about Ray again, recalling their kisses, reliving the way he made her body feel when he laid his hands on it.

Not being around him was a withdrawal of sorts, leaving her shaken and sickened by her choices. Not being around him made her feel deadened to the world, and she wasn't sure if it was better than feeling wounded.

Seeing Trent every day made things worse. He reminded her of Ray. Every day was a jab to the heart, especially since she was still tutoring him, going places Ray would've enjoyed sharing as well.

She had a choice to make: either she'd continue this mere existence, pining away for a man and thinking about what could've been, or she could jump into the game, running the risk of tears and pain. But the risk would also include moments of joy so profound they made her throat burn.

Her head cheered the first choice, her heart lobbied for the second. She had no idea what to do. Nora turned over every solution in her mind. But, in the end, it came down to indecision again.

Nora rolled to her side, seeing her jewelry box waiting on the dresser. Her diamond bracelet would be sparkling inside. She shut her eyes, conjuring every ounce of trust she'd ever stored up. It still wasn't enough.

After she'd drifted off to an early sleep, the phone rang, jarring her awake. She mumbled a hello.

"Ms. Murray?"

She sat up on her bed, rubbing her temple. "Trent? Is that you? Is something wrong?" She'd given him her phone number for just-in-cases.

"No. Everything's cool. I was just wondering if you were busy."

Sure, she was busy obsessing over his dad. "You know I always have time for you."

"Excellent. Want to come over to help with my social studies project?"

Oh, my. He'd invited her over every day since they'd started this tutoring strategy, but she'd always declined. Usually he was asking her over for dinner, but this was different. She assumed Ray was sidestepping invitations for any more beach dates as well.

"When is it due?"

"Tomorrow."

"Great planning, Trent." But at least he intended to turn in a project. And on time.

He broke into her thoughts. "Brody's working at the restaurant tonight, and I really need some help."

His calling Ray by his last name didn't really surprise Nora. He'd done it for weeks now. When he was ready, he'd call him "Dad." Nora was sure of it. "Okay. Do you need me to bring anything?"

''Just your brain. Say, Ms. Murray, thanks a lot. You don't know how much this'll help.''

She sighed, rubbing her neck. ''See you soon.''

''Bye.''

She hung up, holding her head in her hands. If fate was kind, it'd keep Ray busy at the Clubhouse for the entire night. But, just in case, she'd put on some makeup: red lipstick to ruby her lips, a touch of mascara to darken her lashes, and blush to make herself seem like one of the living—not someone who just watched life go by.

Not for the first time, she wondered who was pulling the strings of her existence. Her or her past.

When Trent opened the door that evening, Nora almost didn't recognize him.

He'd slicked back his blond hair and wore a crisp, blue-and-white-checked button-down shirt with jeans. An angelic grin rested on his mouth.

Right away, Nora felt uncomfortable. ''Hot date?'' Was there some sort of dance tonight that she didn't know about? Should she have been somewhere chaperoning?

''No, Ms. Murray.'' He shuffled his feet in an ''aw, shucks'' moment.

While she walked into the house, remnants of what smelled like a TV dinner wafting through the air, she asked, ''Where are your T-shirts and baggy shorts?''

''In the wash. This was the only thing I had to wear.''

So much for that glimmer of hope. She'd thought maybe he'd found some button-down friends who wore loafers and spent nights studying at the library. Then again, she had to respect Trent's individuality, if his independence didn't lead to a stay behind bars.

''Where's the project?'' She tossed down her purse on the couch, expecting Trent to whip out a colorful time line or a report he didn't plan to invest much time in.

He motioned her into the kitchen. What she saw on the table astounded her.

He'd created a model of samurai warriors in full battle dress, attached to a board explaining Bushido, the code of the samurai that valued honor above life itself. Trent had even started a section detailing the lives of these particular samurai warriors. Overall, it was still crude but an awesome feat for a seventh grader.

"Whoa," she said.

"Is it okay?" The question loitered in his eyes, begging for a positive answer. "My dad was helping me, but he had to go into work. Someone called in sick."

She spread out her arms, gesturing to the project. "It's incredible, Trent. I don't even think you'll need my help."

"Could you check my writing?" He pointed to the paper explaining the fictional warriors' lives.

She felt honored that he'd asked her to do this. Obviously, he hadn't really called her over to his house to help him. He took great pride in this project, and he wanted her to know how hard he was working.

"You bet I'll do it." Before sitting in a chair, she put a hand on his shoulder. He looked at her fingers, then up at her, smiling. "I'm so proud of you, Trent."

He shrugged, and she took her hand off of him. Not that he'd admit it in a million years, but she'd bet he was proud of himself, too.

They settled at the table, Nora, reading Trent's work, Trent, putting the finishing touches on his model warriors. The stillness of night chirped and flowed from the open kitchen window, cooling the room. They worked in companionable silence, no radios or TVs blaring to make her feel less lonely.

She had no idea how long Ray Brody had been standing in the kitchen entrance. When she felt the hair on her arms stand at attention, she looked up, pulled out of her contented daze by his loose-limbed stance, the sight of one broad shoulder wedged against the door frame. Emotions she couldn't quite define mingled in the blue-green of his eyes—longing, tenderness, joy, loss…maybe something more. She looked away before he could read her as well.

* * *

When Nora had casually glanced up, then just as easily dismissed him, Ray felt his hope sap. He'd been standing here for mere seconds, taking in the sight of Nora and Trent working arm to arm on his son's social studies project. He'd even been able to pretend that they all belonged together, a trio of lost souls, combining to form the family he'd always needed.

Nora, her hair held up in a barrette, exposing her peach-cream neck, was a vision of quiet beatitude in her soft pink sleeveless shirt. He loved watching the light play off the smooth skin of her arms, glowing like a dusky pearl. And she was wearing those jeans again, the ones that accentuated every dip and curve. Not many people could've tolerated Trent and his outbursts, but Nora wasn't just another face in the crowd. Not by a long shot.

He'd missed her these past days. Trent talked about Ms. Murray all the time, giving Ray no opportunity to forget her scent, the gentleness of her touch, the hunger beneath her kisses.

Yet, like a dream materialized, here she was. Refusing to look at him.

He kept his voice low, unwilling to disturb the scene's serenity. "How go the samurai?"

Trent stood up, just noticing his presence. "Almost done. Ms. Murray almost fainted when she saw it."

She placed a slender finger on Trent's story to mark her place. "Now, I think we're practicing a little hyperbole. But I did almost shoot through the roof." She winked at his son. "It's absolutely incredible."

"Brody gets a lot of the credit, too. Don't you?"

Ray wanted to ignore how his son addressed him, but it was impossible. Every time he heard his son call him by his last name, he felt like a stranger. Cold, stranded, watching a loving family through the frosted panes of a window from outside. "I didn't do that much. You're the idea man."

God, he wished Nora would just look his direction again.

He'd promised no more kisses, no more steamy contact. Why did she have to be so standoffish?

She'd gone back to reading the essay, playing the part of teacher to the hilt. Ray didn't know if he could take the tension much longer.

Trent piped up again. "Brody built the board and helped me with the warriors. I thought he'd yell at me for starting this late, but he was okay." He addressed Ray. "You were cool about it."

Nora lifted her head, eyes seeking Ray. Uh-oh, not a good expression. He wondered what he'd done wrong now when all he'd wanted was to help his son with homework. Hadn't that been their deal? Spend more time with Trent, help him out, attempt to establish some sort of bond?

Or maybe he'd given him too much aid. He wasn't sure, but he knew he'd hear it from Nora, judging from her demeanor.

"Why don't you sit down, Brody." Trent dragged a chair out from the table and placed it right next to Nora.

As his son busied himself with his project, Nora shot Ray another mysterious glare. Did she want him to sit across the table? Not if he could help it. Riling her, stirring up the sparks in her eyes, sounded like a pretty entertaining pastime. Ray sat down next to her, scooting his chair even closer.

She peered at the space separating them, as if saying, "That's a little too close for comfort, buckaroo." He grinned at her.

As she resumed proofreading, Ray started work on one of the samurai, all too aware of Nora's presence. He could barely keep his mind on even the simplest task when she was around.

Trent went to the refrigerator and returned with two frosted cocktail glasses, which he placed in front of Ray and Nora. Without a word, he went back to work.

Red-tinged liquid bubbled around maraschino cherries. Both Ray's and Nora's mouths gaped at the same time.

"What's this?" Ray finally asked.

Trent talked while he worked. "It's not booze, so don't

stress. It's just Sprite with cherry juice. A Shirley Temple, right?''

As if the froufrou drink was Trent's number-one favorite. Ray opened his mouth to say something…anything, but the only sound he heard was a sharp ''ding'' from the oven.

Trent scooted up again, slid a mitt over his hand and withdrew a cooking sheet piled with little pizza snacks. While Ray and Nora just stared at the sight, his son shut off the oven, dumped the hors d'oeuvres onto a china dish and clanked the plate between the adults.

This was not looking good to Ray. What the hell was his son trying to do?

''Ms. Murray, how's my samurai story?''

She gulped, head down, face pink. ''It's great.''

Trent stepped back from his project and surveyed the results. ''Cool. I'll finish it up in the morning.'' He waved and ambled out of the room. ''Good night, guys.''

Heavy silence. The sound of Trent's door shutting seemed like the boom from a starter's pistol.

Ray looked at the pizza snacks, slightly burnt at the edges, but giving off a tomato-cheese aroma. Hell, why not. He tried to take one, but it was hot to the touch.

Nora stood up. ''I think that's my cue to call it a night.''

''He's being Trent.'' Ray actually laughed. ''Don't be nervous, Nora. I won't let the romantic atmosphere overtake me.''

She crossed her arms. ''I came over here to help him with homework, and he springs the parent trap. Isn't it enough to make *you* jumpy?''

He thought of Cheri, and how they'd never had such a courtly setup. He had to admit, pizza snacks and Shirley Temples weren't exactly caviar and champagne, but it was the intention and the company that mattered most. Things didn't get more ideal than Trent's crystal-clear approval of Nora. How could he be nervous, considering the circumstances?

''Relax. It's not like we're on an actual date, although I don't think it's a bad idea.''

''You know it is, Ray Brody.''

"Why?"

Her eyes dimmed, amber to murky night. "I've explained. Teachers don't date parents." She shook her head and walked to the other side of the table.

Ray wondered if she believed her own excuse. "All right, no more of that talk. But wouldn't it be a shame to waste this setting? I feel like we're at a Parisian restaurant. Not that I've ever been, of course."

She ran a finger over a samurai, hesitated, then strolled back to her seat. Much to Ray's surprise and pleasure, she sat down again. Good, now the world had returned to the beauty it had when Nora was near.

"How much of the project did you do, Ray?"

Casually, she picked up a snack, tentatively bit into it. Steam seeped from the pastry as she held it away from her mouth. She took a quick drink. Lucky glass.

His mind came back to her question. He thought about this afternoon, how he'd purchased supplies, helped decorate the models, cut and sanded the board. "Let's just say I was a willing volunteer."

She still held the glass to her mouth, letting it linger as she absently rubbed the rim against her lower lip. She watched him, speculation in her gaze. Ray could feel himself growing aroused.

Breaking the spell, she set the glass back on the table. "It's great that you were here for him. Helping is wonderful, checking over his work, leading him in the right direction. But it might be better if, next time, he could do his own work."

Oh, great, the teacher returns. "He wouldn't have been able to turn in his project on time if I hadn't helped." The excuse sounded lame, even to his own ears.

"Then Trent needs to be accountable for that. He needs to plan ahead. If he knows you'll take up his slack when he's too lazy to take responsibility for himself, why even bother?" By now, she was leaning on the table, hands grasping the edge with apparent conviction.

Sure, he'd wished for her advice before, but that was in

times of trouble. When Trent was smiling, pulling cute little jokes like this pizza-and-Sprite picnic, Ray could handle his son. He didn't need Ms. Murray's input at the moment. "Any other unsolicited opinions before you leave?"

Now he'd done it. Once again, his mouth had spoken before his brain could catch up, just as he'd done on more than one occasion since he'd first met her. She stood up, smoothed down her pink top, making Ray's gaze wander to her breasts. He remembered the beach, and how her lacy white bra and the curves beneath had driven him to distraction. Like right now.

"One last thing. I adore Trent, but he's an expert at manipulation. If he's got you wrapped around his pinkie finger now, just think of how you'll be worked over for the rest of your life."

"I don't plan on anyone controlling my life." He grinned, leaning back in his chair, allowing his gaze to take a long, lazy jaunt down Nora's body. Who was trying to control whom here?

She stood, crossing to the other side of the table to hide behind a samurai. "You're like a brick wall sometimes. You know that?"

He tried to look innocent. "What do you mean?"

Yeah, right. He knew exactly what she was talking about. His stubbornness. His eighteen-wheeler-thick head. And, from the sight of it, Nora was about to read him the riot act for not admitting when he was wrong. Good. He liked when her face bloomed pink with passion, her eyes sparking clusters of gold fire.

She shook her head, narrowing her gaze. "You know what I mean, Ray Brody. If the truth whacked you in the rear end, you'd grit your teeth and say, 'Thank you, sir, may I have another?'"

Okay. He couldn't dispute that. "Has anyone ever told you that you're beautiful when you're all riled up?"

"Oh, please. Have you heard a word I'm saying?"

"Definitely. You're raising the roof."

She held up her hands, her eyes turned toward the heavens. "Why do I waste my time?"

Something about the way her voice balanced between a tremble and a laugh plucked at his heartstrings. He rose from his seat and walked to her side, his skin pricking with heat with every step that drew him closer to her. "You have the heart of an angel. That's why you're here."

"Do *not* sidetrack me. I was in the middle of a good diatribe." Her breath chopped the words, diced them into tiny bits of tension.

So much for ending her holier-than-thou speech. "Sorry. Go right ahead with your scolding."

Nora locked gazes with him for a moment, then shook her head. "You just don't get it, do you?"

Unfortunately, he did. He was well aware of his failure as a father, and how, even now, he could be blowing it with Trent. With her. He stepped away from Nora, leaving her a clear path to leave his home.

Maybe she expected him to apologize, to bow down to her wisdom. At any rate, he just stood there as her jaw locked and her hands fisted. Mule that he was, he couldn't think of a thing to say.

Without another word, she stomped from the room, grabbed her purse and left, leaving a wave of citrus as a remembrance of her presence.

He'd blown it once more. But what else was new?

When Ray checked into work a few days later, he found a phone message from Nora Murray dated earlier in the morning.

Nora stopping by after school. Joan

Now what? More back-seat-driver advice? Or had Trent pulled another unthinking stunt at school? Ray was in no mood to talk about negativity today. It was Friday—a day for making his brain into a tabula rasa—a blank slate. He just wanted to relax.

He thought he'd done the right thing when he'd helped

Trent with his project, but in hindsight, maybe he was coddling his son, making up for lost time by catering to him. Nora was right about not allowing Trent to take advantage of him. But what about the way he and his son had gotten along these past few days? If Ray had to bribe Trent, maybe it was worth it.

Or maybe not. She was right. He wanted to raise a responsible boy, a good citizen. Spoiling him wouldn't accomplish that. He could help Trent, but his son would have to be accountable for his mistakes from now on.

Yet one problem remained: he missed Nora, jerky leg, honey hair, fruit-spiced scent and all.

Joan, beaming with purpose as the manager of *his* bar and grill, elbowed him. "Here to check up on me again, huh?"

"You haven't run the place into the ground yet," he said with a wink.

"Ray, you just concentrate on that demon child of yours, and I'll concentrate on making this the place to be in San Diego. Deal?"

Running his hand along the bar, Ray walked to the jukebox. "I guess I'm trading one baby for another."

Yes, he had shaped this Clubhouse into what it was—it had grown up well. Now, Trent…he'd see about that child.

He was already in the weekend mood, that driving need to live life like an ad for sexy jeans or American-made cars. Searching the jukebox for the right song, he picked a down-home seventies anthem and wandered around the pre-happy-hour murmur of the Clubhouse.

He missed this place: the watering-hole gossip of the regular customers, the excuse to watch every game the satellite TV could afford him. Being in here lately had only reminded him of how much he enjoyed it. He missed the strong aroma and sizzle of grilling meat, the clatter of silverware. Then again, he had so much more time to be with his son now. They still weren't fishing buddies, but they had come a long way since his son had moved here: Trent actually removed his ball cap without being asked, and their nightly rounds of basketball provided a tacit bond that Ray didn't understand, yet didn't question.

What would've happened had Nora not intervened? Ray had no doubt that Ed Sanchez or his fellow officers would have been involved. Imagine, his son, a criminal. Robbing houses. Getting high on alcohol. Tagging the school. He had never pictured his life like this.

A streak of bitterness surfaced as Cheri crossed his mind. He shut his eyes hard, leaned against the jukebox and tried to "tabula rasa" his brain.

When he opened his eyes again, he saw Nora approaching. Her hair was twisted up, and featherlike tendrils blew around her neck. In spite of the mild heat outside, she seemed cool in her blue outfit. Her entire face felled his heart, and he realized her glasses were gone.

"I wasn't aware that jukeboxes made comfortable beds," she said, stopping far enough away to be appropriate.

Nora talking about beds. It was almost too much for Ray. He grinned. "It's not so bad since I get to wake up to the sight of you."

An awkward silence. Had he offended her?

Finally, he spoke. "I didn't expect to see you again. Not after Shirley Temple night."

Shuffling her blue flats, Nora looked down. He knew that he had embarrassed her yet again. But when she looked back up, she had a melancholy smile on her soft mouth. He breathed a sigh of relief and longing, then recovered by rubbing his chin with his hand.

She casually looked at the selections on the jukebox. "I'll bet you're wondering why I'm here."

"I sense an explanation will be coming my way sooner than I think."

"It's nothing Trent did. Well, except that he's doing well in class." Her touch was as light as a patch of warm sun as she brushed his forearm in a mock punch. "But you already know that."

"Yeah. I know." Silence again. "So why?"

"An apology. I've got no business telling you how to raise Trent and, now that I've said so, I can have a clear conscience."

"And that's the only reason you're here?" There had to be something more. She could've tried to reach him by phone if she hadn't gotten a hold of him this morning.

Her hand spidered the blue neon covering a coin slot. "Yeah. That's it." He cocked his brow, causing her to lift her hands. "That's the truth," she said.

"You have an honest face. I guess I'll have to believe you."

He watched her struggle with herself; she peered at the jukebox a little too intensely. She started to say something else but stopped.

Before she could run off on him once again, he grabbed her sleeve. "I don't want to cause any trouble…"

Laughing softly, unconvincingly, she said, "Helping Trent is no trouble at all."

"I'm talking about something else entirely, Nora."

There was a long pause as the jukebox switched selections. A wistful love song and its mellow twangs floated between them. The singer crooned over Ray's thoughts, sang about dreams and whispering into the ear of the one you wanted.

Now, this was a little eerie. Or was it just that every love song seemed to hit the nail right on the head when you stood next to the person you craved with every beat of your heart?

Nora put her hands next to her eyes, like blinkers on a horse. "See, this is what…this is the thing." Her hands pushed out in front of her while she widened her eyes. "I don't think I can do this anymore. It's just…too strange. I know I have to tell it like it is, so—" She squeezed her eyes shut. "Oh, God. How can I put this?"

"I wish I had you alone in a shady room right now, Nora Murray."

Her eyes flew open, black pupils almost eclipsing the sunlight and amber. "What?"

His voice was soft. He couldn't believe he'd just said that. "You heard me."

She nodded nervously, almost comically. "See. This is what I was afraid of."

Exactly what was she afraid of? His finger directed her chin into the line of his gaze. "Only a blind man wouldn't have been able to tell what's been happening between us every time we see each other. And then, that blind man would have been able to *feel* it."

"I'm not your type of girl, Mr. Brody."

She was trying to distance herself by using his last name. He'd caught on to that trick by now. By instinct, he gripped her chin tighter, but loosened it after her mouth opened in surprise. "Don't call me Mr. Brody."

"All right," she said, her voice lowering to a husky undertone.

He wanted to climb over the wall between them, or take it down brick by brick. "You're exactly my type of girl precisely because you go against the idea of every woman I've been with before. Now, I know I'm not perfect, and probably more trouble than I'm worth, but what if we could forget all our disappointments and go out to have a nice dinner somewhere?"

It was out there. He'd said it. Ray let his hand slide down her chin to the column of her neck.

She paused, cheeks reddening. "What about Trent?"

In spite of his happiness at her answer, the comment was like a splash of ice water over his face. And other parts of his anatomy. Yeah, what about Trent? She was the voice of reality. Did he really want to get involved with Nora while he was killing himself managing Trent? How could he possibly have time for both?

He'd find a way. Even if this date was based on the victory of body over mind, he'd make it work. He was determined not to mess up like he had with Cheri.

"You want Trent to chaperone us?" he asked, grinning.

She actually looked as if she were considering the idea. "Maybe."

"Hey. I thought that you weren't afraid of anything."

Out of the corner of his eye, Ray saw Joan casually wiping the bar. She was a little too close to be subtle. He put his hands in his pockets and leaned toward Nora, whispering, "Let's blow this pop stand."

Biting her lip, Nora paused, watching the lights on the jukebox. As if in a daze, she said, "Let's go, then."

Ray could have jumped to the moon. "How about doing this right? I'll pick you up at seven tonight. All right?"

"My word." The jukebox neon reflected the fright and excitement on her face. "This has to be low-key, Ray."

The intensity of her eyes burned the message home. He had to admit, the idea of secrecy appealed to him as well—it was a necessity. A little testosterone devil voiced its opinion in his ear: *We can pull it off,* it said. *Just look at her standing right here in front of you. You want her, Brody. Keep it undercover, if you know what I mean.*

Ray gave in with all of his heart. He would be careful to protect Trent, to keep his boy from thinking that he was deserting him by stealing out with another person just when father and son were growing closer.

"I swear myself to secrecy. Blood oath?"

She grinned. "No more *Tom Sawyer* for you, Ray Brody."

They clasped hands in a very un-Sawyerish manner.

Chapter Twelve

After returning home, Ray had made arrangements with Ed, who lived across the street, to watch Trent for the evening. He could hardly believe Nora had said yes to going out with him.

He tried not to act like a teenager on his first date as he shaved, showered and pulled out of his closet some dark blue chinos with a short-sleeved cotton shirt. Lesson learned from Trent's comments at the beach, he splashed on a minimum of aftershave. At least his son wouldn't be around tonight to make jokes about his attempt to smell desirable.

Peering in the mirror, he decided that he looked ready for a first date. He slid a comb through his tawny hair one more time and went into the family room where Trent was hooking up a computer. Ray had purchased it this morning, hoping that his son would use the complicated network of machines for word processing or educational purposes.

But, as he spied the open package of a popular star-fighter game he'd impetuously thrown into the shopping cart earlier, he grinned to himself and thought, *All work and no play make Ray and Trent dull boys.* They had to have *some* fun, for crying out loud. He also wondered if the computer was another attempt to cajole Trent into loving him.

"How's it going?" he asked.

"It's easy. Can't you stay? If you don't, I'm going to be able to beat you at saving the galaxy when you get back." His eyes looked half-serious, half-pleading.

Ray felt guilt punch his gut. Maybe he should stay....

He pictured Nora. Smiling, prim Nora in a tight red dress. *My sex drive should be that lucky,* he told himself. He only wished he could invite Trent to accompany them, to take this heavy secret away.

"I'd love to, but I've already committed to something else, son."

Trent returned his attention to the computer. "Is it a date?"

How could he be so perceptive? Ray wondered if Trent was just taking a shot in the dark. Should he lie?

A little white one wouldn't hurt. If things went well, he could be entirely up-front about Nora. "Just a friend." There. That wasn't too far from the truth. He and Nora were on friendly terms. Very friendly.

"Where are you going?"

Wasn't it the parents who were supposed to give the third degree? "Old Town, I think."

"Oh. I've never been." He continued to fiddle with the computer. Then he stopped and watched Ray. "Why don't you go out with women?"

The question took Ray by surprise. "Well. I, ah, I used to, Trent. But I like to spend time with you now."

Trent nodded sagely. "And time with Ms. Murray."

Laughing uncomfortably, Ray back stepped toward the door. "Sorry, buddy. Ms. Murray is your teacher. She's part of the education package."

"Bummer," said the boy. "She'd probably be a good girl-friend. Don't you think?"

Ray thought he felt sweat bead on his upper lip. He gave

an exaggerated shrug. "Who knows? I've never given it any thought."

The boy went back to work. "Have fun."

Acting as if this appointment was more of a chore than a pleasure, Ray said, "I'll try. Ed's just across the street if you need him."

"Okay."

That had been interesting. Almost like a parent-child body switch.

He climbed into his Range Rover and drove to Nora's apartment according to the directions she'd given him. She lived in a modest complex about two miles from the beach, ivy creeping up the building's tan stuccoed walls.

Touching his hair one last time, he knocked on her door and waited. A commotion sounded inside. Finally, Josie answered, dressed in pink sweats.

She looked him up and down, much like she had in the Clubhouse during their first meeting. "Hi, Ray. Nora's still adding the finishing touches."

The thought of red lipstick skimming over Nora's lips made Ray light-headed. "Thanks."

"Nor!"

A muffled "Just a sec!" was the response. Ray scanned the apartment while Josie ran into the hallway. Ballerina prints hung on the walls, two bookcases of movies framed the TV, modest yet matching furniture and curtains decorated the room, and a peachy smell hung in the air. It was…female.

Come on, Nora, he thought. Let's just get out of here. He impatiently tapped his foot. Josie appeared, a big smile on her mouth.

"Here she is," she said, proud as a parent presenting her prom-queen daughter.

Nora hesitantly stepped around the hall corner. Ray's heart began to pound, and in response to his prom-queen analogy, he felt like the corsage-wielding, pimple-faced date.

An ivory-and-gold-print vest and a matching long skirt covered her tan skin in a prim, yet provocative manner. Every time she lifted her arm to tuck hair behind an ear, the vest would ride up to flash a glimpse of her flat, peach-toned belly. He attempted to act as if he was in utter control of himself.

"You look beautiful," he whispered. He cleared his throat and adopted a stronger voice. "Ready?"

"Heaven help me," Josie said, her voice almost choking with happiness. "I feel like I should take a picture or something!"

"Oh, please, Jos," Nora said through her teeth.

"Let's go." Ray dashed to Nora's side, lightly held her arm and led her to the door.

"Off like a bride's nightie!" Josie waved excitedly as the couple left.

Outside the door, Nora and Ray smiled at each other: head-dizzy, summer-sun smiles.

He offered his arm and she accepted.

Nora Murray, he thought, I want to treat you like a queen.

The feeling of being on a date was so foreign to Nora that she moved with the steps of a sleepwalker. *This can't be real,* she kept thinking, her arm snuggled in the crook of Ray's much larger one.

She loved the feel of a man's arm; her small hand couldn't circumvent his biceps, and she felt that he could protect her under the warmth of an embrace. She imagined sinew, smooth muscles and skin beneath his clothes.

Oh, underneath those clothes. She felt wicked just thinking about his shadow in a moonlit room, moving close enough to tickle her ear with promises.

What would happen at the end of the night? Would he try to kiss her, to come into her apartment, sneaking in the dark…

Into her room?

The thought occurred to her that neither of them had complete privacy. She would have to play roommate games to achieve solitude, and he would have to send Trent to a slumber party.

Nora subtly fanned her face. Listen to her, composing a plan of attack. Ever since she'd gotten a taste of Ray's tantalizing kisses, she'd been completely hormone-fixated. Just walking next to him, matching him step for long step, was enough to warm her all over. Even at this moment, if he did have her in a shady room, she thought with a smile, she wouldn't hesitate to unbutton her vest, rub up against him, feeling the material of his shirt scratching her bare breasts.

Oh, it would feel good to be bad.

She tried not to trip down the stairs as she peered out of the corner of her gaze, thrilling at the way the dark blue and olive of his shirt brought out the island-water color of his eyes. His skin was tan and fresh-shaven. He smelled of clean and soap: that aftershave again. My word, did she love that scent.

He helped her into the Range Rover, and as he walked to his side of the vehicle, she took the opportunity to glance at herself in the side view mirror. Red lipstick: check. Hair: check. Bedroom eyes: check. Ready to fly.

Before he started the car, he watched her, a slightly boyish grin on his face. Did he feel as awkward as she did?

"I mean it, Nora. Every guy in the place tonight will be green with envy."

She nodded stiffly and folded her hands in her lap. God, help her accept his compliments with grace. She just wasn't used to them. She'd never heard her father compliment her mom, and Jared had been stingy with them as well.

His hand insinuated itself onto her thigh. She gasped as warmth zinged through her…oh, she couldn't think about where it zinged.

"Promise me." His fingers danced lightly, massaging her skin. "Tonight we're just Ray and Nora, two people who met at the…at the beach. No guilt, no worry. And no school talk."

She rested her head against the seat and tried not to be aware of his hand. She was dying, truly dying the little death. Gathering her breath, she softly said, "All right. But let's get out of here before Josie brings out the videocam."

Hesitating, he smiled knowingly and removed his hand— much to Nora's disappointment.

They roared out of the parking lot and rode silently to Old Town, commenting every so often about the nice weather or current event topics.

For a moment in the past, she remembered herself in the passenger seat of a Jaguar, watching the yellow road lines zip by because the driver floored the gas pedal. Tires screeched just in time to avoid a valet booth. Jared would enter the restaurant without opening the door for her. Alone, dressed in a confining green silk dress, she would stumble into the restaurant, trailing behind Jared. She would order the appropriate dishes, burrowing into the folds of the restaurant booth. Wishing she were home.

"Nora, you're not supposed to wrinkle your eyebrows tonight."

She looked at Ray and memory fell to dust. "I'm trying to be endearing."

He laughed, and Nora admired his genuine cheer. "I prefer your smile."

And she imagined that, if he touched her in all the right places, she'd smile a lot tonight.

But what was the purpose of this date? To have dinner once, savor a last kiss, and never talk about the emotions between them? Or would it lead to something more…tangled limbs, shared dreams, entwined lives? Nora couldn't predict the future and, even if she could, she didn't want to know.

She'd just take a chance to see if taking the risk was worth the reward.

Ten minutes later, twilight settled over San Diego as they walked into Old Town, a landmark of the city's Hispanic history. Ray touched her hand and held it to his heart for a moment. The gesture pounded her head, making her wonder about the events to come.

They walked, hand in hand, jasmine and wisteria floating in the cooling heat, mariachi music coursing through the air, gay fiesta colors decorating the shops and restaurants.

He led her to a hacienda that had been converted into a restaurant. As the aroma of salsa and chimichangas swirled around her, she made a concerted effort to keep her stomach from grumbling. Just you wait. When there would be a pause in the conversation, then it would grumble. Her body had that sort of impeccable timing.

The traditionally costumed hostess seated them outside, where a fountain splashed and a mariachi trio strolled from table to table. They ordered drinks and sat back, allowing the water's spray to mist their faces.

She surreptitiously admired Ray, the way the outdoor colors with yellow, green and red banners framed his lean body. Women from other tables cast sly glances at him, and she couldn't help thinking that they wondered why a man like Ray would be on a date with such a prim miss. She'd left her glasses at home in the hope that she'd seem more carefree without them. After all, that's what this night was about— tinkling fountains, lingering glances and decadent desserts.

But she wasn't sure the ploy was working. To add to her discomfort, she felt the build-up of a huge growl in the pit of her stomach. Panic in her throat, she looked around for chips and salsa. She dipped a tortilla chip—in the hot bowl.

As her face flamed, Ray leaned on the table. "You all right?"

Nora nodded quickly and tried to smile. Her stomach growled, anyway, the sound thundering in her ears. She just put her hand on her belly, as if to say, "Bad stomach."

"It would have been nice if Trent could have been here," she mumbled, just to cover the rumble.

His look was probing. "You sincerely like him, don't you?"

"Of course!" She sat back again, shocked that he'd even asked. "Why wouldn't I?"

Sighing, he said, "I ask myself the same questions. He's coming along, but I feel this anger inside him, in the way he looks at me. I know he resents the divorce. I resent the divorce, or at least, the marriage."

He looked so sad that she scooted her chair closer to his,

the scraping sound drawing attention to her proximity. She felt herself blush. *That was subtle.*

Yet all she wanted to do was comfort him. "Cheri? That's her name, right?"

"Yeah." He looked at her askance. "I forgot. We can't talk shop."

"I don't mind." In fact, she wanted to know everything about Ray. She already knew that he'd led a less-than-perfect life; what else could he possibly say that would shock her?

She fidgeted with the red-glassed candle on the table, wishing she could touch Ray as easily, without fear of consequences. "She was not a nice person, was she? This Cheri."

Ray paused as he watched the couple at the next table. They were in the middle of a fight, obviously: both silent, the woman eating her food with a vengeance, the man giving her testing looks every second or so.

"Do you think they're on their fifth date?" he asked in a voice close to a whisper.

Strange question, Nora thought, realizing that maybe this was how Ray avoided a subject. "I can't tell. Certainly not their first. No, they've definitely been going out for a while. She already knows how to control him."

Ray laughed, and Nora sighed at the crinkles around his eyes. He looked at the table and played with his root beer glass. Without really thinking, she ran a finger over his knuckles. Before she could take her next breath, he'd slipped his large hand into hers, rubbing his thumb over the sensitive cleft at the base of her palm.

Nora lifted her shoulders, goose bumps prickling her skin. His ministrations made her lethargic yet ready to spring from her seat. He kept caressing, voice lowered until Nora needed to lean closer.

"Cheri was a great gal when I met her in college," he said. "She always came to my games—this was very important back then. Baseball was *it* for me."

"And she was your cheerleader," Nora said, feeling a spark of envy.

"Yeah. We got married in school. I was only about twenty, too young to really be thinking. But I thought that I would make my money on the field—there was no question of 'would I or would I not be set for life.'"

Nora imagined a young golden Ray, his lithe body fielding hits. It was an immortal picture; it reflected the way he'd felt about himself, she guessed. The photograph in her mind made her long to touch his hope, to encourage his naive passions.

He frowned, fingers tightening on her hand. "Then came the accident, and a baseball career was out of the question. I couldn't stand myself—I thought I was worthless." He looked over her head, as if Cheri stood behind her chair. "She started staying out late, partying, smelling like other men's cheap aftershave. But, at that point, I just didn't care."

"You care now." Nora smiled, eliciting one from him. She moved her knee, making contact with his under the table. With a small adjustment, she maneuvered her thigh so it touched the length of his. Warm, taut, lean. She imagined stretching along his solid body—skin to skin.

His eyes were hot pools of blue heat. "I've done a lot of growing up."

She leaned toward him, drawn by his parted lips. Suddenly, the waitress stood by the table, ready to take their orders. They stilled their movements. Nora counted the seconds until she left, then watched Ray expectantly.

He took her cue, this time watching the fountain. Much to Nora's disappointment, he let go of her hand, choosing to fiddle with his silverware as he avoided her gaze. Would both of them ever be on the same wavelength?

He lifted one shoulder in a half shrug. "All of a sudden, Cheri became a shrew. A very pregnant shrew. And I had no hope for the future, at least, not the future I had hoped for."

"I hate to be cynical," she said, "but it sounds like Cheri was trying to get her claws into you before you hit the big time."

"That's what I believed for a while. But maybe, somewhere, sometime, there had been a spark of…I don't know…affection. I'm not sure it was love.''

"And then came Trent?" asked Nora. She hated to see his pain as he relived it, but maybe he needed to talk with someone who actually understood Trent.

Ray's smile of remembrance looked genuine. "It was the best feeling of my life, having a son. As he grew up, I thought we would be close, that he'd look up to me, ask me for advice about everything from girls to college choices. But then Cheri started wandering again.''

Nora held her breath. Trent had talked about his "impersonal mom" in his paper. He'd talked about her coming home late at night, eyes unfocused, hair smelling of cigarettes and leather jackets.

"She was very resentful about the hand life had dealt to her, so to speak. She came to hate the sight of me, and she wasn't much better with our son. 'I should have never given you the time of day'—that's what she always said to me right before she left for the evening." Tearing his napkin into little pieces, Nora was afraid that Ray would tear into the most convenient object when he finished, namely her.

"Did you ever have good times? Besides the baseball days?" she asked. She could very well imagine a marriage of unhappiness. She'd seen one firsthand with her parents.

Ray thought for a moment. "No."

"Oh."

His laugh was biting. "Well, I'm sure there were a few chuckles here and there, but the bad memories cloud the issue.''

She wanted to kiss the lines from around his mouth. He just seemed so sad. She'd seen eyes that sad before. They belonged to his son.

With a casual flick of his wrist, he balled up the napkin. "The busboys are going to love me here." He tossed the trash to the table. "You know the rest—the divorce, the flight. Trent wrote all about it in his essay. It's the part he remembers.''

"Why did Cheri take Trent if she wasn't able to care for him?"

"The million dollar question. To this day, I believe that she did it because she knew it would kill me." He all but wilted in his chair with relief when he saw the waitress coming with their food.

He seemed relieved to have finally gotten his emotions off his chest. Nora admired his candor, his strength in taking back a son who probably expected the worst of his parents. Most of all, she admired his ability to take the risk of loving Trent again.

Their legs still burned against each other beneath the table-cloth. She moved hers slightly, just to see if he'd respond.

He did, slipping his hand where no one could see, cupping a knee, massaging it until Nora wanted to slide out of her chair.

"Nothing like unburdening the spirit to make a man hungry."

She wondered what sort of hunger he referred to. "Shall we dig in?"

The pressure of his grip on her knee increased, making her surge against his touch. In response, he moved a little higher, between the inside of her thighs, fingers tracing against her thin skirt material.

She wanted to die of embarrassment or desire. Either way, she reached under the table, grasping his hand, stopping his progress. "The meal's on the table," she reminded him, looking around the courtyard to see if anyone was watching.

No. Safe for now.

A mischievous smile told her that he knew very well how much he was flustering her, stoking her need. "You can't fault a guy for trying."

She laughed, more from a fun sense of frustration than prim-and-properness. "You're insolent."

"Next thing you know, you'll have slapped my face with a kid glove."

"You watch too many old movies."

He smiled, a touch of guilt seeming to tinge his mirth. "That's what I do late at night when Trent misses curfew. And when he does something ill-advised, and I can't sleep."

She could think of a few ways to cure his insomnia. It made her blush just to think about it. She nodded at the food, crossed her leg over the other to discourage any more under-the-table games. "Your food's getting cold."

He grinned. "That's the only thing."

"Shape up, you flirt."

"Now, Nora," he said, putting banter aside. "I think we have a deal. When I reveal my innards, you must retaliate." She balked, and he raised a finger. "The precedent was set at the beach. You show me your epiphanies, I'll show you mine."

How could she possibly tell him about Jared and her upbringing? It was bad enough he knew about Tommy's death and her father's part in it.

She stirred her vegetable fajitas around her plate, watching the steam rise. "My life isn't half as interesting as yours."

"I certainly hope your war story isn't quite as bloody." He paused, probably remembering Tommy. "I'm sorry. Bad choice of words."

He had no reason to be sorry. That was her dad's department. "Aren't you supposed to avoid talking about past relationships on the first date?" asked Nora, hoping to get out of it. "You seriously want to hear about my nightmare of a past?" She said it lightly, but wondered if she meant it.

"Of course."

She couldn't. If she said too much, she'd just drive him away, causing him to disappoint her. She sat still for a moment, conjuring up memories of embarrassment and bad decisions.

Maybe she could edit her story, give him the PG-13 version. "Okay." She poked at her food until he reached out to caress her cheek.

He said, "I was joking. You really don't have to say anything. I could just look at you all night instead."

"And have you perish from boredom? I couldn't take that responsibility." She smiled shyly. "So here it is. When I graduated from college, I met Jared Jacobs at a Cinco de Mayo party, and we started to go out."

"The man of your dreams?"

Nora laughed uncomfortably. "You decide. Jared and I dated seriously for a while. He was independently wealthy. Which, of course, meant that he wouldn't lower himself to take a job." She felt the sarcastic smile weigh down her face. "Daddy was loaded."

"I can't imagine you with a guy like that."

"It was a bad choice. But I did learn to foxtrot and be seen and not heard."

Nora didn't like the expression on Ray's face. Pity.

Tucking her hair behind an ear, Nora smiled sheepishly. "I believed every word he uttered, this clench-jawed rich boy. At least I did for a while. Then he started to do silly, immature things. Tossing peanuts at me across a party and throwing them harder when I asked him to stop. Making fun of a new dress I'd buy, calling it 'trailer park.' Stupid stuff."

"What was his problem?" Ray was leaning on the table, his expression intense.

"The problem." Nora leaned back, her mind a cloud of memories. Rude chuckles, inappropriate jibes in front of his family and her co-workers, a disgusted sneer when she'd try to fit into his world. "The problem was that gold didn't run through my veins."

Ray's voice was rough, menacing. "And money made *him* a perfect catch?"

If Jared had been there, Nora knew Ray would defend her, be her knight in shining white button-downs. She felt more comfortable now that she knew Ray wouldn't make fun of her, validate her feelings of worthlessness. "Little did I know he had a girlfriend on the side, too, during our engagement. He brought her to parties, and people told me she'd sit on his lap when I wasn't looking. Meanwhile, he'd be laughing at me across the room, his corn-fed, Midwestern fiancée.'' Nora laughed, entirely without joy. ''He was like Pygmalion, the guy who wanted to mold the perfect woman. Emphasis on *pyg*.''

Ray all but exploded. ''He was a bastard to treat you that way. How could he not see you're perfect as you are?''

He looked down, leaned back from the table, while she caught her breath. Then, slowly, as if doubting her reaction, he reached for her hand. She took his, cupping it in her own, smoothing her lips over the strong veins on the back of his hand.

Softly, ''Why didn't you leave, Nora?''

Against his skin, she said, ''I did. Eventually. But he'd already taken away my pride, and I've spent years trying to get it back.''

She felt tears gather in the corners of her eyes, but fought to suppress them. Moisture trickled down the side of one cheek, hot and unwanted. He gathered her tears in his hand, clenching his fist, making her sadness disappear.

Now that she'd told him about her dirty little secret, she was able to relax a little. Should she escalate things, let him know she wanted him? What if he spurned her, told her that he wasn't interested in her *that* way? She knew how a male must feel asking a woman out on a date.

Be honest, she decided.

Subtly, softly, she ran her lips over his knuckles. His hand skimmed to an ear, to the collar of her vest.

Hoarsely, he said, ''You don't know what you're asking for, Nora.''

Tell him, said a voice in her head.

''Believe me, I do.''

They stared at each other as she ran her hand along his arm, feeling his muscles bunch. He hadn't told her she was stupid for staying with Jared. He hadn't laughed at her misfortunes as she'd feared he would.

She whispered, "I want to go back to my apartment." She almost dreaded his answer.

His eyes lost their glow. As Ray started to rise from the table, he said, "I'm sorry you're not having a good time."

Oh, no. He thought she meant she wanted to end the date. "It's not like that at all, Ray. I want to go back with *you*. So we can be alone."

He hesitated for only an instant, then helped her out of the chair, his touch feverish. "What are we waiting for?"

Chapter Thirteen

Ray ran a hand through his hair as he waited for Nora to come out of the kitchen with their drinks. He couldn't believe he was actually nervous, for Pete's sake. Hadn't he ever been on a date before?

Not with Nora. And he'd never reclined at the foot of her couch, heart thumping to the beat of soft reggae music, breathing in the aroma of peach potpourri. It seemed like she was getting a kick out of entertaining him. Right when they'd walked in the door, she'd dusted off a pair of stately crystal glasses, inquiring if he wanted to drink ginger ale or grape juice. She apologized for having no alcohol in the apartment, but it was fine with him. Ray only wished she had some root beer.

He scratched his chin, checking to see if his stubble was unbearably rough-edged. At the very least, he planned to engage in some serious kissing with Nora tonight. If he wasn't mistaken, the look in her eyes ever since they'd departed the restaurant symbolized a woman ready for a lot more than cuddling.

She swept back into the room, long skirt swishing against her shapely legs. "Grape juice made to order," she said, presenting him with the glass.

The dark liquid nearly splashed over the top as he took the cup. Take it easy, he thought. You've got all night.

Josie had left a note, telling Nora that she was visiting her folks in Long Beach. Yes, even fate was on their side tonight.

His hormones were ready to scream. As she eased down next to him, propping her back against the couch, he watched the way her sleeveless vest hugged her body, molding every luscious curve and indentation. She'd taken off her shoes, her toes tipped with red polish. Red that matched her lipstick.

"Thanks." He took a swig, careful to make sure the juice didn't leave a purple mustache.

"So…" they both said simultaneously. They laughed, cutting through the anticipation.

"You go first," he said.

She cradled the glass between both hands. "This is so awkward."

"It doesn't have to be." He followed suit and set aside his drink as well.

They watched each other for one tense moment, one of her eyebrows slightly cocked as if considering the consequences of their dinner flirtation. Her amber eyes, rimmed with a band of black that made them stand out in the muted light, told him he'd have to make the first move.

Ray swept a finger over her bare arm, noting the skin's softness, readiness. He noticed her nipples puckering under her vest, receptive to his overture. Was he willing to carry through with his desires?

She took a breath, exhaled. "I can't believe I did this."

"Did what?" Did she regret her decision to bring him here?

An embarrassed smile, accompanied by reddened cheeks. "Invited you over. I don't do things like that."

"Never?" He kept his voice low, as if he were soothing a small, wounded animal.

"I guess I've never really wanted to ask a man to my apartment. I mean, what would I do? I don't live at *Melrose Place*." She rubbed her arms. "I'm not used to this."

He leaned closer, cupped her jaw in his hands, got close enough to bury his nose in her freshly shampooed hair. The world turned into a shower of stars, bright bursts of light buzzing behind his eyelids. He touched his lips to hers, gently, tasting a trace of grape juice. He thought he heard her sigh, but couldn't be sure. All he knew was that it was the eighth grade in review: giddy and life-altering.

She made him feel full of possibilities, just the way he'd felt running on the open grass of a baseball field. Nora was just as fresh, just as confidence inspiring.

His hand butterflied from her hair down the front of her throat, stopping just shy of the soft swell of cleavage. After a stunned moment, she responded by pressing closer to him, wrapping a slim arm around his shoulder, the heat between them causing friction. If only he could feel this good every day for the rest of his life....

Ray rested his lips in the warm space between her neck and ear, smelling orange spice. His mouth lingered, and he groaned as he realized that he could feel her wild heartbeat with a touch.

Nora shivered and pulled back, eyes as wild as a golden explosion. Her words came in gasps, matching the pace of his. "You're a great kisser, Ray Brody."

"You're not so bad yourself."

They caught their breath, hands leisurely exploring safe places like arms and backs. Ray traced the area between her neck and shoulder, feeling her tense muscles. "Here," he said, "turn around."

She tilted her head and gave him a sidelong glance, quickening his pulse even more. "You won't stab me in the back?"

He became deadly serious. "Never."

She seemed to read the promise in the one word. He'd never

betray her. He knew this because he'd never allow this relationship to go that far. The young boy who waited for him at home was top priority; their developing trust needed all the attention he could spare. There was no time for distractions like Nora, no matter how tempting she was.

Apparently satisfied, she nestled between his legs, which he braced on either side of her. He moved her hair so it fell over one shoulder, using his hands to knead her back and shoulders. He ran his thumbs down her spine, applying tender pressure, stopping at the small of her back to rub away the stress.

Neck arched, she moaned softly. "You'll put me to sleep."

"We'll see about that." He loved that he could make her feel good. It'd be nice if he could do this to all her worries and bad memories—rub them out, perish them to the black hole of nightmares.

He continued for a while, enjoying the way Nora's body swayed with every move of his hands. But he was growing edgy, wanting more than just an innocent massage. What would she do if he performed the same therapy on more than her back?

Pure, unadulterated lust blinded him. His hands moved of their own accord, ignoring protests of his brain, an organ that knew better than to start something that would definitely have to stop soon.

She relaxed a bit more, allowing Ray to slide his fingers around her waist, flexing on her ribs. Nora shifted restlessly, her hand sneaking over his to guide him to her stomach.

He rubbed circles, feeling her stomach muscles constrict beneath the thin skirt material, causing her to smooth her lips over his biceps. She used her teeth to nip at him.

Ray could feel himself getting ready to burst. Didn't she know he'd find it all but impossible to stop with her?

He glided both hands over her torso, then reached up to cup her breasts. They were firm, yet soft, the tips hardened with passion. She gripped his arm, and he ran a tongue over the shell of her ear, taking it into his mouth to suck on a lobe.

They moved together, surging up against the couch, down

to the floor, Ray hard against her hip. Summer flames burned around them, making him feel hot, unable to be controlled.

He slid a hand into her vest to tease a bare breast, taking the crest between two fingers, squeezing gently, rolling, palming. She was so damned soft, so warm and welcoming.

Then she turned to face him, straddling his body with her skirt hiked to her knees. They kissed again, tongues testing, mouths devouring. Before he could stop himself, he'd unbuttoned the vest, baring her breasts in the soft glow of new moonlight coming through the window.

He tore his mouth away from hers, feasting his eyes on the sight. "You're so perfect, Nora." And he meant it, her waist stem-thin, the full flower of her breasts exposed. He couldn't help touching her again, rubbing his mouth against them to taste the sweetness of her skin.

"Ray, I'm not ready to—"

"—I know," he said, almost choking on his words as he kissed her neck. Slowing down. Chugging to a stop before they crashed.

He'd never forgive himself if he made love with Nora. They were two damaged people who needed to get their lives back in order. They didn't need each other to derail their progress.

Sweat mingled, breaths ripped out of them. He held on to her for dear life, not knowing when—or if—they'd ever touch each other again. It was probably best to stay away, to fold this memory like a cherished gift and secrete it in a corner of his life to be unwrapped when he wanted to recall some sense of joy.

Unfortunately, Ray was wise enough to know that happiness was short-lived. Times like this couldn't be stretched to fill a lifetime. Reality intruded on joy, tarnishing it until there was nothing left but a black reflection.

Nora couldn't believe she'd let it go this far. As she cradled his head, heart beating against his firm jaw, she almost felt ashamed of herself. But she felt too alive to feel the stain of regret, too flushed with need to let him go.

But she did.

They backed away from each other, and she buttoned her vest, her skin still burning from his stubble. Silence hovered over the reggae music, which she'd forgotten about until now. Everything was a blur of his soap-cologne scent, his thick, wavy hair, his hard body. Everything had gone much too fast. Why did it have to end?

Because it was time. Time to cut off a good thing before it turned bad. Maybe, just this once, she could hold a memory like a bright candle, watching the forever-flame, knowing the beauty of it would never burn out. If she and Ray never touched again, perhaps it'd be for the best. She'd always have a wonderful, soul-shattering keepsake of him.

She turned away, watching him out of the corner of her eye.

He peered at his watch, ran a hand through his sun-and-sand hair. "Would you mind if I called Trent?"

"No. Go ahead. You can use the kitchen phone."

He kissed her before rising, sweeping fingertips against her cheek. "You have no idea how much I want you, Nora."

She heated up. "The same goes for me."

He stood, looking down at her with an intense sheen to his gaze. Then he left to use the phone.

As she listened to Ray's muffled voice carrying on a one-sided conversation, she drew her fingers down her arms, tingling with the remembrance of Ray's touch. Was she crazy? If she hadn't wanted to get involved before, she sure was involved now. Where would their "relationship," if they indeed had one, go from here? The bitter part of her demanded things go nowhere. The optimist cheered for leaving the past behind and embarking upon a new future.

Problem was, Nora didn't trust her judgment when it came to making choices.

Ray walked back into the room, hands in pockets. "I'd better head home."

Maybe he was having second thoughts, too. "Oh. All right."

"It's not because of you." He shook his head. "It's getting late and I want to look in on Trent."

They shuffled to the door. Nora kept her head down to avoid a big farewell scene. He opened it, a brisk coastal breeze shivering her skin.

"Goodbye for now, Nora." He tipped up her chin with his index finger, and she closed her eyes, waiting for a kiss. Hoping for a kiss.

He touched his lips on an eyelid, making her wonder if he'd cooled off so much as to regret their earlier embraces. Her lashes brushed his jaw as he moved away.

She watched him walk down the stairs and climb into his Range Rover. He held up his hand as he drove off, leaving Nora feeling foolish for standing at the door like a sad puppy.

Heaven help her, she wanted more.

Nora's loving hung over him like a tropical moon. Heat hovering over his limbs, the taste of fruit lingering in his mouth. He wanted more.

Ray drove around his neighborhood one more time, almost shaking with conflicting emotions. Finally, he cruised onto his own street, swinging into his driveway and cutting the headlights.

He walked into his house, noticing that the lights were already extinguished. That's right—Trent had decided to call it an early night.

After quietly unlocking the door and slipping inside, Ray moved to his son's room to crack open his door. There, still in his clothes, lay Trent, sprawled on the carpet with an open journal pillowing his blond head.

Dismissing the temptation to read the journal, Ray kneeled on the floor, minding his bad knee. A slight throb from his baseball accident was beginning to bug him, but it wasn't anything major. He could be walking around with a stump and still not notice. Nora's kisses had healed some of his pain. But not enough.

He tucked a blanket around Trent's shoulders. This was a kid who could use a woman's guidance. But not just any woman's. Nora's. Would it be so bad if he were to bring Nora into the family? Was it even a possibility? The thought jarred him.

It was possible, but only if he made it happen. He shouldn't have ended their date so abruptly. He needed to see her again, if only to convince himself that he hadn't imagined the pain in her eyes as she'd watched him drive away. He couldn't stand to leave her like that, wondering why he'd vacated her apartment so soon after their intimacy.

He ran a hand through his hair and watched his son.

It seemed hours had passed when Ray stood and left the room. He continued out the front door after locking it and walked across the street to Ed's house.

He could see his friend through the screen door, blue TV light playing over Ed's features. "Hey," he half whispered. "Sack out on my couch, would you? Watch over Trent."

After very little coaxing, Ed ambled across the street, too tired to even ask questions. Satisfied, Ray hopped back into the Rover, feeling so conflicted he almost raced back into his house.

He should never have been to Nora's in the first place. It had sent his libido all out of whack. But he had to know. Was there a possibility of them being more to each other than Ms. Murray and Mr. Brody?

The streets, dry and empty, rushed by his window in a blur of closed-store lights and fluorescent telephone booths. He couldn't bear to turn on the radio and ruin his concentration. Or maybe he felt that a song could talk him out of this insane Casanova act.

When he drove into Nora's apartment complex, he almost turned back home. This was childish, giddy stuff only a hormone-captive kid would do. And, he was ashamed to admit, he loved it, loved the freedom.

He knew that Nora's room would be in the back of the apartment, so he walked through yuppie foliage and into the pool area. Balconies surrounded the blue glow of the water, and he calculated which room would belong to the woman he wanted.

There. The one with candles glowing in the window, behind sheer curtains. He took his chances and grabbed a fistful of pebbles.

Wait. Wasn't this too silly? He considered a moment, wondering if a woman would welcome the romantic cliché of pebbles awakening her sleep, or if she would scorn him. Hell, he'd take his chances.

He tossed up a small, rounded stone, his baseball-aim true as it tapped the lower part of the paint-chipped sill. The only answer was a flicker of the candles. He tried again. And again.

A light flashed on, like a giant opening its eyelid. Ray floated another pebble. After it hit, he saw the curtain draw aside slightly, enough to allow a peek of honey hair to enter his view.

Her entire face appeared from the corner of the window, mouth in an O. A soft screech filled the air as she pushed open the glass. The candles danced, and one blew out entirely.

"Ray, what are you doing?" she asked in a stage whisper.

As her body filled the sill's picture box, he saw the white of a thin gown clinging to her body. A peek of darkness told him that she wore nothing but skin beneath the material. His mind flip-flopped, a heavy wind changing directions.

"I have no idea what I'm doing!" He tried to whisper, but his deep voice made it impossible. His voice carried around the courtyard, rippling on the walls like the light waves reflected from the swimming pool.

He could see her piling hair on her head nervously, as if she were taking cover. "I thought you needed to get home. This isn't home."

Right now, *she* was home. "Come with me, Nora."

"Are you bonkers?"

"Yes!"

As she hesitated, he could sense her struggle. "Where are we going?"

"Anywhere."

She turned aside, offering a profile while she bit her lip.

"Say yes, Nora." He held out his hand, grinning, hoping. "Just for tonight."

Forever seemed to pass by as she mulled over his words, leaning against the windowsill like a moonlight-glow statue, frozen in place. A million doubts ran through his mind. What if she said no? Hell, what if she said yes? He'd only get himself in trouble with her.

But, he loved trouble, loved it since he'd run around the neighborhood as a little kid, shooting stones out of slingshots, throwing baseballs through neighbors' windows. He still hadn't learned how to stay out of hot water.

Thrusting hands in his pockets, Ray smiled smugly. "So, what's it gonna be?"

But she'd already closed her window. He could see the pucker of her lips blowing out the candles. Closing his eyes, he imagined her room before he'd summoned her: candlelight bathing the walls as she lay in bed, hair spread out like wheat on a field, Nora staring at her ceiling, thinking about him.

It was too much to ask. Maybe she liked to sleep with candles burning, like a night-light.

Then again…

In five minutes she stood before him, dressed in her faded jeans and a clinging beige top under a brown leather jacket. A blossom of red lipstick colored her lips as they grinned.

"I can't believe you," she said. "I thought we were done."

"Let's go for well-done." He tried not to think of the problems waiting for him at home. Just for this one night.

They walked to his car silently. He thought that anything he said would shatter the moment like a snow-filled crystal ball exploding on concrete.

As he held open the door for her, she laid a hand on his arm, his skin rippling with the touch.

"Wait." An unrecognizable glint slanted her amber eyes. "Can we just walk?"

"We can do anything," he said, nestling his palm over the small of her back, under the warmth of her jacket. The leather lent her a slightly musky scent, and he couldn't help guiding her nearer to him.

From where they stood, he could discern the seashell-mute sound of waves from nearby La Jolla Shores. Automatically, the pair strolled toward the roar.

"We're doing the right thing," she announced, voice shaky. "Right."

The way in which Nora looked at him—heart expanding in her eyes—told him that maybe this wasn't so right. Damn it.

Beneath the crash of waves, a thick, drumming beat pulsated. The air blew dry and soft, like the feel of a woman's hand against a feverish forehead.

She laughed and shook her head, fists stuffed in the pockets of her jacket. "This was the last thing I expected tonight."

"I think I needed this little extra bonus to keep us on speaking terms." Actually, he'd been surprised that she even wished to speak with him again, much less walk with him under a jewelry-box velvet sky. She'd looked so disappointed when he'd left earlier.

Ray resisted the urge to tug down her jacket, wrap her in its bonds and hold her tight for a captive kiss. "I apologize for the way our date ended. It didn't exactly go as planned."

"And what was your plan?" There it was again, that devilish gleam. Or could it have been the shape of the moon casting a white speck of mischief in her eyes?

"You're asking a guy this question?"

"Yeah."

A sly grin lit over his lips. "My plan was to give you a chaste kiss on the cheek and go home to take a cold shower." Ray laughed to himself. His mind was dominated by cold showers nowadays.

"How do you see me?" she asked, catching him off guard. He could've interpreted this as flirty bait, an invitation to a seduction, but Nora's earnest expression told him that she was serious.

Now drumbeats thumped the air. They had reached La Jolla Shores with its waterfront cottages, playground, lifeguard stations and dark-jewel water. He could see the silhouette of a three-piece percussion band against a bonfire on the beach. The black sparkle of ocean water glimmered behind them, reflecting the moon. The group had a small audience of admirers balancing beer bottles between fingers as they listened, reclining in the sand, barefoot. Shirtless, the male musicians worked under a slick of well-earned sweat.

Ray and Nora halted on the grass by the skeletal playground, just on the fringes of beachside activity. Aside from the orange-lit entourage, only a few scattered groups lounged on the shore. The tang of salt water and fire-heat made him shiver.

He slid his hand into her pocket, seeking her warmth over the nippy coastal air. Fingers coiled around fingers. "How do I see you?"

She looked away. "Never mind."

A finger tilted her chin so their gazes met. "I see a princess who looks after her people. In red lipstick."

Her lips rubbed against each other, making his itch. "Like a dress-up dolly?"

"Like an old-time movie siren."

Rounded eyes met his compliment. He could tell he hit the mark, scored points. But he'd meant every word. What he saw in Nora was everything he wanted but felt he wouldn't dare hope for: apple pie, Mary Jane shoes and that infernal hot lipstick.

By now, the drumbeats had crept under his skin, causing goose bumps to prickle and dance. The cadence struck him on an almost primal level.

Suddenly, he was holding her waist, grasping her hand, leading her a dance. After the initial tenseness of her body, Nora flowed into him, watching his eyes, gauging his play.

"You're one big bundle of carpe diem," she said, holding back a laugh.

Seize the day. Yes, he had. He feigned innocence by furrowing a brow. "That wouldn't be a brand of fertilizer, would it?"

Closing her eyes with an ''oooh,'' she flopped her head onto his chest. His hand instinctively cupped her hair. So soft and fine.

''Okay,'' he laughed. ''So I'm not a comedian.''

The shine of her eyes told him that she wouldn't have had him any other way.

Chapter Fourteen

What was she going to do about these cornball jokes of his?

Drums and waves pounding her mind, Nora tried to look away from his gaze, but it proved impossible.

When Nora felt that extra second of eye contact, she finally managed to turn her head to watch the drummers. Several of the audience members were now being entertained by her and Ray dancing.

So maybe they did look a little dorky, swaying by firelight on the beach to a bunch of drums. They weren't exactly sipping cocktails in a dimly lit dance club. But she liked it that way, the anonymity, the nobody-ness of the blurred flamelight. She didn't feel like a professional out here, a teacher running from eyes and judgments.

She was Nora. Just Nora. And she liked the way her name growled in Ray's throat like a husky engine.

There were a million questions she wanted to ask him: What was Cheri like? How many women had he loved?

But she couldn't bring herself to throw a wrench in their

moment. Tonight wasn't made for monsters in the closet; it was made for slow dancing and the smell of wood smoke over beach salt.

And she would be with him only tonight. To think, this magic might not have happened. After their date had ended, she'd gone to her room, grabbed a good book, tossed her skirt outfit in a limp pile on the carpet, slipped on comfort in the guise of a linen nightdress and lit the candles in her window. Usually, she used the peach-scented objects to calm herself, to shut out her emotions. But tonight they represented what could've been.

She would've lit those candles if Ray had come into her bedroom to make love with her as his lean body had promised earlier. Yet she'd entered her room alone.

Not that she would've invited Ray into her bed tonight. Her body had been more than ready. But her mind rebelled. She wasn't comfortable with speedy intimacy; she hadn't built up her store of trust yet. Instead, she'd fantasized, lying on top of her coverlet with the warm glow of muted light casting shadows over her framed prints of Egypt, Greece, places untraveled.

What would it have felt like to have Ray's long body next to hers on the bed? Would he have cuddled her into a spoon position, murmuring into her ear? Or would he have tried frisky male moves and sneered if she asked him to leave?

The drummers had stopped, and the audience applauded. As they began their next song, steel drums joined in, giving the beach a Caribbean hue.

Through Ray's shirt, Nora could hear him speak. "You've got that sad look again. It's easier to see it without the glasses."

She attempted to laugh off his concern. "It's nothing. Really."

Leading her over to a swing set, he said, "Can you see without those granny specs?"

A swing wiggled in the air, inviting her to lean into it. She grasped the chain, smelling rust and well-used metal. Her derriere barely fit into the leather seat and, suddenly, she felt every shred of innocence leave her being. "Actually, I just wear those things to look older." She sighed, rising on her toes, slanting back her body. "But I should go to the doctor for real reading glasses."

He positioned himself behind her, pulling back on the chain so her head was level with his. "Very clever, Nora. Those glasses add at least...two years to your presence."

Placing a hand on the back of her hipbone, Ray pushed, sending Nora bolting on an arc toward the stars.

Cold air whipped through her hair when she swung near him again. "Cute," she said, flowing past him.

And that's all she could say before his hands sent her higher. For a moment she wondered if the drummer audience would think them idiots for romping on a playground. Then she decided that she really didn't give a flying fig.

After all, tonight was a night to throw caution to the wind. She wasn't the type of girl who usually had men lining up to throw pebbles at her window. She wasn't the type of girl who frolicked with men on playgrounds as if they were in a shampoo ad.

She was Nora Murray and, finally, she was enjoying life. For a little while at least.

A streak of whimsy stole through her. As she flew upward once again, she let go of the swing, taking wing like a small child who does not believe in mortality.

For a brief moment, she flew, heart in her throat, light as a daffodil on the wind.

She landed on her feet, bending down to absorb the blow. Then, standing, she calmly turned to face Ray.

"Are you crazy?" he asked.

"I think I asked you the same thing earlier in the night." She brushed off her jeans, sucking in air when she made a quick move.

He sprung to her side, holding her arms. "Now you've done it. You're hurt."

She was touched by his concern. "Nah." She held out her

arms in a "tah-dah" position. "Those college ballet lessons really paid off. I've still got some balance." She grinned.

Her smile was infectious, spreading to his face. He cupped her jaw and back-stepped her into the shadow of a ginger-breadlike playhouse, thus blocking them from the view of the drum spectacle. The steel drums still danced over the shore, making the surrounding palm trees all the more exotic.

Once he had her out of sight, his lips dipped down to meet hers.

At first, he kissed her softly, rubbing her mouth, teasing. Still dizzy from her swing free fall, she responded, tease for tease, by inching out his shirt from the rim of his pants. Then, slowly, her fingers crept under the light material to flit over his back muscles, up, over to the front, where his ribs felt like bumps of smooth wood.

She heard his breath catch, and he paused, probably waiting to see where her hands would venture next. He had obviously not anticipated her sense of adventure out in the open, an audience waiting not one hundred yards away. As if in retaliation, his own hands slid under her leather jacket, pressed Nora's body into his and molded over her rump, into the rear pockets of her jeans.

A startlingly husky laugh caught in the skin of his neck as she leaned her nose and mouth there. Here was that scent again: clean laundry and soap and aftershave.

A spark caught somewhere in her chest, goading her to nail her fingers to his washboard stomach ridges. Then she ran an index finger into the space between denim and flesh.

Bad idea, but she felt unable to resist the urge to please him.

He responded by joining their lips again in a hungry promise of twisted sheets and humid nights that could never be. Her breasts swelled as they pushed into his chest and, in a flicker of thought, she was amused to discover that one of her feet angled upward as if they stood in the steam of a train in a black-and-white film.

Then he wrenched her clingy top out of her jeans, his thumb

inside her belly button, meandering up the line of her stomach, palming a tender breast.

They breathed so heavily that Nora could imagine the drumbeats keeping time to their gasps. "Maybe we should…" She trailed off as his mouth sought her neck. Her knees buckled, and he scooped her up by placing a hand on the back of a thigh, straightening her with a zing.

He whispered in her ear, "Maybe we should stop now?"

"Well…" She shut her eyes tight as he dusted kisses down her neck, over her collarbone, to the swell of her breast. "Either that or maybe we should go somewhere else."

He looked her in the eye. It was all she could do to be straight-faced because his hair cropped up in tufts. Maybe her hands were busier than she thought.

"Don't say that unless you're absolutely serious, Nora."

So, did she mean it? Or were her hormones merely dirty dancing, overriding her common sense as they had earlier in the night?

She abruptly pulled away, turned her back and tucked in her top. Behind, she could hear him gathering himself. He had to be disappointed. Jared would have been. He would have called her a "blue baller" or something equally off-color.

"I don't know what to do, Ray," she said, keeping her back to him until he hovered at her side.

She expected anger, frustration. But when she looked up at him, the seascape eyes shone with understanding, patience. Doing a double take, she decided to wander closer to the fire, to recheck his reaction.

As they walked near the band, a couple of men leered at her, obviously fully aware of what had transpired in the back of Hansel and Gretel's playhouse. She turned up her nose and used the opportunity—and the light—to watch Ray.

Shadowed by moonlight, he stood tall and gorgeous, seemingly carved by athletic prowess and the loving hand of nature itself. He had a smile stuck to his mouth. Without looking her direction, he held out his hand, and she grabbed it.

After they had traipsed down the sand a few hundred yards

from the fire, he bent down and picked up an object, examining it.

"What is it?" she asked. "A message in a bottle?"

He laughed, fiddled with the dark matter and finally turned to her, slipping a string of kelp around her wrist.

She watched for a minute, stunned. In her heart, the kelp was more beautiful than even Gran Murray's bracelet, waiting for her wedding day in the confines of a ballerina jewelry box. In the moonlight, the sand sparkled on the kelp like diamonds.

"I'll treasure this. Always." She held out her wrist and admired it. Tears gathered in the corners of her eyes, blurring moon, shore and man together.

As he engulfed her in his arms, Nora hoped that he hadn't heard the emotion shaking her voice.

"Always," she repeated.

The Brody household was dark except for the eerie light cast by Trent's computer. Ray found Ed sleeping on the floor. Trent had moved to the couch to sleep, lips pouted like a cherub.

Something inside Ray told him to just let his son sleep. To deal with his tardiness after he'd recovered from the afterglow of Nora's presence.

Nora. She *had* tasted like peaches and sweetness. She'd even surprised him by responding so ardently to his overtures: leaning into him until his stomach tightened, heart pulsating like liquid fire beneath his lips on her neck.

Trent stirred on the couch, and Ray held his breath. The boy's eyelids fluttered to a squint.

"You're late," his son said, sleep in his voice.

"I, ah, need to talk with you." Ray sat on the couch next to Trent's legs as the boy sat up.

What was a euphemism for betrayal? "I told a little white lie to you tonight, son. I really did go on a date."

Trent nodded like a wizened old crone. "That's not exactly news to me. But if you're going to be my dad, you can't lie to me again."

I guess he told me, Ray said to himself, feeling duly chastened. He attempted to lighten the conversation. "Who's the grown-up here, huh?"

"I'll give it to you straight," Trent said, blue eyes taking on a jaded sheen. "You probably think I'm just a hellish kid or something. But I'm not dumb. Cheri acted more immature than I ever did."

Ray was silent. He didn't want to interrupt the most revealing conversation he'd ever had with his son. Pride and shame welled within his throat.

Trent continued, the glow from the computer making him look like a moonbeam child. "She was always out, and when she came in, I had to put her to bed. I was the one who cooked. I answered the phone and talked to the bill collectors." He yawned and shattered the illusion of an adult. "If you're going out on dates and stuff, you should just tell me. Nothing shocks me anymore."

Wanna bet? He wished he could tell his son about Nora. But he didn't want to risk alienating Trent from his teacher. Trent needed her.

And Ray needed her.

"I wish I had known life with your mother was so bad," Ray said, putting a hand on his son's shoulder. Oddly enough, Trent didn't shrug it off or even flinch.

"Would you have raised me if Cheri had left sooner?" asked Trent, fear of rejection in his eyes.

"Son," Ray's voice cracked with emotion. "I wanted you with me the minute Cheri asked for a divorce. The courts, your grandparents and your mom never gave me a chance."

An unbidden tear sprinted down Trent's face. He angrily wiped it away. "She told me that you didn't love me. She told me lots of bad things."

Ray drew his son into a hug. Trent clung to him for dear life, then pushed away.

"Crying is for babies," the youngster said, scrubbing his face with his shirt. He looked up at Ray, almost all evidence of sadness gone. "So are you going to get married again?"

"For heaven's sake, Trent. It was a first date."

Shrugging, the boy said, "You guys will probably get pregnant and have to get married." He paused. "Did you know that some of my friends have already gone all the way?"

Birds and bees flew by Ray's vision. He figured he'd have to have this talk with his son sooner or later. Ray closed his eyes in mental agony. Later, it would have to be later. At this moment, he was tired enough to sleepwalk to his bed.

"How about this," Ray said. "We'll go to the batting cages tomorrow and talk about all that stuff." He looked over at the still-slumbering Ed. "And maybe Sleeping Beauty can join us."

Ed's only answer was a fitful snore.

"I don't want to talk about that stuff." Trent scrunched his nose. "Stacey Pickens is the only girl who bugs me, and I hate her, anyway."

So he thinks, Ray thought.

"Besides," continued his son. "We're talking about you, not me. I don't want you to date some bimbo."

Ray's voice grew level with anger. "I don't date bimbos." Not anymore.

"I think you should date Ms. Murray."

He almost choked on air. "What makes you say a crazy thing like that?"

"Why not? She'd be a perfect mom." The boy's mouth was a line of stubbornness. "I don't like any other women for you."

Ray longed to tell Trent about Nora, but he'd have to avoid the truth without lying. His relationship with Nora was too shaky to mention right now. Telling his son about their night out would raise the boy's hopes, only to smash them if things didn't work out. Lord knew that Trent had known enough heartbreak to keep him in armor the rest of his life. His son didn't need any more disappointments.

"You think about it, Dad."

Trent darted up to his room. Ray heard the door close, leaving him with his conscience.

Dad. Trent had finally said the magic word. A warmth so strong suffused his soul that Ray thought he'd stepped into the sun, all brightness and love. They were finally getting back on the right track—father and son. Maybe they'd have a good life after all.

Now, if only his heart would stop battling against being with Nora, he'd feel more at peace. Somehow, he knew he was in for a bigger fight. One he suspected he'd already lost.

Chapter Fifteen

Eyes a-glaze with faraway fairy tales, Nora sat on her bed, brushing her damp hair. The breezy aroma of a citrus bubble bath rose from her skin as she remembered the feel of Ray's fingers skimming her body.

Every inch of her tingled and blushed. How good it was to feel a man's rough skin once again. Even if her body was still buzzing after a few days, the feelings were fresh. Alive. She'd wanted him near her, on her, *in* her.

She flopped back on the bed, the towel she wore pressing against her breasts and riding up to reveal a length of thigh. So why had she stopped Ray? Why had fear pulled her under like a riptide?

Because she needed to remember her resolve, her promise to stay away from men because of her horrible choices. She'd only end up hurting herself.

The excuses were sounding lamer and lamer. But it was all true. She was well aware that she had poor judgment. Josie always teased her about it—how she could catch a kid whispering across a crowded auditorium and, yet, be totally un-aware of a person's obvious flaws close-up. Maybe it was because Nora tried to find the good in most humans when others immediately sought the negative. Naiveté had its price. She'd fought hard to preserve it.

She sighed, absently running fingertips over her collarbone. Seize the day. Yeah, in her dreams.

No, no more carpe diem for her. Nora could barely stand the little love-starved hormones chanting the Latin phrase, goading her, convincing her that choosing Ray Brody wouldn't be such a bad thing at all.

A sunset-beach kiss, moonglow caresses. The longing for more, more, more racked her emotions.

When she'd returned home today, she thought that maybe taking a bath would be a fine reward for her hard work in the classroom. Oh, to feel like one of those decadent women in a massive Roman pool, luxuriating in bubbles. Fortunately, as the school year wore down to a close, her homework was getting lighter. She suddenly had time for the wasting.

The bath had only made her more aware of her body, and more aware of the fact that she *liked* being touched by Ray. She couldn't think of anything else.

In a half daze, she rose from the bed and sauntered to her washed-pine drawers. Running a hand over the top, she stopped at her jewelry box. Looking inside, she sighed as she did every time the brilliance of Gran Murray's diamond brace-let winked up at her.

As if waking a slumbering baby, she gently lifted it out of its resting place, then led it over her wrist. Before her bath she'd taken off her kelp bracelet, but it'd snapped in two, having dried to the point of total disintegration. This felt dif-ferent—the gems heavier on her skin, like responsibility.

She sat on her bed again, rubbing citrus lotion into her arms, dreaming of other hands on her body.

The door swung open. "How do I look?" Josie asked, turn-ing around in her spaghetti-strap dress.

Nora turned on her side and leaned on her elbow, glad to

be relieved of her lovelorn angst. "You're a hot mama. Where are you off to?"

"Concert by the bay. A reggae band. Are you sure you don't want to come?"

Her roommate stuck an unlit cigarette in her mouth, and Nora gasped. "What are you doing, Bailey! You don't even smoke."

Josie held up her hands. "It doesn't add sophistication?"

"Oh, brother. Didn't you read the warning label?" Nora narrowed her eyes. "And I don't want this place stinking like the 'boy's room.'"

"Nor, it's not like I'm really going to smoke it." She crammed the cigarette into her purse. "Not that the smell matters, anyway—I give off antipheromones."

Laughing, Nora fell back onto the bed. "One day Mr. Right will come along." Someday.

"Oh!" Josie opened up her purse again, fumbled and threw a brightly colored wrapper at Nora.

"Josie!"

"Hey, from what you told me today, Murray, it won't be long before Chief Brody swims with the sharks. Every time you two inch a little closer to taking that dive."

Speechless, Nora could only stare at the condom in her hand. Finally, she looked dubiously at her friend. "First of all, why are you carrying this around with you?"

An innocent grin was Josie's reply. Nora's mouth fell open, and her roommate laughed. "Just joking. It's another sophisticated prop." At Nora's silence, Josie said,

"I'm serious! I can't believe you don't trust me, Nor. You know I only wish that I were that kind of girl." She winked.

"Second of all," continued Nora, "I'm not going 'swimming with any sharks,' Miss Metaphor."

"Oh, please. You and Ray are meant to be."

Nora stood and clutched her towel, feeling it slipping away from her breasts. She was having enough trouble dealing with the voices battling inside her head without Josie adding to them. "Can I please decide what's best for me? Remember, career first, nookie-nookie next." How hollow that sounded.

"Then I guess if Ray were on our living room couch right now, you'd tell him to get lost."

Great, another one of Josie's games. The thought of Ray made her want to run her hands over her body, a poor substitute at best. "Of course not."

"You'd just want to jump his bones."

Her roommate wasn't helping. "Bailey, don't you have some sort of concert to go to?"

"All right." Josie pointed to the condom, nodded her head and shut the door. Nora merely laughed, walked to her dresser and opened her pajama drawer. Maybe hopping into her jammies and cozying into her couch with a good book would capture her attention from thoughts of Ray.

Her eyes strayed back to the condom. She sighed. "Be strong," she said, riffling through a drawer.

She felt, more than saw, the door open. "Forget something, Jos? Maybe one last tease for the road?"

Silence. How unlike her roommate.

She looked over, finding Ray filling the doorway, a stunned expression on his face. Springing to attention, she twisted her towel over her breasts, feeling vulnerable. But excited, too.

He slowly pointed toward the living room. "Ah… Josie said you were ready to see me."

In the background, Nora heard a wicked Josie-like giggle. Then the door slammed, shivering the walls. Shivering her. She was alone with him.

Attempting to be casual, she backed toward her dresser, hoping it would cover her uncovered state. "Yeah, my roommate. What a joker." Oh, boy, was Josie going to get it when she returned from the concert. Now it was war.

When Nora looked at Ray again, he was averting his eyes like a gentleman, his blue-green gaze focused on the ceiling. "Maybe I should leave."

Nora didn't say anything. She could only produce a sound that could have been a yes or no.

"I, ah, just wanted to come over to give you an update on Trent. He and I had a real good talk last night, and for the first time since he's been here, I've got hope for us...." His voice trailed off. Just as his eyes had.

Hunger. That's what they held. Her leg started jerking.

"Ray..." His name sounded huskier than she'd intended, more like an invitation than a warning.

He moved toward her in what she would have called a daze. "So this is what a cameo looks like without the veiling," he said softly, stopping just inches away.

Taking a step back, her spastic leg hit the wall...again and again. *Oh, great,* she thought, her heart ready to take five more steps backward. He looked as if he were ready to devour her.

"What are you doing?" she whispered. Her hand reached out to stop him, but instead, it rested against his broad chest. His heartbeat echoed through her fingers. Their eyes locked.

"My being here is a bad idea, isn't it?" he murmured.

"*Very* bad. Awful and evil." All she wanted to do was give into her wild-girl musings and whip off her towel, but she came to her senses and pulled away.

He reached out to stop her, catching a bare arm. "Come back."

Was she afraid of the longing in his gaze? Part of her wanted to flee, because if they never made love to each other, there would be no bond to painfully break when he finally decided to hurt her. And they wouldn't have to hide anything from his son. But another part of her wanted to sling the towel around his waist, roping him in, then wringing him out.

He clenched and unclenched his hands. "This is what I've been waiting for ever since I laid eyes on you, Nora Murray. Ever since you breezed into my restaurant and left me standing there like a drooling jerk. *This* is what's screwed up my mind."

He spread his hold around her waist, over her back, drawing Nora to his body. His mouth covered hers, cutting off words. As she pressed into him, squeezing her eyes with the joy of his clean scent, evidence of his desire pulsed against her stomach. His fingers crept beneath the towel, rubbing the backs of her inner thighs.

Her lips gasped free. "You liked me when you first saw me?"

He chuckled. "Damn straight."

She smiled, remembering the humiliation of running out of Brody's Clubhouse with the speed of a fleeing bird. She'd been so wrong.

Her voice was a breath, a raggedy, wavering breath. "Maybe we should just wait." She felt herself losing the battle of staying away, ignoring her needs and wants.

Ray kissed her ear, bit it playfully until it burned. He pulled her away from the wall and leaned against it himself. His whisper echoed like the ocean lapping onto a tropical shore. "I'm beyond waiting."

A moving wall of relief thundered through Nora's chest, almost breaking in a sob. *Don't ever leave me,* she thought. *I couldn't stand the sight of you walking away, your son looking back at me with regret.*

His hands stopped. "What's *that?*"

He looked at the bed. *Oh, please, no,* Nora pleaded. *I forgot about…*

Lids lowered, she said, "Josie's idea of a dirty, ribbed joke."

"I'm not offended," he chuckled, placing a soft kiss on her forehead. They both laughed, releasing tension, then stopped. His lips traveled down her nose, rubbed against her own lips, and blossomed into a deep, searching stab of need that warmed Nora to her core.

As she dug her hands in his thick tawny hair, her leg stopped dancing, and she seared against him, urging, almost groaning with need.

He walked around the back of her, trailing kisses as he went. Over her bare bath-beaded shoulders, between the middle of her blades, on the nape of her neck. She opened her mouth to ask him where he was going. Nothing came out.

Carpe diem. The phrase sang through her head from the

mouths of angels. Or chickens. She wasn't sure, but now her stomach was jumping instead of her chicken leg.

As her neck veins vibrated like humming guitar strings, Ray's breath warmed the back of her neck. She heard a whoosh of his shirt material, and his bare chest rubbed down her back. His corded arms encircled her, hands moving over her collarbone, the terry of the towel, and down between its front folds.

This really isn't happening to me. I'm not so lucky.

It was almost an out-of-body experience. But not exactly. Out-of-body souls couldn't feel his fingers sliding over her most private spots. Couldn't feel his fingers inside of her, slipping in and out as her own hands tore into his hair. As her own teeth bit into his shoulder.

"Sorry," she whispered. A drawn-out moan followed.

He laughed softly in her ear and used both hands to slide up her quaking stomach to her swollen breasts, cupping and kneading tenderly. His thumbs rubbed over the center of them.

"I'll consider that mark a badge of honor," he said, sliding the towel from her body.

She heard the soft thump of the material as it slumped to the floor, and she stiffened, realizing that her body was without a stitch of clothing. And the lights were on. What if he laughed at her? What if he found dimples in her thighs?

Gently, Ray turned her around, exposing her body to his famished gaze. Slight blond hair dusted his broad, sculpted chest, tapering into a thin funnellike stream that wandered past the washboard muscles of his stomach and into the rim of his pants. Without thinking, Nora eased two fingers over the hair and into that hem, pulling Ray closer.

Now I'm going to pass out, she thought. But she had to find out where this downy trail led....

She looked up as his Oahu eyes washed over her and back up again. She exhaled as he smiled, drawing her closer into his arms.

Her bracelet scraped against his shoulder blade. As he

pulled her wrist into his eyesight, he said, "Don't tell me I'm seeing things."

"The kelp broke, and my fairy godmother replaced it with this." The lightness of his smile warmed her through and through.

She drew the jewelry from her wrist, bringing him with her to the ballerina box since she couldn't bear the thought of separating their skin.

With it safely tucked away, Ray said, "I sort of enjoyed the picture of you wearing only diamonds."

"How about wearing only you?"

Then they tumbled onto the bed, Nora on top of him, working at his belt. Nothing could stop her now—not even the thought of past ghosts, past hurts. This was her future, this man and every emotion that came with him.

Once and for all, Nora shook off her doubts and threw Ray's pants to the floor. He was beautiful, his lean hips framing proof of his desire for her. Nora went weak for wanting him, needing him inside her. Her heart beat a little faster.

From her open window, the breeze carried the sounds of children playing in the pool and the smell of leaves, chlorine and coastal air. And Ray. As a parent told his child to play safely, the chill of wickedness urged Nora on. She reached for the condom.

They lay skin to skin, ready for each other. When he entered her, Nora shuddered, inviting him to relieve her tightness.

"*This* is what I've been looking for, Nora." He thrust deeper.

The children splashed and roared, "Marco!"

Nora bit her lip, holding back a swell, a threatening moan. "Polo!"

Her hands bunched the sheets, yanking them off the bed corners as intense pleasure coursed through her. She was going to scream. Please, don't let those kids hear her....

"Oh, Go-o-o—" Ray's mouth silenced her, absorbing her passion. The world whirled like the passing of a bullet train.

As the last of it flew by, she focused her gaze on the storm-swept eyes above her. He smoothed back her hair.

Something shy within her wanted to tear her eyes away from his. But she couldn't. Couldn't distance herself after a moment when his fingers had touched her body and soul.

Did he love her? He hadn't said so, but from the way in which he gazed down at her, she wanted to believe it was true. She'd never been looked at this way.

And what was love anyway? Rolex watches and fancy-restaurant dates? No, not by a long shot.

Love, or at least part of it, was laying out your entire being for another person. Inviting rejection, and being flung to the nearest star when the other person took your vulnerability and wrapped it in the cocoon of his heart.

Love was being held by Ray, feeling safe as he stroked her hair, being warmed with his emotion-slicked skin.

She closed her eyes to revel in his scent, his arms as he rolled to his back and drew her to his wide, hair-sprinkled chest. She thought her racing heart would never calm itself, and her breath refused to mellow.

Maybe this was love.

And maybe this time—if she left her affections in Ray's capable hands—she'd come out whole. Cleansed.

But maybe she was simply carried away by the heat of the afterglow, the memory of his hips as he'd filled her whole, the rush of her blood as he'd taken her to heights she'd only grasped through the haze of a dream before now. Maybe she shouldn't be thinking of love at all.

They didn't talk for a while. Just listened to the pool play outside. The splashes. The music from a neighbor's room. The children.

Children. Trent. Suddenly, she felt a part of his family.

She must have dozed off because it seemed as if, in the next instant, he was hard against her thigh again.

"A long time between ports, captain?" A saucy laugh, one she had no idea had been hiding in her collection of emotions, floated from her soul. Surely, no one was allowed to be this happy.

His answering chuckle muffled into her shoulder as he bent to kiss it. "How can you blame me?"

She tried to put herself in his position, to think of herself as he thought of her. No. That was too hard. It took too much confidence on her part. "I guess death by kisses isn't a bad way to go."

His head had already disappeared beneath the covers, so she doubted he heard her.

The phone rang, and she could feel his body tighten. She let the machine pick up the call. As they listened to the salesman pitching a wonder vacuum cleaner, Ray resurfaced.

She knew their ghosts had not been exorcised, if they ever would be. But she would take control. Now.

"Junk messages," she murmured, flipping her body on top of his, holding his arms crooked overhead.

He seemed surprised, but a pleased grin broke over his face, lighting his eyes.

She pulled the covers over their heads. "No more interruptions."

As night settled over Ray's world, he quietly got out of bed, trying not to awaken Nora. She stirred and sighed in her sleep, coiling his heart. As he gathered his clothes and watched her, he couldn't help feeling a mixture of intense joy and loneliness. The weight of the universe fell upon him. Why had he let Nora into his heart? They'd reached a summit with their lovemaking already, bonding both body and soul, and now there was nothing left for them but heartbreak. That's how love had worked for him in the past.

He buttoned his faded jeans, standing over Nora. Her arm hit the headboard with a dull thump as she rolled to her side, making Ray wince with empathy.

The bed sank softly as he sat down to rub her red fingers. The tip of one breast peeked out from the sheet; it rose and fell, covered and uncovered, as she breathed. He strained against the jeans.

He needed to get out of here—now. Ray leaned over, allowing his lips to linger a pout away from her lips. "My Nora," he whispered, enjoying the taste of both words. He kissed her, but she remained sleeping.

Damn, he needed to calm his raging pulse. He ambled to Nora's kitchen and grabbed a glass of water.

He found a plastic mug with a giant heart stamped on the outside. Satisfied, he stopped in front of her refrigerator, noticing the pictures held captive by Snoopy magnets.

One featured Nora and Josie, sunburned cheeks gleaming as they smiled, heads resting against each other's. Ray grinned, running a finger over Nora's image, glad she'd recorded a moment when her eyes sparkled. An instant to keep forever.

Would he ever have pictures like this with Trent, the two of them caught in a minute of unforced appreciation for each other? He wondered if Nora would ever join them in such a photo.

No, it'd never happen. He'd have messed up her life by the time the shutter clicked. With Cheri, the relationship had disintegrated in little more than five years. With Nora, he couldn't give it a chance to start.

So, Einstein, what'd you do?

He'd made love with her, and he'd enjoyed it. Hell, he'd more than enjoyed it. What was wrong with him? Say he did try a relationship with Nora. Say things were going well— Trent loved her, they were getting along great, no arguments or petty mind games… What would Ray do if Nora broke his heart first?

That's what he was afraid of, was it? Yes, he was concerned about taking care of Trent. He was even genuinely worried that he wasn't capable of carrying on a healthy association with a woman. But he couldn't handle it if he had to face rejection one more time. Especially from Nora.

There were times when he saw gleams of a potential heart-

breaker in her eyes. Shards of memories he couldn't grasp for
fear of bleeding. Somewhere along the line something had
gone terribly wrong in her life. Those recollections affected
her, he knew, made her wary and as unwilling to commit as
he was.

But what if Ray was the one man on the face of this earth
who could heal the wounds left from those cutting remem-
brances?

He shook his head. There was so much he still didn't know
about the woman he'd just caressed, kissed, made love to.
These feelings of protectiveness were disconcerting, to say the
least; he wasn't even sure what Nora's demons looked like.
How could he fight them for her unless she told him?

He moved his fingers past pictures of Josie and a myriad of
guys to one hidden, peeking from beneath the roommate's
toothy grin. Nora's. The refrigerator's coating felt hard and
cold as he touched the sharp edges of the picture.

In this photo, the colors were muted, the people stiff and
formal. Ray assumed they were father, mother and daughter.
Nora couldn't have been more than five in this image—the
age Trent had been when Cheri had taken him.

Ray's face warmed. He couldn't help it—she was precious,
clutching a fuzzy teddy bear, wide eyes stoically staring at the
camera. The man and woman stood ramrod straight, not touching. Something wasn't right.

He leaned closer, inspecting more details. The man's iron
jaw, his dispassionate gaze. The woman's perfect hair and
dress, the slight puffiness of one eye.

Brow furrowed, Ray backed away from the pictures and
opted for tap water. He filled his glass, hoping his suspicions
were wrong.

What kind of childhood had Nora endured?

Not wanting to disturb her, Ray took a seat in the shaded
living room, shadows of blue-tinged ballerinas dancing eerily
from the framed prints decorating the space.

How was he going to protect Nora from her past?

While he mulled over the question, a soft padding sound

entered his perception. Nora, standing next to the chair, a long white button-down shirt covering the body he'd loved mere hours ago. She clasped her hands together, cradling them beneath her chin, watching him with a lowered gaze.

Heart clenching, Ray thought she looked as lost as the little girl in the refrigerator photo.

Chapter Sixteen

"I thought you'd disappeared," she said, voice husky, barely above a whisper.

Ray absently rubbed the dull ache in his knee, then spread out his arm in an invitation to join him. She complied, snuggling on his lap, leaning her forehead against his.

She smelled so good, well-loved, contented and sleep-warmed. He rested a hand on her knee, cozying his fingers between her inner thighs. Toned, sleek muscles. Smooth, toasty skin. He wanted to take her again, right now. Instinct told him to slow down.

"You really think I'd desert you?" he asked. He wondered about it himself.

She laughed softly. "I've been deserted before." A long drawn-out breath, an extra wiggle in his lap, molding herself to him. Making herself an extension of his own body.

"That's right. Daddy dearest." How could he forget, now that he'd seen the stone-chiseled man in the picture? He wanted her to tell him all about her troubles, her fears. He wanted to shield her from the lingering pain.

But how could he go about this? Ask her straight out about his nagging feelings that something was off about her mother's puffy eye? No, that'd scare Nora away for sure.

She beat him to it. "*Dearest* isn't a term I'd use for the man. In fact, I wish I'd never have to think about him again."

"But you do."

Their voices were quiet, intimate. Soft as the down of a feather pillow. Ray liked this closeness, wished it could last forever outside the bubble of this instant.

"Nora, somehow I think you'll never forget about your father."

She shivered, causing him to hold her tighter. "Every time I talk to you, all this angst comes out. I've got to be a real downer."

Was this the right time to tell her that she was one of the few bright spots in his life? "I think if you tried me, you'd find I can help you feel better. Like you've helped me."

He kissed her gently, forehead coming back to nestle against hers. Evidently, it was all she needed.

"I'm not sure what to say, Ray. None of it's very pretty."

"And my past is rosy, right?"

She played with the hairs on his chest. "Maybe not."

He waited, trying to be patient, trying to believe a conversation like this would cleanse them whole.

Her voice grew even softer. "So much happened when I was a girl that I can't go through every horrible story. What I remember are images, really. Mom's bruises, my father's screaming fits. There came a point when I would try to distance myself from every fight. I'd give names to his moods. Ragin' Rowdy, Drunk Deadweight, Sobbing Sorryhead, Silent and Sullen… Mostly I recall what I saw and heard as if I'm locked in a box, or under a table. Hiding."

He could hear her teeth grinding, and it took all his strength to just hold her, comfort her. There wasn't much else he could do.

She continued. "I can't even cry much anymore. The tears all dried up after my mom died. I couldn't even feel sad when I found out my dad passed away from a heart attack."

He hated to ask, but the image of her mom's faded black eye haunted him. "Did he kill her?"

Deep breath, followed by a sigh so pitiful, Ray wanted to wrap her in his arms forever, protecting her. But the pain came from the inside. How could he defend against her memories?

"No, he didn't physically end her life, even though he's killed almost everything that mattered. It was cancer. And I couldn't do anything about that, either."

Tommy, her childhood friend, her mom, and... Ray turned her words over in his mind. *Trust.* Her father had murdered her trust.

She laughed again, an entirely ironic sound. "The kicker is, I went out and got myself a man just like my father."

"Jared?" Had that bastard laid a hand on her?

"Sure, but to blame anyone but myself for the decision would be weak. I was perfectly aware that Jared was all wrong for me. But I thought I could change him. Just like my mom thought she could redo my father. We were both wrong."

Ray had always wondered why women didn't leave in an abusive situation. It was harder to ask why when one of those women had sought solace cuddled next to him. He still didn't understand the reason Nora had become engaged to Jared, not when she'd told Ray the stories about how her ex had made her feel worthless, how he'd played her lack of self-confidence to his own ego's advantage.

He asked, "What made you decide to leave?"

She paused. Would she answer him at all? Maybe he'd asked too much of her, so he couldn't blame her for clamming up. Not long ago, he'd been nosing around her kitchen, while questioning his commitment to her. Why should she believe in him at all?

With an awful clarity, he realized that she'd placed a lot of trust in him tonight. It must've taken a great deal of courage to take a chance with him. Ray's heart felt like wood—a thing once alive, but hardened after being cut to pieces.

He felt even worse when she began speaking again.

"I left when Jared raised a hand to me."

She must've felt his body tense, because she lifted her head from his and placed a calming hand on his cheek. "Don't worry," she said. "He missed."

"I would've kicked his butt if he'd laid a hand on you." His anger overwhelmed him, raised a sheer red curtain over his gaze, bathing Nora in steam and rage. "Even if I'd had to hunt him down—"

"Violence is what I want to avoid, Ray." She pressed her lips to his, putting a stop to more threats.

Shame, a different shade of red, cleared his vision and made him want to slink away. But he wouldn't leave as her father had. Nora needed someone to stay in her life, for all time. Now, he didn't know if he was the man who could make her whole again, but he could alleviate a little of her pain for at least tonight.

He spread his fingers through her hair, bringing her hard against his lips. They tested each other, teeth nibbling, tongues tasting until Ray moved the hand that nestled between her thighs upward, sliding along the moist valley until he came to the juncture of her legs.

She breathed against him. "Yes…" Took hold of his hand, leading it, stroking it against her lacy undies. Her hips ground against him until he was hard, pulsing against the curve of her rear end.

This woman fulfilled him in so many ways, reading his mind, his desires. As if sensing what he craved, she straddled him, lean legs clamping against his. Caging him.

He ran his palms over her stomach, feeling the flatness under the cotton shirt. Up, up over her rib cage. She arched her neck, moaning, writhing on top of him until he broke into a groan.

"You're beautiful," he said, tracing his thumbs over her breasts, feeling the crests peak, puckering under the shirt.

Using one hand to support her back, he unbuttoned her blouse, clenching his jaw when she used her fingernails to lightly scratch his arms.

He wanted to possess her, lay claim to every curve. Finally, he finished with the shirt, delving a hand inside to part the material. Her breasts, budded and firm, popped out. He took one into his mouth, laving it with attention, taking the warmth of it into his body like a healing potion. He swirled his tongue around the nipple, then lavished the other one with sucks and nips.

Nora cupped his head, moving with him, her breath hot in his ear. Her hair, scented and soft, fell over one of his shoulders, intensifying the sensitivity of his skin, making him painfully aware that he could never be enough to complete her.

But he would try. He stood, taking her with him, wanting to make her comfortable by pillowing her on the bed. Besides, he still had enough presence of mind to note that Nora had a roommate—one who could walk in at any time.

"Ray, I want you now," she breathed.

Maybe she didn't care, but Ray didn't like the notion of being caught *flagrante delicto*. "Slow down, sweetheart, slow down."

It was as if she was releasing every repressed ounce of yearning she possessed. With a burst of strength, he lifted her onto his body, leading her legs to wrap around his thighs.

Too much—her undies rubbing over his arousal. He made it as far as the wall, driving her against it.

He hoped he hadn't hurt her, but before he could manage to ask, she panted, "Yes," slipping off the shirt, smoothing her breasts against his chest, hardened nipples parting his hair. Burning his skin.

He swept his hands over the toned muscles of her back, pausing over her waist, scooping up to feel her shoulder blades. So small, so vulnerable.

She started sliding down, her hair leaving looped trails of darkness against the moon-white wall. Her hands followed, caressing, memorizing every turned-on inch of him, stopping to circle the bulge in his jeans.

He propped his forehead and hands against the wall, his breathing erratic, as she unbuttoned his fly, slipping inside to free him from the material's constraints. She tugged down his pants, and he stepped out of them, clenching hands into fists as she looked up, running her fingers over his thighs.

He groaned again while she took the length of him in her palm. He couldn't take much more of this.

She stood again, trailing her hand along his stomach, obviously relishing his enjoyment.

"I want you, Ray."

It was his ultimate undoing.

He turned her around until she hugged the wall, her cheek resting on an arm. He dipped inside her undies, feeling lace and dampness, stroked her until she fanned her hands on the wall, rays of a dark sunset.

She moved against him as he brought her to ultimate gratification, her sweet moans filling his ears with song.

But he was still aroused, still in need of her.

They sank to the carpet, and he helped Nora wriggle out of her panties. He'd never been with a woman who could keep him going for so long. Having him so enthralled must have given her some confidence, he hoped.

He entered her, closing his eyes in ecstasy at the sense of heat and slickness surrounding him. As they moved in rhythm, he whispered, "You drive me crazy, Nora. Only you."

She locked her legs around his even tighter, nails raking his back. He didn't mind the burn.

She bit her lip and threw back her head, exposing a neck ripe for his kisses.

This was pure. It was complete fulfillment. But could it last beyond tonight? Ray didn't want to ask himself any more questions.

He climaxed, remembering too late that he hadn't worn a condom. In the heat of the moment, he'd absolutely forgotten. Damn it all, what had he been thinking?

He wanted to apologize, but, instead, was swept back into the moment when he realized Nora still hadn't reached her peak.

Later. He'd think about it later. He helped her, leisurely running his hands over different dips and turns of her body, until she turned her face away and convulsed, eyes shut, hand over mouth.

It'd have been better if she could've looked at him, sharing the intense physical pleasure of release. But she'd shut him out again.

Part of him was still buzzing with enjoyment, part of him felt empty. If only life was different. If only they could put their faith in each other's hands.

He palmed a breast, feeling their mingled sweat, using it to explore the rest of her body. He wanted to ask more questions, talk about what they would do if they'd just made a child together.

God, what *would* they do?

Maybe he should worry about it later, when she was ready to talk, to give him answers more illuminating than what he'd gotten earlier. Chances were, Nora hadn't even begun to reveal her soul to him.

Would she ever be able to? He couldn't bring himself to ask.

Nora wanted to hide away from the rest of the earth. Stupid, stupid, stupid.

She hadn't really been thinking about it at the time, but they hadn't used a condom. No protection whatsoever. How could she be so thoughtless?

The last thing she wanted was to drag Ray into a relationship he probably didn't intend to pursue. A baby would do that, play on his guilt, make him a part of another tense fatherhood situation.

Stupid. She wished she'd waited to make love with him. Even lying here now, night air and Ray's gaze mingling to wash over her, she felt sad because when he left tonight, he'd most likely leave forever.

"Hey," he said, hand snuggling against the exposed skin at her waist. "What's wrong?"

Actually, everything was right. And everything was wrong. The stillness of the moon peeking through the window, the companionable way he touched her... Then again, that same moon was only a cold reflection of the sun, his touch a final farewell. "Nothing's the matter." She brought his hand to her mouth, kissing his knuckles.

They sat in silence, broken only by the too-loud pounding of her heart.

He leaned on an elbow, silvered by moonlight, looking down at her. "I'm sorry, Nora. I didn't use anything."

There, he'd said it. Her turn. She almost wanted to sag against him, hiding her fears. "I'm not on the pill. Nothing. What if—"

He cut off her words, kissing her. Emotion swelled over her, leaving her speechless as he pulled away.

"I can't make any promises, Nora, but—"

"If you can't promise anything, don't dance around the subject." She flushed, drawing away from him, immediately regretting her sharp words. No way she'd force Ray to commit himself right now, especially during the afterglow.

He stiffened, then stood and walked away. As she stared at the blank wall, she heard him pulling on his pants, the rustle of jeans material like the sound of nails screaming down a blackboard. Now she'd done it—driven him away. He'd had his fun and was content to leave.

What had he been about to say before she'd interrupted him? She'd hurt his feelings, obviously, so asking him wasn't going to do any good.

Nora rose, went to her room and wrapped herself in a robe. She gathered Ray's clothes, pausing an instant to bury her face in his shirt, wishing things could go back to being the way they were before they'd made love.

When she returned to the living room, he was staring out a

window, arms crossed over the bulk of his chest, his face chiseled and shaded by the night's glow. Her heart ached as she watched, knowing he'd be leaving soon to go home to Trent.

Wordlessly, she handed his clothes to him. He finished dressing, then faced her.

"Am I going to see you again?"

Was he asking her or himself? She wanted to see him every day for the rest of her life, if she could convince herself it was a good idea to trust him with her heart.

"Sure," she said. "But could we...I don't know..."

"Slow down?" he supplied.

"Yes." Was she asking too much?

"Whatever you need, Nora."

He smiled, making her believe she hadn't been out of line in asking. Relief flooded her, weakening her knees. Just as she thought she might collapse, he drew her into his embrace for one last kiss.

She melted into him, hanging on to his clothes so she wouldn't fall any farther into a pit of emotion.

As he left, looking back with one of those wry, boyish grins, her body started missing him. She caught his clean scent on her skin. She wrapped her tongue around the thought of his kisses. Her skin was ultra-aware: she could feel every bite of wind, every prickle of goose bumps. She was lost, all right. And she couldn't wipe the crazy smile from her face.

Maybe things could work. Couldn't they?

After he'd driven away, she climbed in her bed, the space next to her feeling very empty indeed.

When Ray had asked Nora if he could see her again, he'd meant every word. For better or worse, he did want to feast his eyes on her petite figure, her soft beauty. Now, time would tell whether or not being with her was a good idea, but every male cell in his body begged for her touch. He couldn't deny it.

The day after their lovemaking found him replaying every

caress, every word. Sure, they hadn't parted on the best of terms, but maybe things would seem all right when they saw each other again. As friends. That would be the best solution. They'd gotten all that simmering sexual tension out of their systems, so why couldn't they remain on civil terms?

He scrubbed at some crusted sink remains in his kitchen. Food, of some sort. Damn, he hated cleaning. He hated cooking. He hated a lot of things about being a single dad. Then again, he loved many aspects: watching his son surfing, hearing the title "Dad" slip from Trent's lips more easily and easily as the days passed... There was much to enjoy.

"Hey, Dad." Speaking of the little troublemeister. "Wanna play some catch?"

Ray couldn't drop the cleaning products fast enough. He turned from the sink to find Trent holding two leather gloves and a smooth white ball, red stitches beckoning. "Let's go."

Trent, a knowing glint in his eye, led the way to the backyard. A rust-colored fence, in need of a fresh coat of paint, pointed to the late afternoon sky. A barely used barbecue grill guarded the small grass lot. Before Trent had come to live with him, Ray hadn't really used his backyard. Now he felt the need to decorate the area with soccer balls, go-carts, or whatever preteen gadgets were popular these days.

His son tossed a glove his way, and Ray easily caught it. They faced each other across the springy grass, and Trent threw the ball, cutting the air with a graceful arc.

Ray grinned, proud his son was a natural athlete. He'd have to check around the community, see if there were baseball teams to develop Trent's abilities.

They fell into a groove, a tacit connection, father throwing, son catching, and back again. The pattern allowed Ray's mind to free itself from worry, to relax.

Until Nora entered his thought one more time. Dammit, she was never far, not as long as the memory of her body fitting itself to his remained fresh on his skin.

And that brought him back to Trent. Should he say something about Nora to him? Was he ready to hear that Ray wanted to break their new peace? Although Trent had said Nora would make a "good girlfriend," was he really ready to share his father with someone else? What if Trent felt replaced, shoved to the side? The boy had felt that way most of his life. Ray couldn't imagine putting him in the same situation again. It'd shatter all the hard work he'd invested in getting Trent to love him again, and he wasn't about to let that happen.

He plucked the ball from its free fall, wound his arm back to return the sphere to Trent. As his son imitated his actions, Ray saw the specter of a five-year-old boy tripping all over himself to catch a Wiffle ball.

Ray's throat burned. So many things had changed. That little kid who lived in the scrapbook of his mind wouldn't have gotten drunk or broken into someone else's home to steal. He wouldn't have talked back to his dad. The child's big blue eyes would've reflected adoration, complete trust.

Could Trent's life turn out the way Ray had always envisioned? Was it too late?

He missed the tiny boy, but he saw so many glimmers of him in this young man before him. Sure, Trent's legs were longer, his gaze a bit more cautious. But wasn't that the case with most adolescents? It was their time to question the world, to wonder if everything would be so crummy for the rest of their lives. Ray wanted Trent to know the universe had a beautiful side—a side Nora had revealed to him.

God, Nora again. Did all roads lead to the woman he'd made love with yesterday?

He wondered what it'd be like to have her here right now.

"Dad?" Trent watched him, head turned sidelong, ball poised in the air to throw.

Damn, he probably looked like a dumbstruck idiot. He held up the glove to signal his readiness.

Trent folded his arms, a tilted grin on his face. "You aren't concentrating."

"It's catch, not brain surgery."

"I know."

Ray would have to be careful around his perceptive son. Trent probably knew much more than Ray thought possible.

The young man continued. "I'm hungry."

Wasn't he always? "More mac and cheese?"

"Ugh." Trent made a corny face, causing Ray to laugh. "How about real food?"

Ray hated to break the news, but neither one of them really knew how to cook. "What do you suggest, since I assume you have a plan."

"I'll bet Ms. Murray knows some good recipes."

His heart fluttered. Butterflies. Other men would laugh if they knew. He looked at Trent's expectant expression, his brows forming two curves of a question mark.

If Nora joined them, how would he keep his growing feelings at bay? How would he hide those emotions in a secret place where Trent couldn't find them? As it was, whenever he thought of Nora, he became a drooling nut. Then again, he wanted to make his boy happy, keep the peace. Would a visit from Nora do much harm?

Trent won.

"If you call her, I'll run to the store to buy a few steaks."

"Are you sure you can cook steaks?"

Ray threw his glove to Trent, dismissing his son's horrified grimace. "I can manage."

As both Brodys slid open the patio door, Ray cast a glance at the ancient grill, shrouded by a plastic black covering. He'd check it over, but he thought it might work.

Trent sprinted past him to the phone, making no secret of his excitement at having Nora join them.

As Ray ran a hand through his hair, he wondered how he could keep his own happiness a secret.

At the Brody house, the aroma of grilled rib-eye steaks wafted through the patio's screen door, making Nora feel sublimely content. Minutes ago, Trent had wandered into the kitchen, watching in his much-too-observant manner while she'd sprinkled garlic salt and pepper onto the pieces of meat, laving them with melted butter and olive oil to add flavor.

When Ray had picked up the plate of steaks on his way to the grill, they'd barely looked at each other. It'd been the same when she'd first arrived. The only indication that they'd been intimate yesterday was a secretive smile he'd flashed her before disappearing to grill the meat. As he'd left she'd smiled, her gaze raking everything from his long legs to his wide shoulders, remembering his skin pressed against hers.

She'd gotten the hint—Trent shouldn't know about them, and she couldn't agree more. Even if her body flared up every time she looked at Ray's hands or lips, she'd stay quiet.

She didn't know what exactly was running through his thoughts, but hers were filled with indecision and a rekindled joy at being invited over for dinner.

Dinner. It sounded so normal, so fifties sitcomish. A family gathered around a Formica table to catch up on their days. Nicknames like "Kitten" and "Beaver" highlighting the conversations. Could she ever be a part of something so ideal?

Maybe. Trent had pulled up a chair to the counter, sitting on his knees while watching her grate Parmesan cheese over sliced garlic-salted tomatoes. She slid the cooking sheet into the oven to join the tin-foiled baked potatoes.

"I like how you cook, Ms. Murray." He tested an already-chopped chunk of zucchini, mugging after tasting it.

Nora eased the cutting board, teeming with the zucchini, mushrooms and onions, away from his curious fingers. "These are pretty good when they're sautéed."

"Do you want kids?"

The question came at her like a lightning bolt. "I, uh… maybe someday."

"Someday? Like how soon?"

What could she tell him when she wasn't sure herself? She wanted to be positive she was ready to raise a child properly, to make no mistakes in life's most important career. When she and Ray had made love yesterday, she'd taken her first step in realizing that maybe she was ready. Maybe she'd even be forced to be prepared if she turned out pregnant.

Oddly enough, the possibility didn't sound all that terrifying now that she'd had a day to think about it.

"Trent, I don't know how soon I'll be ready for a child. Sometimes grown-ups are never ready."

He nodded, lips pursed. "Cheri wasn't ready. Dad's ready. I know what you mean."

Nora smiled at the word *dad*. Relieved that one of Ray's obstacles had been overcome, she set to work melting some butter in a sauté pan. It sizzled, filling the air with a heady, comfortable scent. She could almost believe right now that Trent was her son, that they were part of a perfect family, one in which she and Ray could live worry-free, as happily ever after as possible in this world.

"Can I help?" asked Trent.

"Sure." Her heart warmed as she instructed him to wash his hands with antibacterial soap, scoop the vegetables into the pan and lightly shower them with more garlic salt and pepper. Working together. Wasn't this a cog in the well-oiled machine of a family?

When he'd finished, he set the table with two beige candles, modest chipped-blue plates, silverware and paper napkins. She watched him, proud of his involvement, his full-force throttle into what was probably his first good home-cooked meal in years.

A whiff of steaks turned both their heads to Ray's entrance. He laid each cut onto a plate while Trent and Nora loaded the table with the side dishes—baked potatoes with all the trimmings, the zucchini-mushroom mix, Parmesan tomatoes, warmed French bread and a tossed green salad. She'd gone for overkill, that was for sure, but to bear witness to two starving men digging into the food as if it was a treasure hunt made her feel needed. Appreciated. She loved the thought of cooking for more than herself and Josie.

They didn't talk much as they ate. Instead, it seemed they relished one another's company. A couple of times she caught

Ray eyeing her across the table, a sexy smile spread across his handsome face. He was remembering it, too—yesterday, the touching of their bodies and souls, the fact that they'd laid themselves bare to each other. Only Josie knew about her family and how they'd affected her life. Now Ray was a member of her exclusive agony club. And, the miracle was, he hadn't been driven away from her as she'd feared.

She longed for some time alone with him, if only to stroke his muscular arm or press against his magnificent body in a quasi-innocent hug.

After a while, they all made small talk—school, TV programs and the like. Nothing deep. But long, candle-warmed family dinners seemed a certain reality for Nora. Cloud nine for now.

At nightfall, Ray allowed Trent to go to a neighbor boy's house, leaving them alone to clean the dishes.

She stood at the sink, once again planning which curtains would complement the stark view of the neighbor's house. "You guys are getting along well." Her voice almost caught in her throat. Did this have to be so awkward?

"Yeah. I can't hardly believe it. I'm not sure if this is how our lives will be from now on or if he's planning something evil and trying to divert my attention."

She laughed, rinsing a dish and then handing it to Ray for drying. Their teamwork felt natural, functional, just like dinner, when she'd watched father and son, loving the way Trent shot adoring looks to Ray without Ray's knowledge.

"Maybe we're just discovering that Trent's basically a good person."

He said, "I'm mad at myself for even doubting that. But I can't ignore your influence, the great meal you made, the time you've been spending with him. It's made all the difference."

This forced casualness was making her edgy. As she handed him a bouquet of silverware, their fingers connected, causing her to drop the utensils with a loud clang into the sink. He kept hold of her hand, rubbing, heating. Her breath had a hard time finding release.

"Nora, I can't stop wanting you."

She wanted to pull away, but not really. "I know. I…" She lost the words.

He said, "I almost hate that I can't stop thinking about you. And every time you leave, I tell myself that we should just be friends, but then I see you again and my mind gets all fuzzy and nutty."

Just friends. He wasn't going to commit. The only reason he wanted her was because he couldn't control his hormones, not because of love.

She smiled, trying to pretend it didn't matter. "I understand."

"Do you?" He drew her into his arms, where she could feel his heart beating against her cheek. "I've convinced myself that we shouldn't be together because Trent needs my full devotion, that he wouldn't appreciate me dividing my attention. He deserves all my affection."

"Yes, he does." Was he going to tell her they'd never see each other again as lovers? She steeled herself for the pain.

He continued. "But, I don't know, Nora. He loves you."

Trent loved her. Ray didn't. He rubbed her back, making her shut her eyes.

"What am I trying to tell you?" he asked, giving a soft laugh. "I don't know. Maybe, considering that I'm a wound-up, scared-to-death jackass… Can we see how this plays out? If I'm worthy of you?"

She looked up in shock. Him, worthy of her? He had to be joking. She was the one with the horrendous past, with the drunk of a father who'd killed her best friend. He was the courageous one, the tender one, the man who could take an estranged child back into his arms and fight for his love. She hadn't even been able to protect her mom from her father's abuses.

"Ray, I think you have it backward."

Now it was his turn to be surprised. His blue-green eyes mirrored shock. He embraced her again and softly said, "We both have a lot to learn about each other and ourselves. Don't we?''

True, very true. She only hoped he wouldn't break her heart in the process.

Chapter Seventeen

The knock on his door was timid, barely saturating Ray's perception as he puttered around the nook in the hallway that served as a laundry room. It'd been days after he'd last touched Nora and he was still stumbling around with his head in the clouds.

He wondered if he had heard anything at all as he tossed a red shirt into the batch of white laundry in the washer and strolled over to answer the summons.

Nora. He smiled unthinkingly, arms aching for her.

"Hello, Mr. Brody," she said.

Ray's blood froze solid at the mention of his last name. What the hell… Of course. He'd asked for a civil association, and she was gladly providing him with one. But that didn't keep him from stroking her with his gaze.

Her eyes widened, and she looked past him. Once again, he felt as if he'd never be privy to her thoughts, and that's the one part of her he really ached to touch.

She whispered, "Is Trent here yet?"

He hesitated, then laughed. *Phew.* Maybe she didn't want to act cozy with him because she was afraid Trent might be home from school to see them acting all Valentine-y together. "No, he went surfing with his little friends from the beach."

She smiled, amused and still strangely distant, testing. "Those fifth-graders?"

"One and the same. They came here this afternoon, asking if Trent could come out to play. Then one of the moms drove them to the surf." He reached out, dragging her into the house and shutting the door. His hand brushed against her diamond bracelet, and she quickly drew away from him. He tried not to make his disappointment obvious.

They hadn't made love that long ago, yet she was acting as if he'd burned her. Couldn't she understand that he wanted her? It was just going to take a little time, if he could indeed bring himself to commit.

He nodded toward the bracelet. "Ah, I see you're feeling like a princess again."

She blushed. "It went well with my outfit."

Good try. He hadn't noticed her wearing it when she'd come over for dinner the other night. What was she doing wearing that thing, anyway? It was jewelry for a black-tie affair, not work. "That's a pretty piece of sparkle."

"Thank you." She ran a thumb over it, the light catching a diamond, winking at him. "My grandmother gave it to me."

"Some present."

She hesitated, getting that look that told him she was wondering if she needed to tell him more than he knew. He hoped she'd enlighten him, because everything about her was interesting—all-encompassing, as a matter of fact.

A soft smile preceded the explanation. "This is my wedding gift from Gran Murray. A sort of symbol of hope, I guess."

"The Hope diamonds?" He grinned, closing the front door and ushering her inside, placing his hand on her back. She didn't stiffen up, thank goodness. He didn't know what he'd do if she rejected him with even colder body language.

"You could say that, I guess. At any rate, I'm supposed to

wear it at my wedding.'' Her face heated a deep red, the shade of I-wish-I-could-take-that-back regret. "It's silly, really," she added, turning away to plop her purse on the couch.

A paper stuck out of her bag, drawing Ray's eye momentarily. A shadow passed over the image, probably just a cloud smothering the sun for an instant, but he couldn't shake the bad feeling.

He shivered and stepped nearer to her. Obviously, weddings were a sore subject for both of them right now, so he'd best not follow up on her last comment. "Well, it's a good-looking bracelet, Nora." He didn't add that he hoped, one day, she'd have the happiest wedding in the world. With or without him.

"I really need to show you something, Ray." She grabbed the paper from her purse, whirling back around to face him. Golden fire lit her eyes, and he was glad to see she'd regained some of the spirit that'd fascinated him in the first place. His stomach began to churn.

Ray, just stay casual. Maybe she wants to show you Trent's first A+ in school.

If only. He reclined on the couch, cautiously, propping an ankle on his knee. As she came closer, he could see that the paper seemed a lot like Trent's original life-changing essay.

Damn it.

She said, "This piece of work is called 'The Criminal Jest: A Midsummer Night's Tale by Trent Brody.''' She waved it in front of his face. "I'm sure it will engross you, Mr. Brody."

Something heavy and black splashed into the pit of his stomach. "What did he do this time? Bomb the locker room?"

"Just read on." Nora began inspecting everything from kitchen to work den, pacing the way she had when he visited her in the classroom. Jeez, it seemed like ages since he'd been there, watching her slide a slender hand over her collarbone, smelling her citrus perfume. He enjoyed watching this woman: the smooth skin of her legs under stockings, the sheen of her honey hair under a slant of sunlight.

Standing in front of him, Nora glared for a moment before bursting out, "Can you believe this? This is not good. Not good at all.'' A faint smile crept onto her lips, but before he could be sure, it disappeared.

''I haven't gotten far enough to know.'' Ray tried to seem casual, if not amused, but he felt panic welling within. The paper he held suddenly felt like lead. He wanted to drop it in a deep body of water, getting rid of the evidence, like villains did with guns in the books he read.

She grabbed the paper and waved it around, emphasizing her speech. ''Let me put it in a nutshell, Ray. This is a creative writing assignment, a fairy tale. It is also a lethal weapon, disguised as the adventures of Brent Giantfan.'' When Ray lifted an eyebrow, Nora spread her hands, exasperated.

''Remember the infamous 'I am the lone wolf of the New York streets' essay? The one that started all this trouble?''

He rubbed his jaw, thinking that Trent would listen to a lecture from a fireball like Nora. ''Sure.''

Nora shoved the story at him again. ''In his own brilliant way, Trent is telling us that he *lied* about getting drunk, burglarizing houses, being a bad boy in general. He's laughing at our gullibility with every word of this paper.''

''What?'' He retrieved the essay and skimmed it. Nora was right. But why would Trent have lied to them? He read some more and found his answer.

Burying his face in his hands, Ray didn't know whether to laugh or cry. He was, first of all, relieved that Trent was not as much of a troublemaker as he had feared. Then again, it scared him that his son was very clever—too clever. And he had used that mental slyness to bring together father and teacher. ''How does it feel to be manipulated, Nora?''

''Too much like a puppet. That's how I feel.'' Nora sat next to him, and they both sank back into the cushions. They waited in silence, shaking their heads at themselves every few moments. Then they laughed, giggles exploding into slumping belly shakes.

Twenty minutes later, after the amusement had worn off, Trent scrambled in the door. When he spied Nora and Ray sprawled on the couch, he didn't seem surprised. In fact, he merely threw his hat on a nearby chair and stood in front of them like a defiant, condemned prisoner. His damp hair fell over his eyes, as usual, his expression undefined.

"So," he said. "I guess I'm in trouble again."

Trouble isn't the word, Ray thought. You're grounded for life.

"It's not like I killed someone or something," Trent said as he slumped in a chair. Ray and Nora stood over him, arms crossed over chests.

Ray looked ready to string the kid up by his thumbs, Nora thought, looking at him. He stood rigid, tall and intimidating, with fists working open and shut. She felt much the same way. Imagine, while Trent had been watching her in the classroom, it was because he was *assessing* her, matching her up with his father. Maybe he'd never heard a word she'd taught him in class. The thought sunk her heart. But Trent...how smart this kid was.

The initial essay had been a cry for attention. And also a matchmaking scheme. She could understand why Trent would attempt to play matchmaker; the boy didn't remember having a real family. He'd only been a young boy when Cheri and Ray were together. Then he'd lived with an inadequate single mother. Now he'd been shipped off to a single father he knew only from scant memories and a few pictures. The boy had obviously seen Nora as a rock, a stable influence.

She could empathize with the kid. After all, she'd always wanted a real father, too—one who didn't slap around her mom, thundering her ears every time his hand connected with her soft skin. But, at this moment, she burned like a fool. A student had gotten the best of her. She wouldn't stand for it, even if his plan had been inspired.

A few months ago, she would have gone out of her way to discipline such a diabolical student act. But with a tiny spark of shock, she realized that her pre-Jared Jacobs humor had returned today. Ray had done this for her: put her back on the path to self-respect.

After the steak dinner, hadn't he said he wanted to "see how things played out"? Wasn't that a positive sign that, someday, maybe he'd want to be with her? She was still scared to death that he'd hurt her, but every day he proved otherwise. A man who had such courage and tenderness in handling a wayward son couldn't be all that bad. Chances were, he might treat her with the same gentleness.

That's why she'd decorated her wrist with the diamond bracelet today. Sure, it'd been a flippant decision, and she'd gingerly tried to avoid getting it caught on anything during work, but she felt good wearing it. As Ray had said, the bracelet was hope, a shining question mark that glimmered brighter every time she caught Ray watching her with softness in his water-colored gaze.

Yet, she had to deal with the situation at hand. "I thought we could trust you, Trent," she said, trying on her best hurt demeanor. "And now I find that you've been lying to us? I still don't understand why you would risk getting into trouble like that."

Throwing his sunburned leg over the chair arm, he mumbled, "I guess I wanted to see if you would do anything, Ms. Murray. And I wanted my dad to meet a nice girl."

"Am I to understand that your lies were a test?"

The boy peered under his hair and caught the disappointment in her gaze. "Aren't you glad that I'm not a drunk? Or a crook?"

"Of course," she began, realizing Trent was about to manipulate her. "But I'm also concerned about your need to pull the puppet strings."

She expected anger in return, but if his face burned red, it was with a sunburn, not rage. In fact, the boy seemed pretty smug.

"I don't care how I did it, just so it got done." He swung his leg, grinning.

Ray leaned over so he was face-to-face with his son. "Don't be too satisfied with yourself."

His tone caught Nora's attention. Deadly serious, not at all amused.

Trent shrugged. "It's not like she's Cheri, Dad. Ms. Murray would be a most excellent wife."

Ray clenched his fists, and Nora wished Trent could take the words back into his mouth and eat them for dinner. His son was putting an unbelievable amount of pressure on Ray, basically asking him to commit to Nora right that moment. She wanted to hide behind the couch, to shield herself from an answer she didn't want to hear. But what if Ray agreed? Looked her in the eye and said, "Yes, you're right. She'd be the perfect wife."

Could it happen?

She couldn't believe the Hallelujah Chorus her heart was singing as she merely thought about it. Maybe her bracelet had been a good-luck charm, bringing them to this moment.

Ray put his hands in his pockets. "Trent, you know marriage isn't in the cards."

Something reached in and tore Nora's guts apart. It'd happened. He'd rejected her, in front of Trent, no less. Tears welled in her eyes, her throat choked up.

God, she could either crawl away, out the door and over the state line, or she could stand here and take the disappointment with all the strength she had. She'd always possessed a core of steel, and she'd never failed herself. Now would not be the time to shrivel and die like a neglected flower.

"Right, Trent," she said, crossing her arms. She almost reached up to adjust her glasses, but realized she hadn't worn them today. The lack of protection made her feel just about naked. "Your father and I don't have a future together."

She felt him staring at her, as if he was surprised at her written-in-stone attitude. Well, if he wanted to discard her, she'd up the stakes. If she was hurting, maybe he was, too.

Many people would've been satisfied with her comeback, but she felt empty, filthy with dishonesty. Damn it all, she did want to be with him for the rest of her life. She'd fallen in love, and it was too late to stop herself. Trying to avoid the emotions hadn't helped, remembering how she'd ached in the past hadn't stopped her. As usual, she'd have to learn the hard way—with plenty of pain and scars. Although, she wasn't sure she'd heal this time.

Her diamond bracelet felt like blocks of cement chained together, dragging her down into misery.

She wouldn't look at Ray, couldn't look at him, for fear she'd burst into unwanted tears, revealing the extent of her pain. Even when he spoke again, she stared at a spot just above Trent's head. A black mark on the wall just beneath the window, visible only if you peered hard enough.

"So I trust you won't be interfering with my life again?" She gathered enough courage to look at Trent, who had clamped his mouth into a straight blade of anger. He seemed just as upset as she was.

"Why can't you be together? Can't you see you guys are perfect?" His eyes filled. "Ms. Murray? Dad?"

"It's unreasonable, Trent," said Ray. "You need to drop the subject."

"No."

"Go to your room, Trent." Ray's voice crackled with anger as he loomed over his son, shoulders stretching his shirt until the seams trembled.

Out of the corner of her eye, she glanced at him. She wondered if he'd bust a vein trying to repress his emotions.

The two Brody men stared at each other with looks that could either burst into violence or dissolve into tears. Finally, Trent spoke.

"Fine. Send me away. Why would you want to listen to my opinion, anyway? I'm just a stupid kid. A stupid kid nobody wanted."

"Trent, you know that's not true." Ray reached out for his son.

"Don't touch me!" Trent squirmed away, and Ray put hands on hips, breathing heavily, watching the floor.

Trent sneered, and Nora realized that tears stained his

cheeks. ''I *hate* you. I hate you so much, Brody. I wish I'd *never* come here to live with you.''

The world snapped into a picture-still halt.

''What did you say?'' whispered Ray.

Nora's hands covered her mouth. A dry sting twisted in her throat.

Trent shrugged, and a stray sob tore out his mouth before he collected himself.

Ray looked at Nora, as if expecting her to confirm Trent's statement. All the blood had rushed out of his face, and he seemed like a boy who had just heard the truth about Santa Claus.

The boy continued. ''I'd have been better off living with my drug addict mom. At least she wasn't as mean as you are.''

Without a word, Ray calmly walked outside, letting the front door slam softly. Nora saw Trent flinch. He sputtered, collapsing onto the couch as tears welled freely.

Her first instinct was to follow Ray, but she knew that these were a momentous few seconds for the boy. She sat next to him, cupped his head and led it to her shoulder. He was like a bag of cloth as he sunk into her embrace.

Trent's words had sliced a gaping wound into this household. How long would it take for that wound to heal? Would it ever?

She stroked Trent's head and whispered, ''Shh.''

When his sobs lessened, Trent stuttered, ''I didn't mean what I said to him.''

''You don't mean to say a lot of hurtful things, I know. Just remember how powerful words can be.''

''I didn't want to hurt him, Ms. Murray. But I was so angry at him.'' He rubbed his eyes, and his face scrunched as another crying spell seized him. ''I want him to be my dad. But I also want you to be my mom.''

She didn't know what to tell him. *I want the same thing?* ''You know it isn't possible. Wishing won't make it a reality.''

His eyes teemed with regret as he looked up to her. "I just want a real family. Is that so bad?"

"No, Trent, it's not." Nora hesitated, wanting to ask the question, but afraid to. "Want to tell me what it was like living with your mom?"

Swallowing, he stared into space. "She wasn't home much."

Nora smiled and held back the burn of her throat. He was definitely like his dad when it came to avoiding certain topics. "I see. Was that a better situation for you, leaving you the freedom to run around New York drinking and stealing?"

He shot her a knowing grin, which she took to mean "no."

"When Cheri got mad at me, she always used to tell me that she never wanted me, anyway." He cleared his throat and latched onto Nora's arm, drying his tears on her blouse. "She said that's why my dad left us. Because of me, because he didn't love me."

"Do you believe Cheri?" The name choked her like poison. "Did she ever give you a good reason to believe in her?"

"She's my mom." The explanation was simple, unconditional.

"I think you need to tell your dad how sorry you are, Trent."

"Do you think he'll come back?" She could feel his body shiver.

She knew he would; it's just that he wouldn't be coming back to *her*. "He'll be here. Just you wait."

"Why can't you just marry my dad?" asked the boy, obviously not as weary of the subject as she. "You'd be good for him. And you're smart." Trent hiccuped. "I know he likes you."

"I'm your teacher, and dating parents is against the rules." She wondered if the words sounded as weak to him as they did to her. The excuse had always sounded lame, but she realized that her job was all she had left to keep her occupied now that Ray had pushed her aside.

"Maybe you'll change your mind, Ms. Murray."

With those words of confidence, Trent bolted up and ran to his room. She was touched by his persistence, the simple acceptance she felt just being near him. Nora stifled the urge to follow him and instead went outside to wait for Ray. Just to say a final goodbye.

The cool of night stung his nose, but Ray didn't care. He thought his heart had been healed. But now it was torn out, cleanly and expertly by a master of words—his son.

And not only was there soreness between him and Trent, he'd gouged Nora as well, having to admit out loud his fear of commitment.

But what else could he have done? Proposed to her on the spot? Trent had forced him to say something, *anything* that would convince him he wasn't interested in marrying again. At least not any time soon.

He was a miserable failure in the matrimony game.

Ray shook his head, remembering.

When Cheri had become pregnant, Ray felt joy at first, then agony. Would he be a better father than he'd been a husband? After Trent's birth, Ray and Cheri had moved around, living in different cities: she working odd jobs as he drifted around, obtaining work as a carpenter—when he could find it.

Trent had grown older, and, in spite of the niggling uncertainty about his parenting abilities, Ray had lost his heart to the child. Trent looked just like Cheri, and even if he and his wife were at odds, he could still love Trent with every worshipful fiber of his body.

Today, when Trent had spoken the words Ray had feared since his son had returned home, all the emotions he'd suppressed came rushing to the surface.

"I hate you. I wish I'd never come here to live with you."

He'd been waiting to hear this for weeks now, and his nightmare had come true. He'd been forced to leave the house before he embarrassed himself in front of Nora.

Nora. How would she fit in to all of this? In the depths of his heart, he knew.

There was too much pain in his life. He'd already messed up with one woman. What made him think that he was capable of loving another?

Did you see the look on her face when she heard Trent's bombshell? asked his conscience. *She was horrified. Your life affects her, and what is your life but a mess?*

Ray shook his head as his stomach trembled. He wasn't capable of loving anyone else. Making love to Nora had just increased his emotions to the point that he *thought* that he could possibly have feelings for her one day. But there was nothing like a blond troublemaker's truth to give you a good dose of reality.

He would not poison another life. Nora was too special. Let her find someone who had it together, someone who could return what she had to offer.

Ray walked back home, dreading his arrival.

Teeth clicking with a chill, Nora hugged her arms over her knees and rocked back and forth on the porch steps. *All right, Ray. You can come home anytime now. You'd* better *come home.*

She had gone to Trent's room to check on the boy once, and he'd been writing in a well-used notebook. He'd looked up from his writing, eyes wide with a smile on his face, but when he'd seen Ms. Murray standing in the doorway, his face had fallen, and he hid the book behind his back. Nora had known better than to ask him about the contents of the notebook—he would have denied that it was anything important—so she slipped out quietly, clicking the door shut behind her.

Her watch told her that it was 10:00 p.m. Briefly, she scolded herself for wasting time. She could have been filling out more job applications or polishing her résumé. Then she took a deep breath and told herself not to be selfish. Her life could wait.

Like fog fading into a tall form, Ray appeared, head down, hands in pockets, footsteps echoing in the night. As he walked up the path to the front door, his head jerked up. He seemed surprised to see her.

Didn't he know that she would wait forever? That she *had* been waiting for at least that long to find the peace she felt when she was near him? Of course, she'd never wait again for him, but that was beside the point. He needed comfort now, and she wasn't about to desert him.

A memory, the kelp bracelet, burned her mind. *Always,* she had promised after he slid it on her wrist. *I'll treasure this. Always.*

Presently, her diamonds rubbed raw over her wrist. They felt like cold stones pressing into her skin, shortening her breath.

It took a moment for her to find the right words, though she had been thinking about them for a couple hours. Then, as she looked into his devastated eyes, her mind went blank. "Hi."

"Hi," he said, looking at a location over her head.

"We weren't sure when you'd come back. Are you all right?"

One hand jerked out of his pocket. "Sure. I'm fine."

"Oh, good." Nora stood, wanting to stroke his sandy hair. He didn't seem as if he wanted to be touched, so she locked her hands behind her back. "Trent's in his room. I talked with him. He didn't mean it, Ray."

His mouth twisted into a bitter grin. "If he didn't mean the words, he sure as hell meant the pain." He brushed past her into the house.

A slap would have hurt less than his refusal to look her in the eye. Should she follow him? she worried, cringing at the possibility of further rejection. Or should she just leave and pretend she didn't care, that it was their problem, not hers?

Remembering the pain she felt when Ray had told Trent that marriage wasn't a possibility, she turned around and started walking toward her car. As she unlocked it, her vision blurred. It was too late to pretend she didn't care.

Stuffing her keys in a pocket, she marched back into the house. When she knocked on Trent's bedroom door, there was no answer. She assumed that they were having a discussion in Ray's room. As she stood before his door, she guiltily rested her ear against the wood. No sound. She knocked.

"Yeah?" was the muffled answer.

Peeking around the door's corner, she saw Ray flat on the bed, arms resting under his head. If she hadn't known better, she would have thought he slept peacefully, but the haunted stare of his eyes betrayed that image. "Where's Trent?" she asked.

"In his room, I guess."

"Oh." She waited a beat. "Have you two talked?"

His laugh was short. *Why is it your business?* it said. "I'm not in the mood for whatever the hell that kid feels like serving up."

Nora sighed. "Trent didn't mean what he said. He's so happy to be here. I can see it every time I look at the two of you."

"Yeah, he seems overjoyed."

Taking two tentative steps forward, she said, "I wish you could see how he watches you. There's love in his eyes, Ray."

His wall of sorrow crumbled a bit. "All I see is Cheri. Her disgust with me. Why should he love me?"

"Ray, why *shouldn't* he?"

"Look, there's nothing more to say on the subject, okay?" Ray snapped.

Taking a step backward, she frowned at his bitterness, though she understood the reason for it. "Well, then. Maybe I'd better go."

"Nora." He sat up, his hair tousled boyishly. Her heart ached for him.

"Yes?"

He swung his long legs over the side of the bed, his broad back to her. "I think it might be best if you don't come back."

It was what Nora imagined a car crash looked like through the driver's side of the windshield: she could see the tree speeding into her window, she could feel the impact, but reality would hit several seconds after the damage. She was speechless.

"Maybe," he continued, hand moving over his hair roughly, "you need to continue with your life and just forget about mine."

Finally, the words formed like cotton balls in her mouth. "Right. I heard your declaration back there in the family room. Forget everything we've meant to each other, Ray. There's no chance for us, right?"

Another harsh laugh. "You deserve so much better than what I can offer, Nora."

How could he possibly know what she *deserved?* Didn't he realize that she might've given up everything just to be with him? "I thought you were different," she said, choking the words out.

He looked away. "I think you should go, Nora."

Brushing away her tears, she sat beside him on the bed. "On second thought, I think I'll stay."

He sighed and shook his head, as if saying *Are you going to make this harder than it needs to be?*

"I'm telling you that we're not going to see each other again."

Nora grabbed the bedspread and crushed it out of frustration. "Maybe we should talk about this at a less emotional time."

"Listen. Every moment around this house is fraught with emotion. Can't you see that?" He locked onto her arm and squeezed it to emphasize his words. "Why do you even want to be here?"

They stared at each other while their wills traded blows. Slowly, she reached up, grabbed his head and brought him to her breast. His arms wrapped around her waist, and he shuddered, breath warming the thin material of her blouse, causing the tips of her breasts to pucker and tingle. She spoke into his clean hair.

"How can you even ask me why I want to be here?"

Hours seemed to pass as they held each other. Then a cool

wind straightened Nora's spine. She pushed Ray upward, but they both looked as guilty as desire itself.

A boy's hand cupped the corner of the door. Trent stuck his head inside the room.

Nora sucked in a deep breath. It was over. There was no explaining this embrace.

The boy's gaze could have been accusing or even hateful, but she couldn't tell. He walked around the side of the bed to where they sat. Man and boy were silent, waiting for the other to speak first.

"I'm sorry, Dad." Trent's face crumbled as he stood back, perhaps waiting for the stinging, punishing words to bullet his way.

Ray opened his arms, and Trent's cry of relief filled the room as he lunged into his father's forgiving embrace. The two held on to each other as if they had found deliverance.

Thank God, Nora thought. She knew they would have many troubles ahead—the life of a teenager was filled with mines of emotion—but they would work it out. They had each other.

She had no part in this reunion. Ray had told her as much. Quietly, she started to stand. An arm encompassed her shoulders. It was Trent's. He pulled her into their circle of comfort as the first of many tears slid down her cheek.

Ray's arm held her as well, but, after a moment, it slipped away.

Chapter Eighteen

Each day that passed was stamped with a heavy heart for Ray. Images of Nora flying on a swing at the beach, her face flushed with happiness against white sheets, her mouth tilted in a smile as she laughed with Trent—the snapshots of his mind were too painful to bear. Especially when he'd come to the conclusion that she had no place in his life. Not now, not ever. Not when he had no idea how to control the hurt that seemed to dog him no matter what he did. And, Lord knew, he didn't want his pain to touch Nora. He'd keep it all to himself if he could, before their relationship got any more serious than it was already.

When the end of the week finally arrived, he knew he couldn't put off seeing her any longer. As he wandered onto Jefferson school's campus, he barely saw the late afternoon sun peeking through the low buildings, the boarded-up lockers, the sandwich wrappers bobbing on the concrete like crumpled lunchtime ghosts. Nora's classroom loomed across a lawn. Her lights were on, indicating that someone was working in her classroom.

He ran his hand through his hair, hating the thought of breaking off a relationship with Nora. First and foremost, he wondered if she knew whether or not she was pregnant yet. Something bright and warm warred with his resolve to stay out of her personal life. He would've welcomed the idea of having a baby with Nora if he hadn't blown his life years and years ago. All he could bring her now was pain. Hell, he wasn't even a very good father to Trent. How could he take care of another little life?

These past days, memories of his bungled past had kept him from seeing her face-to-face; also, the touch and smell of Nora were still too strong in his head for him to see her—he knew he'd have to stay away to remain strong in his convictions. And just the thought of hearing her honey-rich voice over the phone caused a raging hunger within him. When he'd finally decided to visit her classroom for their final heart-to-heart, he'd done so because breaking up over the phone was the chicken's way out. No, Ray Brody was a man—at least, he'd felt like one a few days ago.

In spite of his attempts to keep his distance from her, he knew that he wasn't being fair, keeping her on a string. When she'd left the other night, her parting hug indicated to him that she believed they still had a shot at a relationship. He'd have to end this, once and for all. It would be for her own good. He wouldn't screw up her life any more than he had already.

It was the best thing for everyone, really.

Besides, this situation with Trent consumed his attention. He had no time for her. No heart for her.

No time for Nora. The phrase echoed through the caverns of his soul.

Ray knocked on her door and entered after he heard a muffled "Come in."

She sat at her desk, shuffling through papers. Her fair hair was wrapped in a French twist, and the peach-plaid dress she wore would have made her dull eyes sparkle if they had enough reason. Guilt and longing warmed his face as he watched her.

In that split second of time, he allowed himself to flash back to the first day he'd visited her in the classroom. She'd been so nervous. He'd been spurred by the realization that this was the Cameo from Brody's Clubhouse. In the flesh.

Lollipop-red mouth. Silky-stockinged legs rubbing against each other. Leg bouncing with nerves.

He was an idiot. Maybe she'd forgive him for all his sins. Why couldn't he give her a chance? After all, Nora had the most beautiful soul he'd ever touched, and he needed light in his life. Trent needed guidance as well. So what was the big problem?

You'll only mess it up, Brody. You have a track record of blowing a good thing.

As she looked up anticipatively, her brow darkened. "Oh, hello, Mr. Brody. What are you doing here?"

"Hey, Nora." He sensed hurt and confusion as her body tensed. "I want to apologize for everything…for the other night…"

"Which night?" she asked, uncharacteristically blank-faced.

Over the stale, junior-high smell of the classroom, he caught her fresh scent. It drew him a step nearer. So she wanted to play word games. "Both nights."

The night he had made love with her. And the awful night when Trent had aired their dirty laundry. God, how he wished he could take them both back now.

Didn't he?

"Of course." Nora stood up and leaned against the front of her desk. "I thought you already had your say."

"By the time you left, I didn't think things were clear between us." Ray laughed ironically. Was there anything about his life that was clear?

"Oh, it was lucid enough to me." She puckered her lips at his laugh. "You had to come here. You couldn't have left a message on my machine." Sighing, she added, "Stop playing with my mind, Ray. You can't tell me to get out of your life and then wander back into mine.''

He tried to control himself, but the memory of her skin, the softness of a kitten under his fingertips, boiled his blood. His eyes smoothed over the two splotches of color on her cheeks, down a slender neck, to breasts that strained against her dress. They'd filled his palms perfectly, responding to his touch as if made for the hollows of his hands. When his mouth had tasted the tips, they had budded within his warmth, expanding something within himself—something that had remained dormant until Nora had come along.

He tried to make his voice sound cold and detached. ''Nora, we didn't go into a relationship thinking that things would be perfect. It just didn't work out, okay? We should just cut our losses and continue being friends.''

''Friends.'' She seemed to roll the word around her mouth as if it were a sucker. Her nose wrinkled. ''When were we actually friends? No, never mind. It doesn't matter, anyway. If you came here to confirm that you don't want to see me anymore, just spit it out.''

But he couldn't spit it out.

She watched him with a look caught between fear and hope. ''If this is about what Trent said the other night...''

''Yes, at least, that's what triggered it. I need...to concentrate on him. On our problems. Before I can concentrate on anything else.'' He hesitated. ''And I want to know if...well, if you're—''

''No. I'm not pregnant. You don't need to worry about supporting a mistake.''

He was relieved, but, dammit, that's not what he'd meant by asking her. ''Nora, it wouldn't have been that way.''

She smiled sadly. ''Anyway, I've come to realize that maybe it would be a good thing—not seeing you anymore. The kids catch on, and as I've told you before, it undermines my teaching ability.''

Although he knew it was the right thing for both of them,

he couldn't help feeling hurt that she was throwing in the towel, too.

"So you agree it's for the best?" he said, hovering near her, feeling her glow.

"Absolutely." She watched the front of his shirt, took a sudden breath and straightened her spine.

He knew he made her nervous. And…something else.

In order to put an end to the temptation, he wandered to a Shakespeare poster and perused the student writing samples posted near it.

Here—Trent Brody. She had posted a sonnet his son had written. As Ray read it, his throat stung.

It was about a sea princess who wore a crown of kelp. After she found a prince, the crown turned to diamonds. How did his kid know this stuff?

He turned back to Nora, who still half sat on her desk, watching him. As he spoke, he drew nearer, and her eyes widened with each step.

"It'll take a while before Trent and I come to terms." He allowed his finger to trace her jawline. "But I love that kid. I need to devote myself to him."

She took his hand and removed it from her skin. "I guess that does it, Mr. Brody."

"Yeah. Cut clean. Right?" His hands stayed busy. Of its own accord, his thumb circled the crest of her breast as it hardened to life.

Her eyes darted around the classroom, wide with trepidation. Then they softened as her breathing fluttered against his chest. God help him, he was doing it again. And he couldn't stop himself. He didn't want to stop himself.

As Nora rubbed her lips over his Adam's apple, Ray lost all control.

He slipped under her dress to grip her thigh, twining her leg around his. The desk pressed Nora into his hardness, and their clothing wisped in friction as she rubbed against him. Half her books crashed to the floor when he pushed her back, onto the desk.

"I thought…you were leaving…" she breathed, grabbing his hair, leading his lips to her waiting breast. He had already undone the buttons of her bodice and freed Nora from her bra. "Please—not here—"

"Okay," he said, tongue pushing her erect nipple to the roof of his mouth. The sound she made in response seemed like heat and exotic silk as she arched against him.

Nora put her finger to his lips and held her forehead to his, bringing him to pause. Voice trembling, she said, "I'm not going to be your good-time gal. You leave now or not at all."

Damn it all. An ultimatum. In the past, Cheri had offered him too many of these. He felt as if he had already eaten a big meal, and couldn't stomach another morsel.

Yet, Nora was right. And, after one more week of school, he would have no more excuses to see her: no "Trent needs help with his schoolwork" or "Trent needs someone to watch him after school." Ray realized that if he let Nora go now, she would never trust him enough to return to him. The men in her life had left their dark marks. Would Ray be another brand on her heart?

"Nora," he whispered, holding her head in his hands. He wanted to stay. He needed to go. He wanted the decision to be easier.

Hope seemed to strengthen her embrace. "It can all work out, Ray. If we work together."

Pulling back to look into the amber beams of her eyes, he kissed her, soft as the lyrics of a love song.

Then he walked away.

As the door shut, Nora slumped over the edge of her desk, dress around her thighs, bodice gaping. Shame flamed around her as she slowly fastened buttons, straightened the skirt. She started to pick up books from the floor, placing them as neatly as they had been before.

No. Nothing had happened. She had imagined it. Right? She'd been sitting here working when she had dropped off into a fantasy.

The tingling of her skin told her that this was wishful thinking.

Stupid, stupid, stupid. How could she have lost control once again, in the classroom, no less. She'd never get a job here if common sense fled every time she stood in the same room with Ray.

And, to think, she used to be so together, so in charge of her emotions, but that had been a lifetime ago. And, to make matters worse, she'd lied to him about not being pregnant. She hadn't any proof that she wasn't carrying his child—it was still too soon to tell for sure—but she'd seen the panicked look in his eyes, and had wanted to spare him the agony of committing to her because of a child.

Humiliating. Humiliating to feel the keening of her soul. Crying because, at the moment Ray walked out the door, she'd realized that, yes, she was totally, crazily in love with him. It was no longer a suspicion, it was her reality.

Love had started as a philosophy for her, then blossomed into an emotion. But instead of shooting her to the stars, Ray had crushed her heart between his strong hands, wiping them off afterward as if her pain was so much dust.

Of course, she knew her teaching job was just like a speck of that dust compared to the mammoth world Ray symbolized. He and Trent were so much more important to her than a paycheck, but what could she do? Ray wasn't about to let her into his life. Obviously, he wasn't about to risk his heart for her, either.

The tenderness in his wrinkled brow as he listened to stories of her pain-tinged past, the gentle lifting of her chin when he wanted to look into her eyes to make a point… Naturally she was bound to fall in love with him. It didn't seem fair that he couldn't—or wouldn't—allow himself to spend the rest of his life with her as well.

She ached. Oh, God, she ached for him. And not just physically. It hurt to think she'd never be close to Trent after school let out. She'd never stare back into Ray's eyes after making love with him.

It was over. Even if he felt any memory of the love their bodies had promised, the emotion obviously wasn't strong enough to bind him to her.

God, she hated love.

She went to the sink, turned on the faucet and splashed water over her face. She trudged toward the back office in order to grab her satchel and leave.

But she wasn't expecting Mrs. McArthur.

The older teacher worked silently at a desk. Nora surreptitiously peered into the classrooms that connected to the common office. No one else. Oh, God, what if Mrs. McArthur had heard?

And Nora thought she'd already hit rock bottom.

When the woman looked up, Nora knew that her mentor teacher, Mrs. McArthur, had been audience to something. Her low ponytail swiped the back of her swivel chair, gypsy-red skirt swirling around her Birkenstock-clad feet. "How was your day, Ms. Murray?"

Nora folded her hands behind her back. "It went pretty well."

"I was going to do your final observation today, but I got caught up in a meeting."

"Maybe tomorrow," Nora said, longing to leave.

Mrs. McArthur put down her pen. "Sometimes student teachers don't know all the rules. Or, more to the point, they don't know how to play the game. I'm trying to find the right words." She drummed her fingers on the desk, the noise pounding in Nora's brain.

"There are certain behaviors that will not be tolerated from staff members. These codes are enforced for the good of the students. Do you understand?"

With a sidelong glance, Nora tested her. "Understand what, Mrs. McArthur?"

"I guess I've no choice but to be blunt."

Nothing has stopped you before, Nora thought.

"Through the school grapevine, I've heard rumors about you and a certain parent." Mrs. McArthur cleared her throat and flicked her gaze toward the classroom without mentioning this afternoon's athletic events.

Oh, no. She wanted to sink into the earth and die. If fate were generous, that was what would happen. She shut her eyes and hoped.

But no acts of nature were forthcoming. Mrs. McArthur continued. "You must stop this behavior now, Ms. Murray. It might already be too late."

Though the words were vague, Nora knew that the last statement meant that she would not be hired at this school. And after all the time she had spent busting her rear, with other teachers whispering encouragement. The realization tasted bitter.

As if it mattered now, Nora thought, her mouth quirking up in the corner. It was all too much: Ray's betrayal, Trent's antics, a bad day at work... Her blood stewed, making her head thick. "You know, Mrs. McArthur, maybe this isn't the right school for me."

The mentor teacher's mouth opened, but Nora cut her off.

"I mean, if I can't be myself, how will I be happy? If this is the life of a teacher, I've got to give this a second thought."

While her brain throbbed, Nora's heart followed the beat. *I'm doomed as doomed can be.*

"All right, then," Mrs. McArthur said, pen in hand once again. The older woman's face had drooped into an expression Nora was hard-pressed to identify. "Be thankful you have only one week left. I'm not sure Principal Johnson would appreciate such an attitude during the long term."

Suddenly, Nora realized the impact of what she had said to her mentor teacher. She'd just let a job fly from her fingers, and, she thought, almost laughing at the irony, she'd lost it on the same day she'd lost Ray.

There was no more to be said in her defense. "Thank you," she said lamely as she left, cringing at the words. Thanks for what? For ten thousand dollars down the drain in student loans? Without a recommendation from Mrs. McArthur or the principal, she was as good as faceless when it came to finding a job. The people with glowing reviews would be the ones the school district hired.

She trod out the building, across lawns, into the parking lot. It would be a lonely, awful weekend, not knowing if Mrs. McArthur would talk with Principal Johnson. Not hearing Ray's voice. Not seeing Trent's smile.

And the worst part of it was, she still carried her emotional baggage, a traveler on the endless road to bigger and better pains.

Hey, where was her spirit? The steel core that had gotten her through years of abusive situations?

She stood still, letting the wind blow a tendril of hair across her eyes as she gathered courage. Then the moment passed. What good would spirit do now, when she had nothing to drive her, nothing to protect?

As she unlocked the car, her gaze rested on the graffiti around her. Walls filled with snake-ink filth. Territorial marks.

The eyesores had played a part in her meeting Ray, she thought, the graffiti becoming a blur of spray-can colors.

What did she have to look forward to? She almost wished that she had papers to correct this weekend. It was such a habit that she didn't know what to do with herself.

She'd already figured out grades for the semester, as had most of the other teachers. They planned to show video movies for the rest of the week. Nora decided to follow suit, to go with the lazy flow of summer anticipation that seemed to paralyze the brain cells of the students. What a waste of time. If she could do what she wanted to do, why she'd…

Nora sucked in her breath. Then she hopped behind the wheel and squealed out of the parking lot, a devious smile on her face.

If Jefferson or anyone else wouldn't have her, she would just have to throw herself a heck of a going-away party.

Chapter Nineteen

Days later, the scene could've been straight out of the pages of *Tom Sawyer:* white paint rolling over the wall, children laughingly dedicated to their craft as one individual stood back, admiring the progress.

Nora, ponytailed, a tattered flannel shirt over grubby jeans, pointed to a remnant of graffiti on the wall. "Billy, you missed a spot."

As the student brushed over the dark spray paint, Nora thought that the area looked so much cleaner without the taggers' destruction marking it. Since this morning, she'd escorted each class beyond the school parking lot to paint over graffiti that marred the backs of neighboring stores. Although the task wasn't actual "class work," it was much more constructive than watching videotapes or having parties. And the children were having a great time in the sunshine.

It felt wonderful to be out, enjoying her freedom, trying to forget that she'd gotten her heart broken less than a week ago. She was doing everything possible to fight the space vacated by Ray's attention. And, even if she still loved him, she wouldn't allow the loneliness to swallow her whole.

Decadent hot fudge sundaes, laughing with her students, going on shopping sprees she couldn't afford—she fought the emptiness with all the strength she possessed.

For another diversion, Nora had decided that today would be a perfect time to take her students on this "field trip." She'd talked with the business owners, and they were more than thrilled about the cleaning of their stores' back walls. And the students themselves had been bouncing around the classroom during this last week of school. They weren't content to be indoors, especially on a block-schedule day that forced them to stay in class for approximately two hours per session.

But the children were in their element now, dressed in grungy clothes, putting loads of elbow grease into this endeavor. It helped that she'd promised to feed them popcorn if they cooperated.

Trent, a dry paint roller in hand, wandered over to Nora. "None of the other teachers are doing this, Ms. Murray. In social studies, we watched movies all day."

"You media hounds have seen every movie in the world." Nora strolled down the line of workers, encouraging them. She was dying to itch the tip of her nose, but paint splotched her fingers.

Trent followed her. "Watching videos is good, but I can't stand it in every single class."

Giving into temptation, Nora delicately rubbed her nose, no doubt leaving a slight dot of white. "Why are you taking a break, soldier? There's work to be done." She seized a brush, dipped it into the paint and coated an unbeautified, "graffitied" wall.

Trent worked next to her. When she looked over at him, he grinned. She laughed, shook her head and returned her attention to work. His attitude had improved greatly since last week. He helped her pass out papers and clean the room. He'd stopped acting as if he deserved special treatment because of her relationship—or lack of one now—with his father. Nora didn't know if he was finally maturing or if there was a full moon in bloom. But she liked the change.

In a flash of perspective, she wondered if the school administration would be happy with her community project lesson plan.

Who cared? Nora thought. She wasn't out to please those people—or anyone, for that matter—anymore. She was doing this for herself, because she wanted these kids to learn a practical lesson. Because she wanted the parents and students to say, "Boy, that Ms. Murray was a heck of a teacher. Why didn't Jefferson hire her?" Such a trivial revenge, but it made her feel better in the wake of all the recent rejections.

"This is wonderful work, children," said an authoritative voice behind her. The students dropped the brushes to their sides.

Nora calmly did an about-face, eye to eye with Principal Johnson, a woman who embraced the stereotype of businesswoman chic. Thick black-framed glasses circled small eyes, and she wore a gray linen suit with pumps. Mrs. McArthur, Principal Johnson's gypsy-like counterpart, stood next to her, arms crossed over her stomach and a now-you've-done-it cast to her eyes. Another teacher, whom Nora had seen in the teachers' lounge on occasion, flanked their backs like a bodyguard. Nora didn't think they were here to chip in.

"Good morning, Mrs. Johnson...Mrs. McArthur."

Nora thought she could hear the students' paint dripping from their brushes to the blacktop. Mrs. Johnson and her cronies looked like a SWAT team ready to take her down.

"May we have a word with you, Ms. Murray?" asked Principal Johnson, her smile frigid yet polite.

"Now?" Nora felt light-headed, as if her life was flashing before her eyes. The muscles in her stomach constricted. This was it. "May we have a word with you" was a very civilized way of saying, "May we fire you?"

Mrs. McArthur shuffled toward the administration office. She didn't look back.

"In case you didn't realize it, Ms. Murray," said the principal softly, "you have taken the students off campus. Did you send home permission slips?"

"Well, no. I didn't..." Nora turned her face to the class, smiling encouragingly at them. The children watched, biting their lips, bunching their eyebrows.

"If something should happen to these students, no matter how far away they are from campus, we are responsible, Ms. Murray. Lawsuits could result. And this tagging business...didn't we have a situation earlier in the year in which you showed a tagging video to the students? And then the situation with the parent himself..."

"That was resolved," sputtered Nora. Right. Ray had put an end to the business himself, in a very personal manner.

Principal Johnson shook her head at Nora. Suddenly, she felt like a bumbling fool. Mrs. Johnson was known in the teachers' lounge as a by-the-book principal. She should've expected consequences for taking the students even an inch off campus without permission.

Then again, what did she have to lose?

The principal said, "It's better to ignore this graffiti than to encourage it. To some kids, painting a wall is painting a wall." Then, in a louder voice, "Children! It's time to go back to the classroom. Put down your equipment and let's move." She nodded at the bodyguard-teacher, and he walked forward.

Shoulders slumping, Nora nodded. Sometimes it was better to cut one's losses. She waved a hand in silent request for the students to follow her. Brushes and rollers smashed into paint containers as the youngsters whispered questions to one another.

"Wait!"

Everyone stopped. Trent stepped forward, tentatively at first. Then he took two strides to stand in front of the principal. What the heck was he doing? The boy had that determined look on his face, the one he had when he challenged Ray.

Trent puffed out his chest. "I want to finish this job."

A couple of students agreed. One said, "There's no air-

conditioning in the classroom." Another added, "I like it outside."

Smiling tolerantly under her bunned hair, Principal Johnson
said, "I understand that, children. But you shouldn't be out
here. Not without your parents' permission." She clapped her
hands three times. "Now, let's go."

"Come on," said the other teacher.

Trent sat on the ground and angled his face toward the sun's
glow. "I'm not leaving."

Mouth flying open, Nora couldn't find the words to tell
Trent that they could finish after school if he wanted. He was
purposely trying to challenge the school's principal.

"Trent Brody, you and I have talked about this sort of behavior before," Mrs. Johnson said, steady as an iron warship.
"You will return to class with your fellow students. Come on,
everyone."

Trent looked at Nora, his eyes full of question marks. She
hesitated, somehow unwilling to give up the last vestiges of
her job, and, dammit, painting away the graffiti was worth a
fight. After a glance at the principal, Nora turned to the boy
and sent him a smile of pure approval.

"I'm not moving." Trent looked up at a little red-haired
girl. She giggled, her feet pigeon-toeing just before she sat
beside her Prince Charming. Blossoming love among her children. Wasn't life beautiful?

"Mrs. Johnson," Trent said, "don't you think this is a good
thing we're doing?"

"Of course. But this is Language Arts, not painting. Now
stop playing games." The older woman held out her hand,
entreating him without softening.

"Mrs. Johnson," a boy said, his buck teeth making him
look like a chipmunk, "if this is a good thing we're doing,
why can't we stay? It's just the last week of school."

"I explained that already, Billy. Now, for the last time, let's
go back to the classroom."

Three more students joined Trent on the ground. Then five
more. Then only two students stood.

"Ms. Murray?" Principal Johnson watched her, a veiled threat in the air.

Nora turned toward the class, their show of support making her proud, blocking her words with sadness. She recovered. "You guys are old enough to make your own choices. I've been trying to help you make the proper ones, and I should hope that you do." She cleared her throat and took off her glasses, stuffing them in her back jeans pocket. "If you don't go back to the classroom right now, your parents will be called. If you do, well, I guess you'll have another teacher." She steeled herself. Heck, she could always get a job at a private school. Maybe. "You decide if making your neighborhood beautiful is more important than watching videos in the classroom."

"Ms. Murray," Principal Johnson hissed, "that's more than enough." The principal placed a firm hand on Nora's back, directing her toward the administration building. Over her shoulder, she yelled, "This is your choice, students. A bad choice."

The bodyguard-teacher placed his hands on slim hips and said, "I'll keep an eye on them, Mrs. Johnson."

The two students who had remained standing followed them, avoiding Nora's eyes. "It's all right, you guys," she said to them. One smiled wanly, the other began crying.

"My parents would be so mad at me if I stayed—"

"Don't worry." Nora patted the student on the shoulder.

"You two will sit in the office while I talk with Ms. Murray," the principal said as she pulled Nora along. "Ms. Murray, you will be released today."

The situation was so ridiculous that Nora almost laughed out loud. She was dispirited, yet relieved to finally know her fate. It had been like waiting for a long-ill relative to die.

Losing a job and your true love in the space of two weeks. Wow. And, the funny thing was, she could still walk, even if her principal was all but pushing her. Nora could still smile, even if the expression was wobbly. Not bad for a girl who'd lost everything that mattered.

Heck, she'd maintain her sense of humor and survive the situation. And if she had been blessed with Ray's child, as she suspected was the case, she'd still come out a winner. Fear mixed with optimism. She'd make it somehow, even if she had to struggle as a single mom.

She followed Principal Johnson into the office, ready to face the worst.

Dammit, he was absolutely livid.

Ray had been called by the school to pick up Trent, who was obviously in the midst of some trouble once again.

While pulling into Jefferson's parking lot, he clenched and unclenched his fist on the steering wheel, attempting to calm himself. He'd been in an awful mood ever since he'd split with Nora. Sure, he was somewhat relieved by the fact that she wasn't pregnant.

Yet tiny, gurgling babies haunted his sleep, reminding him of what could've been with the woman he could've loved.

The Cameo flashed into his sight, honey hair glowing, amber eyes wide with consternation. How he'd wanted her, even upon an initial glance. But he'd ultimately blown it. One of the best things to happen to him, and he'd purposely shoved her aside.

What an awful decision. Ed Sanchez and Trent had hounded him about it for days now. His conscience had been equally persistent. Yes, he had made the world's biggest mistake. There—he admitted it. But what was there to do but moon over Nora? She'd never take him back, not after his shabby treatment of her. And he couldn't blame her. He hated himself as much as Nora must've hated him.

Through his window, Ray saw kids sitting among paint cans and supplies. The walls behind them were freshly painted, obscuring the former graffiti. He tried to smile. It was about time the school took some action to help the community, educating the students about the damage taggers did.

He swerved the Range Rover near the group of kids, scanning for Trent. His son popped up from the crowd like a growing weed being plucked from a garden. Mischief-maker. He couldn't help loving Trent even if he was likely to give him an ulcer some day.

"Dad!" Trent loped over to him as Ray got out of the car. "You're not going to believe this! We're just like the hippies, protesting for a cause!"

Ray put his hands on hips, trying very hard to look stern. This situation didn't seem too troublesome. He'd been scared to death, thinking that Trent had set fire to the science lab or something. Still, he needed to be tough, like a father should. "Enlighten me."

As Trent revealed the day's events, parents arrived at the school, one by one.

Ray shook his head while Trent told his tale. Was Nora nuts? Didn't she want to be a teacher anymore? And here he'd thought she wanted a job so badly.

Parents, some merely curious, others steamed at being called away from work, gathered around their children, questioning them as to the reason they were relaxing in the hot sun. Soon, they were drawn to one another, sharing opinions about this odd turn of events.

"I just wish Ms. Murray would get these crazy ideas out of her head and teach my student the basics!" said a mother, her petri-dish glasses magnifying her already bulging eyes.

"Amen to that," another mother said. "I don't appreciate being called out of work by the administration because a teacher can't handle her class."

"Hey," Trent said, springing from behind Ray. His father held him back, placing a finger to his own lips.

"Where is she, anyway?" asked a man in a business suit whose pager kept squealing. "I'd like to speak to the principal about this."

Ray had been listening to enough. Eleven parents had shown up. Most were keeping their thoughts to themselves, listening to their sons' and daughters' opinions about the prinipal and Ms. Murray. If it were up to the students, Ms. Murray would run the school. If it were up to these three loud parents, Ms. Murray would be run out of town.

The frog-eyed woman squawked again. "This is just plain irresponsible. I don't like the way Ms. Murray teaches, anyway. I could do a better job at home."

"Then why don't you?" asked Ray, his voice deep with emotion.

"Wh-what?" the woman said, stumbling back with the shock of a dissenting opinion.

"Why don't you teach your child at home? Teaching's a tough job, and I happen to think Ms. Murray is the best." Ray looked at the crowd, seeing the mottled faces of the annoyed parental trio. He caught nods from other parents and the admiring gaze of his own son.

He could hardly believe this was him—Ray Brody—speaking his mind at a ragtag parent conference. A concerned citizen. A PTA activist. What was the world coming to?

The bases were loaded, and he was up to bat. Trent was the little kid with an autograph pad, yelling, "You can do it, Brody!" The boy's eyes beamed as he watched Ray, and his heart melted. He'd been waiting for this glimmer of love, a sparkle he hadn't seen since Trent was running around with his little-tot belly hanging over his shorts. He had his boy back.

The man with the beeper snickered. "Ms. Murray is only a student teacher, and already she's got this guy wrapped around her finger."

"That's uncalled-for, Horace," a young mother said, arm wrapped around her son's shoulders.

Ray smiled, seeming to go along with the joke. "Maybe I should let you in on something, *Horace*." While the voice was affable, his arm muscles bunched. "If it weren't for Ms. Murray, my son might be sweeping floors in juvenile hall. That woman gives her heart and soul to this profession."

Several eyes looked beyond him, but Ray barely noticed he was so wrapped up in his speech. "I wouldn't want anyone else influencing, helping, raising my son. Heck, you're probably one of those parents who says that the educational system is too impersonal, that they don't pay enough attention to your kid. But when a teacher does reach out, you degrade her."

A parent near the back raised his hand. Ray nodded at him, then flushed, feeling like the teacher. "I just know that, before Ms. Murray, Billy didn't read books. Now I can't get him to stop."

Several voices murmured in agreement. "Thanks, Ms. Murray."

A wild chill ran down Ray's spine as he turned around. Nora stood behind him, tears spiking her long, dark lashes, amber eyes sparkling, white paint spot dotting her nose. White heat shot through him.

This was the woman he loved with all his heart. Defending her in front of these parents and students had only made him realize what he hadn't been able to admit before. Why hadn't he realized it before he'd pushed her away?

He thought of her warmth, the way she fit just right against his body, her sunny smile almost wiped out by his own stubborn refusal to confess his love. Was it too much to hope that she'd take him back? No. He was a fool to even hope for her forgiveness.

Trent ran into her arms, and they held on to each other as Ray merely watched, envious that his son could be so open about his feelings.

Parents and students crowded around Nora, asking questions about her future, which she answered with a quavering voice. She'd been fired, obviously, with no hope of being hired by the school district.

His heart ached for her. She was losing teaching, the one thing that had given her confidence.

As she hugged her students, Ray tried not to look at her with longing. *Work up your courage, man, tell her you never want to let her go.*

Several parents embraced her, while Horace, the beeper man, opened his mouth, but one look from Ray closed it again. That's right, he thought, you'd better not say a damned thing.

Horace led the trio of skeptics to the administration office, their children reluctantly tagging behind, watching Ms. Murray with farewell faces.

Ray could see unshed tears in her eyes. She loved these kids and, just as important, respected them. He felt her loss as painfully as if it were a mortal wound. He'd be lucky to earn her love again.

After more hugs and tears, she broke away from the crowd, waving, walking to her little red car. The remaining parents drove off as Nora watched. Then, as if forgetting he was even there, she started, seeing him waiting for everyone to leave.

His breath caught in his throat. He wanted to tell her he loved her, that he'd always loved her. "Tough day?"

She laughed a bit, then abruptly stopped, biting her lip again.

Ray looked down at Trent, but his son had already run off to the other side of the parking lot, bending down to inspect something incredibly interesting on the ground. Ray breathed a sigh of relief, for once thankful Trent was so astute.

"Nora…" He wasn't sure what to say. He wanted to comfort her, hold her, pour his love out to her. This wasn't right, standing next to her, being unable to touch her.

She took a deep breath, threw back her head, the sunlight warming her skin. "Thank you for the kind words." She looked at him, amber eyes glowing like hot sparkles under the ashes of a fire.

He wanted to shuffle his feet. *Aw, shucks, ma'am, I wish I hadn't been stupid enough to let you go.* "I meant every one of them. You're a great teacher, Ms. Murray."

Her jaw tightened. Silence hung between them like a heavy curtain, blocking their true feelings. He couldn't take this anymore.

"Nora, I love you."

She back stepped. "Stop. Stop right there, Ray Brody."

Stunned, he felt his heart plummet to the ground. "I'm putting my feelings out there, and you're telling me to slam on the brakes?"

Her mouth twisted, and she stared at the ground. When she spoke, her voice shook. "It's really hard to say this, but I love you. I have for a while."

A spark of hope lit his wary soul. Maybe she would take him back. "Then why the long face?"

She rubbed her hands over her arms. Ray noticed the goose bumps, in spite of the warm day.

"As I said, I love you, but it's not enough. You let me down, Ray, and I allowed you to do it." A melancholy smile weighed on her lips. "Disappoint me once, shame on you. Disappoint me twice, shame on me. I'll never let you hurt me again."

He wished he had the courage to sweep her off her feet, paint-spotted jeans, work shirt and all, to take her in his car, drive her into the sunset, and promise her a life of happily ever after. But she wouldn't let him. He was sure of it.

Grief washed over him. Life without Nora... The prospect seemed bleak, like an eternity of dark, foggy nights.

He took a few steps back. Maybe she wouldn't see his pain if he was far enough away. Then again, hadn't he been playing this game his entire life? He looked her straight in the eye. "I wish you'd let me prove to you how much you mean to me."

"Wishes." She shook her head and walked to the driver's side of her car, blocking his view of her, putting another wall between them. A permanent wall. "Wishes are like counterfeit bills, aren't they?"

They just stood there, the wind whistling a melancholy tune, overwhelming him, driving him to the edge of hopelessness. He'd really made a mess of his life this time, losing Nora when she'd been a light in his life. He wanted to punch a wall, to hurt himself as much as he'd hurt her.

He heard her sigh. When he looked up, tears had crept down her cheek. He'd never meant to make her cry. Damn him.

She tried to smile. "Goodbye, Ray."

As she started the engine, she never broke eye contact. She drove away, leaving him to feel as if she'd been waving to him from the deck of the *Titanic*. He wanted her back, needed her back.

With every increasing inch of distance, he realized how much he loved her. He loved her bright eyes, her kind heart, her nurturing spirit. He loved the way she'd survived tough spots in her life and come out a winner. He'd move mountains for a woman like Nora. And he'd have to if he wanted to win her back.

"Nice going, Dad." Trent had come to stand next to him, watching Nora leave.

"You're not supposed to eavesdrop." How could he defend himself when his heart had cracked in two?

"It's called body language. Any dum-dum could see you were blowing it from across the parking lot."

Ray peered down at his son. "Do you know what it means to rub salt in a wound?"

Trent thought about it, then grimaced. "If you have a wound, doesn't that mean you kinda like her?"

Why deny it any longer? Trent was no dullard. "Yes, I kinda like her."

"Do you love her?"

"Yes, I kinda love her. Are you satisfied?" Damn, he'd thought letting Trent know how he felt would push his son back into sullen withdrawal. But the boy actually seemed to light up.

"Good. I like her, too, you know."

He thought of Trent's matchmaking back-street drama essay and ran a hand through his hair. "No kidding. But your old man blew it."

"Maybe not. You just have to kiss up."

This boy needed Nora. *He* needed Nora. If kissing up would win her back, Ray was all ears…and lips. He stared at the blacktop, hoping Trent had more common sense than he did.

"I'm assuming you have a plan, Trent Brody."

His son grinned, transforming his normally wary expression into a genuine sign of happiness.

Ray felt better already.

Chapter Twenty

For the fourth time, Nora tried to slip off her blindfold.

"No you don't!" cried Josie, grabbing Nora's wrist.

Nora felt the car swerve, so she folded her hands in her lap. "Okay, Bailey, don't kill us."

"Don't make me truss you up like a hog."

"Nice image." Nora settled back in her seat, concentrating on darkness and the sound of the car's engine purring, tires spinning over the road. When she'd returned home from work, Josie had been there to listen to her stories about being fired and saying goodbye to Ray one last time. Her roommate had suggested something to cheer up Nora. A night on the town. A surprise destination; Josie's treat.

Nora had agreed, knowing that she might not have a grand meal for a long time to come. Not without a job. So she'd showered, styled her hair until it hung in a straight sheet to her shoulder blades and dressed herself in a dusky-pink cocktail dress.

She'd never worn this one and, truth be told, she'd been

saving it for when she was with Ray. She'd wanted him to run his gaze over the dress's sweetheart bodice, the sheer material grazing her shoulders and arms, the skirt nipped at the waist and flowing down her legs like a twilight-rose breeze.

Wow, and she thought maybe she'd get over him someday. Good luck. She wasn't sure she'd ever stop loving Ray.

She missed him already, now even more than before. He'd said the words she wanted to hear. He loved her. But Nora would be damned if she'd give him another chance at hurting her. She couldn't take any more pain.

If only giving away her love hadn't hurt more than anything she'd ever experienced.

Sitting at home, pining away in front of the TV, wasn't going to solve anything. Avoiding people, dressing in a bathrobe or never eating another bite of food certainly wouldn't help her. Thank goodness she had Josie to accompany her tonight. She didn't feel better about life, but then again, when would she?

The car slowed, came to a stop, squealed against a curb. "If you were a chauffeur, I'd fire you."

"So I shouldn't expect a tip?" Josie cut the ignition.

"Hey, where are we?" Nora had expected to detect sounds and smells of the city: beeping horns, people talking as they milled around on the sidewalks choosing a restaurant, aromatic scents of spiced foods. Instead, a comfortable silence stirred the air, and she smelled grass and flowers. Maybe Josie had taken her to a country club. After all, she'd told her to dress to the nines.

Driver door shutting. Her door opening. Josie's hands clutching hers, helping her out of the car. Stepping on cement, heels clicking as they walked a short distance. Nora waved her free hand in front of her, hoping Josie wouldn't walk her into a wall. She wondered if people were staring at the sight of two young women dressed for a big night, one leading the other blindfolded down a mysterious path.

Josie helped her up a step, then rang a doorbell.

"Where are we?" asked Nora. Were they at someone's

home? God, she wasn't in the mood for a party. Eating a quiet dinner was one thing, but dealing with well-meaning "I'm so sorry" socializers was out of the question.

She heard the door creak open. A familiar creak. Josie pushed her forward.

Garlic, tomato, cheeses. Something good was cooking, but she hoped Josie hadn't brought her to the one place she dreaded.

"This'd better not be..."

Across carpet. A sliding screen door. Back outside.

Someone whipped off her blindfold. She squinted, batting her eyes to adjust to the combination of darkness and light. A blur of starlike pinpricks and smoky moons.

One last blink and it was all in focus. A familiar backyard, yet not familiar at all.

They'd decorated the trees with strings of white lights, giving a festive glow to the area. Candles sheltered by metal covers flickered around the patio, cutouts of half-moons and stars silhouetting the fence, the grass. She was in a fairy-glow wonderland, with a cloth-covered round table waiting in the grass, candlelight wavering from a simple blue-stoned centerpiece, beverage glasses filled to the rim with what looked like grape juice.

Nora looked at Josie. "What is this?"

A voice from her other side spoke up. "It's what you want it to be, Ms. Murray, but don't blame Ms. Bailey. I asked her to bring you."

She peered over to find Trent, dressed in a white button-down shirt and blue tie, khaki pants creased with obvious care. He'd slicked back his hair, making him seem like a choir angel who'd forgotten his halo.

Nora furrowed her brow. What was going on? Nothing made sense. She looked at Josie. "So you're a part of this?"

Josie smirked and stepped back through the entrance. "Exit, stage right." Then she was gone, leaving Nora with Trent.

He took her arm and led her to the table. "Here. Have a seat."

"I don't understand this."

"You will." He pulled out her chair, waiting for her to sit.

Was Trent trying to make her feel better? She wouldn't put it past this creative kid. So thoughtful, so much like she'd thought his father had been.

When she was seated, he disappeared, and the sound of classical music filled the air. *Bolero.* Wonderful, sensual. Entirely inappropriate for a dinner with one of her students.

Ex-student, she reminded herself with a touch of despair. Something, a feeling, really, forced her to turn around.

Ray. Attired in a black-and-white tuxedo, sandy hair not cooperating with the formal atmosphere as it rebelled in waves. Why did he have to look so darned handsome with his broad shoulders and sun-warmed eyes?

He held his hands behind his back, a grin on his face. Her heart tried to slam its way out of her chest.

"You look beautiful."

She started to get out of her chair. "I think I've got the wrong address."

"Wait."

She halted, hand on the table, ready to push away. Did he think a nice dinner and good music would entice her back?

He stepped closer, soft light from the candles and trees giving him a glow. When he reached out from behind his back, he produced her pink blanket from their day at the beach so long ago.

"You've got to be kidding me," she said. Her blanket? How romantic. Now she'd definitely hop right back to him.

He chuckled. "Thought it might break the ice." He set down the symbol of their first kiss on a patio chair and motioned for her to sit again. "Please indulge me. I'm going to do my best to beg your forgiveness."

"I already told you—you're never going to hurt me again." She was simmering inside.

He grinned. "As you'll see, I'm ready to move mountains for you, Nora."

The sentiment took her aback. Curious, she sat again, eyeing him carefully. She'd fall into no traps, no "let's try it again" proclamations. More than a week ago, she'd been abundantly clear that she wanted it all or nothing. And he'd given her nothing.

When they were facing each other across the table, Ray snapped his fingers. "Service, please."

"How typical," she murmured, trying to keep the amusement from her tone. Damn him for being so charming, for being so…Ray.

Trent walked from the house, into the yard, balancing two dishes. Something that looked like Italian food smothered the plate. He plopped his goods in front of them.

When he saw Nora inspecting the offerings, he supplied, "It's spaghetti, very close to mac and cheese. But our neighbor Ed helped us some."

"Thank you, Trent," said Ray, more than just appreciation in his gaze. It seemed as if he wanted his son to scram.

Trent remained, a proud smile on his face. "I know you like garlic, Ms. Murray. Remember the night we made the steak dinner?"

"I remember." She couldn't believe she felt like a part of this family again, even after being discarded. *Be strong, Nora.*

He stood there grinning until Ray cleared his throat and said, "Thank you, Trent."

The boy shrugged and left. How could she not adore him?

They sat at the table, facing each other. She all but screamed with the questions racing through her mind: Why was she here? What were all these decorations? What did Ray have up his sleeve?

She was famished from her long, stressful day, yet unable to eat a bite of the marinara-doused pasta. Unable to stay silent, Nora asked, "Why do you feel the need to move mountains?"

Ray's eyes seemed so blue in the candlelight, a beam of flame beneath the ocean, holding an aching hunger. The intensity of his gaze drew her in, pulled her back, like a night-shaded tide. Surely his feelings couldn't be as strong as his expression indicated.

"I made a huge mistake with you, Nora. Like you said, I let you down, and I let you go. This afternoon, when you were hugging all those kids, and they were hugging you back, I realized something." He leaned on the table and smiled. "I love you with everything I've got."

The tears fought to escape her eyes, but damned if she'd let them. "I don't understand. You made it perfectly clear that you didn't want me. You hurt me, knowing what I've been through in the past."

"And I was an idiot." He leaned back in his chair. "There. I've admitted it. I know that it'll take more than just words, Nora, but all I'm asking for is a chance to prove how much I love you."

What did he expect her to do? Throw herself at his feet, thank the heavens for another shot? If he hurt her again, she'd never forgive herself.

He broke into her thoughts. "You told me you loved me. Has that love vanished?"

"No," she said, feeling the sting of a tear as it crept out the corner of an eye. "But it's been tempered by reality. After that day in my classroom, the last time you touched me, I promised I'd protect myself."

"Isn't that what you've been doing your whole life?"

The words stabbed. The tear flowed down her cheek, unchecked. Yes, she'd been sheltering her emotions most of her life, but the one time she'd laid them bare, they'd been stomped on. By Ray, no less. "Evidently, it's what I have to do. You can't pretend you have feelings for me, then shut down."

"I won't." Voice sincere, gaze direct.

He wasn't lying to her. And she loved him so much, she was on the edge of giving in, but she couldn't. Not if she wanted to preserve her well-being.

She fingered her grape juice glass, avoiding his eyes. "I

think you mean every word you say. Right now, at this moment. Who knows how you're going to feel tomorrow."

"I think I've loved you from the moment I saw you walk into the Clubhouse. I've had a hard time admitting it."

Of course she understood his wariness. His painful past had blocked their paths to happiness from the beginning. "It's unfortunate that I've been hurt as much as you have, Ray. Maybe it would've been easier if I'd had a good family, a nice social life. But I'm too much like you."

"We can heal each other, Nora. Please, give us another chance."

"I…" She shook her head, rose from her seat. "I'm afraid I can't do that."

He also stood, hand inside his lapel, drawing out an object. With long, determined steps, he came to her side, gently capturing her wrist before she could get away. There it was again, his unique scent—the clean male fragrance, the dizzy spice of aftershave, sending her common sense into oblivion.

In two fingers he clasped a ring, its simple diamond solitaire setting flashing in the light. A miniature reminder of the wedding bracelet, the one she'd tucked away in a storage box after Ray had left her alone in the classroom. She'd vowed never to look at it again. Nora's throat closed, more tears gathered. He was going to propose to her.

She would've jumped at this chance a couple of weeks ago, before the strain of their relationship became unbearable. But now, standing under a watchful moon and an audience of candles, she couldn't imagine exposing herself again, saying yes to many more possibilities of pain.

"Ray, please don't."

He tilted up her chin with an index finger, compelling her to face him.

"Nora, marry me. Be a part of my family. Accept my love for the rest of your life."

She closed her eyes, her face close to melting from tears. A sob tore out of her. "I can't…"

The warm smoothness of the ring rubbed against her finger.

As she blinked, she saw a fuzz of gold and crystalline sparkle. It looked like it belonged, like it had been made to remind her of how much she loved this man.

She felt a smaller hand nestle into her free fist. Trent, by her side, anxiously watching her.

Ray's hand slid around her wrist, as comfortable as her bracelet had been. "We want you in our family, Nora."

Trent squeezed her hand. She loved this boy, too, as if he was her own son. Of course, she would've been too immature to have a baby when he was born, but he was the child of her heart. And, in a way, he'd produced the union of her and Ray. They were sort of like his children.

She laughed through her tears at the silly thought. How could she ever leave this place? Every time she looked at one of them, her resolve to refuse Ray faltered. Pretty soon, she'd be proposing to *them*. She started shaking, wondering how she could forgive herself if she walked out of here without a family.

"Ms. Murray?" Trent's eyes had widened to baby-blue tide pools. He smiled wistfully. "You know, I wish I could stop calling you 'Ms. Murray.' I'd like to call you 'Mom.'"

She almost felt detached from her body, looking down at the earth from the height of a shooting star. A star that twinkled like her bracelet. "Mom." She'd be a good one, too. "I don't know what to say to you guys."

Trent gave a tiny hop. "Say yes. Dad needs you. When you're not here, he's cranky, and you can help him make good decisions."

Ray raised his eyebrow at his son. "Are you finished proposing?"

Trent shrugged as Nora tried to hide her grin. "I guess."

"Good." Ray rubbed her hand, sending warm chills up her arm. "As I was saying, we two poor saps adore you. If I could, I'd write my love in the sky for everyone to see. And maybe in fifty years, when we're still together, we could hold each other and see traces of it."

"Jeez, Dad." Trent laughed.

The words had been beautiful, lulling Nora into stroking her finger along the ridge of his hand. She'd missed his touch, his sense of humor. If she said no to his proposal, she realized she'd be hurting herself much more than Ray had hurt her. The thought was staggering, yet so obvious. She could control the pain, take charge of it, rule it.

She loved this man and his boy more than anything on this earth. She was ready to take a last chance.

"Yes."

Ray glanced at Trent, then back at Nora, his eyes wide, unbelieving. "Did you just say yes?"

"Yes, I said yes." Nora could feel herself blushing, her tears turning into signs of joy. Relief washed through her, letting her know she'd made the right decision. She was excited, yet a little scared, to be starting her new life.

"Ye-e-s," said Trent, hopping once more. He straightened his tie, calming his reaction. Nora couldn't believe he'd be her son.

Ray enveloped her in a hug, rubbing her back. She buried her nose into his chest, reveling in the protection he offered. He made her feel wanted, made her feel that she deserved his love.

When she pulled away to look at him, she saw Trent had left.

Ray must've noticed her confusion. "He went across the street to Ed's."

A thrill of delight shot through her. "He could've stayed."

"No." He grinned. "He's perceptive enough to know that I've been dying to hold you." He drew her to him again, his broad chest expanding with every breath, his beating heart a lullaby beneath her ear.

When he kissed her, his lips promised a future, sunrise-soft and tender. She nuzzled him, returning caress for caress. She was ready to be Mrs. Nora Brody.

He swept her into his arms, carrying her to his room, her sheer pink skirt fluttering as they moved into the house, down the hall. When they reached the bed, he let her slide out of his arms, over his hard chest and torso, her dress wisping over him, emphasizing his obvious desire for her.

The mattress sunk beneath her knees as she kneeled, slipping off his tuxedo jacket, unbuttoning the shirt, the pressed pants. Stroking her fingers over his chest, she watched his face as he shut his eyes in pleasure.

She loved making him happy, wild with need. And they could do this every night for the rest of their lives. He'd be her husband, her lover, her best friend.

The buzz of her zipper numbed her mind with dizziness as he undid the dress, warming his hands against the bare skin of her back, tracing her spine with his thumb. She shivered, indulging herself in the comfort of his knowing touch.

He peeled the dress from her body, stretching her arms over her head, his lips following the trail of the disappearing material. Then she was naked except for her silk undies, vulnerable under his hungry gaze. His hands traveled everywhere his eyes did, rubbing, petting, heating her skin. He straddled her, spanning her ribs with his large hands, sliding them upward to cover her breasts.

She flexed her body on the soft covers, running her hands through his silky, windswept hair as he kissed her aroused nipples, tonguing them, gently biting, bringing her to moan in increasing excitement. This was her intended husband, the man who brought her joy and fulfillment. The rest of her life she'd wallow in his practiced, tender lovemaking.

"I love you, Nora," he murmured, drawing his lips up to her neck, her ear.

"Me, too. I love you, too." She cradled his head, toying with his hair as they held each other a moment.

Then he shifted, grinding his hips against hers, reminding her of how he fit inside her body. Perfectly. He slipped off her undies, tossing them to the floor, stretching his length along hers, their skin slick with sweat. The friction lit a spark in her chest, the spark growing with every touch, every kiss.

He entered her, full and hard, rocking against her until she gasped with surging passion. They were a part of each other.

She twined her legs with his while they moved with each other, climbing up, up, until he shuddered in release, holding her in his arms, stroking her face, her neck.

She was ready, almost exploding with built-up ecstasy. Ray moved down her body, adjusting her legs over his shoulders, spreading her thighs, placing his mouth against the center of her. God, yes, she wanted this.

Ray sensed her urgency. He loved her with his mouth and tongue, kissing his way up her body when he felt her tense, then shudder. He tasted her sweat, loving the orange spice and peaches.

"Oh, Ray…" She was ready, and he'd be damned if she would look away like she did the last time they'd made love.

He smoothed his hand over her brow. "Nora…"

She watched him, thank goodness, she watched him. Sharing her ultimate joy with him this time, arching her neck, mouth in an O, eyes slanted with desire and, ultimately, release.

He smiled, bringing her to nestle in his arms once again. For all eternity.

Epilogue

Ray watched as Nora lifted their baby girl, Tina, out of the crib. A sharp sense of gratification overcame him as he saw his wife and daughter side by side—Nora, with her sunny hair and twinkling golden eyes and six-month-old Tina, a child who favored him in so many ways with her curling blond locks and wide blue-green gaze. She was a smiling child, the happiest baby ever. Maybe because she lived with the most loving family in creation.

As he leaned against the nursery's door frame, he languidly rested his arms over his chest. When he'd found out that Nora was pregnant, he'd put all his energy into constructing this room, making sure every angel-lined cloud, every diamond star was perfectly shaped. An old-fashioned white crib adorned one corner, a baby-changing station and a chest of toys filling other spaces in the room. Tina must've been conceived the second time they'd made love, when they hadn't used protection.

Ray remembered worrying about that night, but he'd misspent his time. Baby Tina was a blessing, a welcome addition to their cozy, patchwork brood.

Now, as Nora cooed at their gurgling baby, his heart felt near to bursting. He didn't want to say a word, for fear of shattering the moment.

His wife turned in profile, a flush pinkening her cheeks. She certainly had the glow of motherhood about her.

Another presence warmed his side. Trent looked over at him, grinning, enjoying the sight of his mom and baby sister as well. Ray put his hand on Trent's shoulder, and his son smiled up at him. He'd grown an inch or two and was at the top of his ninth-grade class so far, and just getting involved in school sports. Sure, he still caused Ray and Nora an occasional sleepless night or two, but Ray thought that might be normal for all parents of teenagers. No doubt Tina would make them worry as well, with her heartbreaker eyes and wild blond hair. He couldn't wait, he thought, rolling his eyes.

Not that Nora wasn't busy enough tending Tina. At first, when Nora had decided to become a full-time mother instead of pursuing teaching jobs, Ray thought she might regret her decision. After all, she'd loved being in the classroom. But she had her own kids now, and she greeted him every day when he returned home from the Clubhouse with kisses and smiles filled with promise.

He watched her walk to the other side of the room, to the bureau with the jewelry box on top. As she opened the lid, a song tinkled out. "Wind Beneath My Wings." Nora swayed with Tina for a moment, their heads pressed together. Then, she lifted out a piece of soft material. Ray knew what was inside as she unwrapped it.

Whispering, he said, "Isn't it a little too early for her first prom, Nora?"

She turned around, smiling at him, then at Trent. Softly, she said, "It's for later."

Nora looked at Tina, and Ray could almost see the connection between mother and daughter. He knew she'd felt love for her own mom, and this was her chance to make up for her guilt at not being able to save her. Nora shone as a mother.

He swallowed away the sudden lump in his throat. He knew exactly what the bracelet meant. Dreams for their daughter. Dreams of happiness and a glimmering future. "Right."

She unwrapped it, holding it up in the sunlight. After a moment, she put it back, tucking it into the jewelry box as if it was another baby being put to slumber.

Ray walked to her side, wrapping his arm around his wife and child, overcome by emotion. He held out his free arm to Trent, who shuffled his feet and, finally, ambled into his family's embrace. A grin hid on his face.

Ray looked at the jewelry box, then his family, knowing they all understood. Trent and his lopsided smile. Tina and her wet cherry Life Saver-like mouth. And Nora, her sun-glow eyes shining with joy.

Love had been the hardest lesson for them to learn, but they'd done it. Yes, by God, they'd done it.

* * * * *

SILHOUETTE®
SPECIAL EDITION™

AVAILABLE FROM 20TH SEPTEMBER 2002

ROOKIE COP Nikki Benjamin

That's My Baby!

Working closely with her ex-husband—and lawman—Jake to find the mother of an abandoned baby evoked powerful, passionate longings in Megan. But could a tiny baby give them a future together?

DO YOU TAKE THIS REBEL? Sherryl Woods

The Calamity Janes

Time hadn't dulled Cassie's anger at Cole, the man who'd betrayed her ten years ago and the father of her child...nor cooled the fiery attraction between them. Could she re-kindle their long-lost love?

FORBIDDEN LOVE Christine Flynn

Nick Culhane had come home and Amy could still feel the traitorous heat that had always simmered between them. But how could Amy love the one man her family would never forgive?

MAGIC IN A JELLY JAR Sally Tyler Hayes

Single dad Joe Morgan, and his son Luke, awoke dangerous yearnings in Samantha that she knew could never be fulfilled—unless she could open Joe's wary heart to the magic of love...

SEPARATE BEDROOMS...? Carole Halston

Cara LaCroix married her handsome boss Neil Griffen in name only. But Cara sensed something more in Neil and suddenly she knew she'd risk everything on the chance that something might be love...

STANDING BEAR'S SURRENDER Peggy Webb

Lovely and innocent Sarah Sloan was entranced by wounded warrior Jim Standing Bear. Sarah knew that she would do anything to help him walk again and break the bars over his heart...

AVAILABLE FROM 20TH SEPTEMBER 2002

SILHOUETTE®

Sensation™

Passionate, dramatic, thrilling romances

HARD TO TAME Kylie Brant
THE RENEGADE AND THE HEIRESS Judith Duncan
BY HONOUR BOUND Ruth Langan
BORN BRAVE Ruth Wind
ONCE FORBIDDEN... Carla Cassidy
BABY, BABY, BABY Mary McBride

Intrigue™

Danger, deception and suspense

NEVER ALONE Rebecca York
LOVERS IN HIDING Susan Kearney
SECRET AGENT HEIRESS Julie Miller
ACCESSORY TO MARRIAGE Ann Voss Peterson

Superromance™

*Enjoy the drama, explore the emotions,
experience the relationship*

FOUND: ONE WIFE Judith Arnold
THE BRAVO BILLIONAIRE Christine Rimmer
HOMECOMING Laura Abbot
JUST ONE NIGHT Kathryn Shay

Desire™

Two intense, sensual love stories in one volume

EVEN BETTER THAN BEFORE
THE REDEMPTION OF JEFFERSON CADE BJ James
A COWBOY'S PROMISE Anne McAllister

UNDER SUSPICION
THE SECRET LIFE OF CONNOR MONAHAN Elizabeth Bevarly
ADDICTED TO NICK Bronwyn Jameson

THE NANNY AND THE BOSS
WYOMING CINDERELLA Cathleen Galitz
TAMING THE BEAST Amy J Fetzer

0902/23b

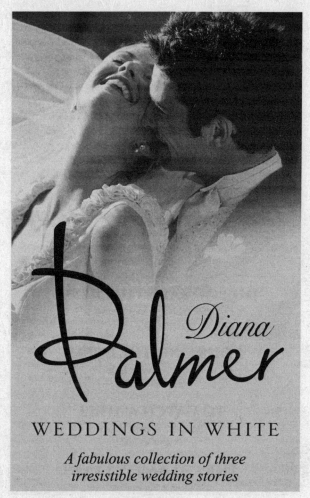

WEDDINGS IN WHITE

*A fabulous collection of three
irresistible wedding stories*

On sale 20th September 2002

*Available at most branches of WH Smith,
Tesco, Martins, Borders, Eason, Sainsbury's
and most good paperback bookshops.*

1002/09/SH34

SILHOUETTE®

proudly presents

five wonderful, warm stories from bestselling author

The Calamity Janes

Five unique women share a lifetime of friendship!

DO YOU TAKE THIS REBEL?
Silhouette Special Edition
October 2002

COURTING THE ENEMY
Silhouette Special Edition
November 2002

TO CATCH A THIEF
Silhouette Special Edition
December 2002

THE CALAMITY JANES
Silhouette Superromance
January 2003

WRANGLING THE REDHEAD
Silhouette Special Edition
February 2003

1002/SH/LC42

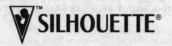

mJ0005

FREE

2 BOOKS
AND A SURPRISE GIFT!

We would like to take this opportunity to thank you for reading this Silhouette® book by offering you the chance to take TWO more specially selected titles from the Special Edition™ series absolutely FREE! We're also making this offer to introduce you to the benefits of the Reader Service™—

- ★ FREE home delivery
- ★ FREE monthly Newsletter
- ★ FREE gifts and competitions
- ★ Exclusive Reader Service discount
- ★ Books available before they're in the shops

Accepting these FREE books and gift places you under no obligation to buy; you may cancel at any time, even after receiving your free shipment. Simply complete your details below and return the entire page to the address below. **You don't even need a stamp!**

YES! Please send me 2 free Special Edition books and a surprise gift. I understand that unless you hear from me, I will receive 4 superb new titles every month for just £2.85 each, postage and packing free. I am under no obligation to purchase any books and may cancel my subscription at any time. The free books and gift will be mine to keep in any case.

E2ZEC

Ms/Mrs/Miss/Mr ....Initials..
BLOCK CAPITALS PLEASE

Surname...

Address...

....

....Postcode ....

Send this whole page to:
UK: FREEPOST CN81, Croydon, CR9 3WZ
EIRE: PO Box 4546, Kilcock, County Kildare (stamp required)

Offer valid in UK and Eire only and not available to current Reader Service subscribers to this series. We reserve the right to refuse an application and applicants must be aged 18 years or over. Only one application per household. Terms and prices subject to change without notice. Offer expires 31st December 2002. As a result of this application, you may receive offers from other carefully selected companies. If you would prefer not to share in this opportunity please write to The Data Manager at the address above.

Silhouette® is a registered trademark used under licence.

Special Edition™ is being used as a trademark.